MW01671521

SWAN BAY

GIULIA TORRE

ISBN 9780692758267

Cover art by Tracy Hetzel.

A note to the reader,

Like *Wolfe Island*, the setting for *Swan Bay* is a fictional representation of the Thousand Islands Region of Upstate New York. Readers will find a different Swan Bay described in these pages than the one they can find in the world. The same is true for the many islands whose names are borrowed for this story – Grindstone, Three Sisters, Grandview, Wolfe and Mosquito Islands.

Swan Bay was written to share the River's beauty, but this book will not provide an accurate map to navigate its shoals.

GT

Thanks to my husband, Christopher, for the inspiration.

Thanks to friends and family who've served as sounding boards, reviewers, cheerleaders, and fans.

Special thanks to Sarah and Katherine for the invaluable brainstorms and beta reads. This book is better because of you.

Thanks, Mom, for reading my books.

And, thanks, Dad, for not reading my books.

1

Grandview Island, NY, September 1893

Chloe Swann remembered burials like photographs of war: black, white, and repeating. She sat cross-legged in the grass. Beside her was a metal bucket of tulip bulbs. She had a thousand bulbs, and she intended to plant every one. Then, she'd hover like a spirit and take aim at the squirrels as they tried to dig them up.

Her eyes narrowed at two bushy tails that scuttled in figure eights around neat rows of stone. Their wily brown bodies were too far away to hit with a rock. What was more, throwing stones at a Civil War memorial was irreverent. Twenty-four Union soldiers were buried there, their gravestones militantly ordered. Set close together, the stones gave the illusion of a dense expanse of white.

The black flannel of her skirt pooled between her legs, and a soft leather boot rested under each knee. Tucked into her skirt was a white muslin blouse with a short collar embroidered in colorful thread. It was a hot September. She'd unbuttoned the neck an hour before, and the billow of her sleeves was rolled up to her elbows. Although the chill of dusk had set in, she kept her skin bare. In the North Country of New York, spring took a long time coming. There'd be enough time in winter to wear layers of wool.

Faced by a slab of marble, she traced the carved numbers with her fingers, feeling for leftover sun in the stone. At the sharp snap of a twig, Chloe leaned to one side for a look. What she saw lodged her heart in her throat.

She hadn't felt fear since she'd witnessed her first burial at the age of six. Her brothers had lowered the coffin into the ground to the sound of a jingling bell. It wasn't a smooth jingle. It rang, awkward and intermittent, as the men lowered the coffin and struggled under its weight. The entire way down, the bell had rung. Then it had been stuffed and buried with dirt. She'd summoned courage enough to look over the edge of the grave and scream at the flat wood as they shoveled on the earth. *Are you alive? Do you want to come out?*

Her bones had grown cold with the realization, even as she'd shouted. Death was being buried alive, underground with a useless bell. Her eldest brother Eric had explained that death was death: final, absolute, and easy enough to recognize. No one ever used the bell; it was only tradition to tie it with string to the finger of the dead. No one was ever, actually, buried alive.

That terror had conquered all others, gotten fear itself out of her system. Chloe hadn't been scared of anything after that. There was, after all, only death to be scared of.

But she felt fear now.

The spit left her mouth. Another twig snapped, and her heart pumped.

It was Michael Low.

And he had already died.

2

Two years earlier

Meredith Wells nudged a marbled red leaf with the slight pressure of her finger. She depressed the leaf again to see the plant bob and return. Tiny leaves that grew in two identical, alternating rows. The nub of her pencil, which had been curled in her palm, spun in her fingers. The point returned to the page in her lap, and the tiny burgundy plant was replicated in her sketchbook, as if by magic.

The purple marble in the dark green leaves fell into shadow. Meredith squinted. A fat drop of water landed and sunk the stem low. She looked up. Though it was mid-morning, the sky was dark. Green clouds had extinguished the sun. Meredith stood. *Green clouds.* She knew what those clouds meant, even if she'd never before seen the likes of the storm that was told to follow. Had she been a landscape artist and not a botanical illustrator, she would have risked her life to paint that sky.

Meredith watched, fascinated, until the clouds swirled in a menacing froth that spurred her into action. She packed her sketchbook into her satchel, and swung it over her shoulder. She was on Bloody Point, a small island that punctuated in exclamation a long island with small cottages, but the cottages were too far to reach in the short time she had to find shelter. She scanned the trees on the rock where she sat. Evergreens were not good protection in a storm. There was, however, a stone outcropping at the base of the island that she might dip into, if the storm didn't change direction. Wind on the river was fickle. She might receive a shifting blast that would make her a fossil in the rock, but with no other option, it was worth a try.

A rumble and crack quickened her descent down the rock face, and her brown leather boots chased the crumbling moss beneath her. But the crack had not been lightning; the mast of a small ship in the distance had been broken in half by the wind. The force of it beat against her face and pressed her back in to the cliff's shallow. She shielded her eyes against the storm and brought the ship into focus.

With horror, she saw it was the *Dreadnought*, Michael Low's boat. She'd been aboard it a half dozen times since she'd become fast friends with its captain two years before. Well, their friendship had not been fast; it had taken time for Michael to trust her, even more for him to give the appearance of enjoying her company. But in the end, sheer perseverance had helped Meredith grow like a barnacle on the underbelly of Michael's boat.

But the *Dreadnought* now twirled unmanned, overcome by the whorl of the river whipped by the storm. Meredith realized at once with an ache of dread that Michael was out there. As soon as the thought entered her mind, she saw him, and all thoughts of her own safety fled. She called once, as loud as her voice would allow, then she plunged into the water.

The shallow bank of Bloody Point forced her to wade in. She tried to submerge her body, but her skirts sunk into the water with a nightmarish lethargy. She pushed with her thighs though the water, and fought with her dress until the shallow riverbed released her, then she swam. Her arms cut through the water in long, efficient pulls.

She heard another crack. She spun in a half circle in the water, and found a twin sailing skiff twenty yards south. It had been hidden from her vantage point ashore by a small island of trees. This boat, too, she recognized. It was the *Flagship*. Meredith had never met Michael's twin, but the boat was familiar enough. Both boats spun unmanned, and she was faced with a choice.

Meredith didn't change course. She'd seen Michael, and she meant to reach him. She continued to pull toward the *Dreadnought*. "Michael!" Over the crash of water, his name travelled nowhere. She swallowed and coughed, then found him again. His head bobbed in the water, alive and afloat.

Her pulls now were more than strong; they were fast. Her arms wheeled without thought of pacing herself, and it was shy of a minute before she reached him.

He'd strayed from the boat, intuiting that in the violent water, the *Dreadnought* would be a threat. If he'd been bumped in the head, it would've been all over, but she'd reached him. Relief filled her. She had him now. Meredith's arm went under his shoulder, then across his chest from behind. "I've got you."

He struggled against her, but his struggle wasn't strong. It had been wrung from him already by the storm. He resigned himself to being carried to shore.

But Meredith's struggle started afresh. She had only one arm, and legs bound by skirts. With Michael's added weight, she sunk once, and swallowed water. She took time to stop and tear at the buttons at her waist. She had no other choice. They popped, and she kicked until the heavy twill sunk away from her feet, leaving her boots and tights free to keep them both afloat. Her pulls moved them now, together, backward toward shore. When her kicks hit the riverbed, she almost wept. When they were both on dry ground, she lay back on the wet rock, and breathed air in long drags. The storm that had raged from above was being sucked back into the morning sky as quickly as it had arrived.

She tilted her head until her cheek rested against the ground and looked sidelong at Michael, who stared at the water, at the sailboats they'd left behind. Meredith pushed herself up and crawled to kneel beside him and put a hand on his arm. She understood what he did not say. His brother was out there. "Michael."

But it was not Michael who turned at the name. It was not Michael's eyes who, wrung empty of emotion, now stared into hers. Meredith blanched and shook. Her shirt clung wet to her neck. Her drawers dragged at her knees as she stood. She stumbled to the shoreline, her fists at each thigh as she called across the water.

"Michael!" But he was gone.

3

Present Day

Simon Low stopped at a gravestone and sat. He retrieved a cigarette from his jacket pocket and lit it with a match, tossed the wooden stick to the grass and watched it smoke. His thumb sunk into the curved stone at his hip, reading the smooth, deep letters with his touch.

Ornamental grasses grew in tufts at each side of his marble seat He pulled off the wheat-colored crowns. He should've been sailing, had he not given it up, but he was here, doing this: looking for his brother's stone at Riverside. He cursed when he saw what the walk had done to his trousers. He was not dressed for this. He pushed cut grass from the leg of his pants.

He scanned the headstones for his brother's grave, not in the least expecting to find it from where he sat. In spite of the scant number of stones, he didn't know where to look. Markers were scattered in every direction. There was no family plot; his father was buried among the Civil War soldiers. His brother's headstone could be anywhere.

Simon scanned the words on the tops of white marble headstones that surrounded him. Mother. Father. Son. Iconography of burial decorated each stone. Crosses and flying birds. Oak leaves and lily of the valley. The symbolism was generic, religious, predictable. A hand with a single finger pointed heavenward. Up. Simon grimaced. Everyone hoped to go up.

"My father carved that one."

The cigarette dropped from his fingers, where it sent up a tendril of smoke between his feet.

"Did you know Mrs. Vanderbelt?" a woman asked.

Vanderbilt? He looked at the stone between his legs. He hadn't known any Vanderbilts were buried there.

"Vanderbelt, with an E. You shouldn't be sitting there, and certainly not smoking. It's disrespectful."

The woman was young, younger than he and his brother. With the sun behind her, she lit up like a star. She had white hair, long and straight. It was all he could see of her face. His eyes squinted into the sun.

"And sacrilegious."

"I'm not religious." He should have stood, but he was in a foul mood. All of his *nots* were on display.

Her head tilted, and the halo of sunlit hair fell to the side as she regarded him. "You're Michael's brother."

Michael's brother. He hadn't been identified in that way for two years. Regret washed over him. He frowned. Yet another loss he'd not yet known to ache for. They took him by miserable surprise.

"You know Michael?" *Knew* Michael, he corrected himself.

She nodded. "Are you here for a visit?"

When Simon frowned, Chloe's smile encouraged him. "I know right where to find him." She held out her arm. "I'll show you."

Her fingers extended to him, pale, small, expectant. Pressing against his thighs to stand, he ground his cigarette out in the grass and took her offered hand.

Simon thought he'd feel differently. *Michael Jennings Low. 1865-1891.* A boat, a small wooden skiff with a half-circle sail was carved into the stone, but Simon could barely see the headstone. His thoughts were blurred, came through faster than a train. It took all his attention to feign focus on his brother's grave, because when the woman's fingers had taken his, everything went white.

White. He'd not felt white since the morning he and Michael had started their race, before that unearthly squall.

White. It was neither heat nor cold. Neither pain nor pleasure. It was an invasion, an entrance into his mind that was only...*white.* And following that brilliant entrance, that bright light invasion, was connection, solid, forceful, tangible. He'd always felt it with Michael. Then, with the single gulp of the river that had swallowed his brother, had not.

Until now.

His eyes traveled to where she stood.

"You knew him?" Though Simon and Michael were mirror images of one another, it was the end of their likeness. As a start, they didn't share the same friends. "We've never met."

She tucked a lock of straight blond hair behind her ear. It fell forward again when she nodded.

Beside her, Simon felt a tingle of electricity. Arousal. He hadn't felt *that* with his brother before. Though the pulse of white when he'd touched her had been familiar, this electric ache was not. If they'd met before, he would've remembered. He would've remembered this. Simon turned to face her full on. He couldn't keep himself from taking stock of her another minute. "Who are you?"

She extended her hand to him. "Chloe Swann. My family buries," she hesitated, then both hands opened in a wide gesture that took in the lawn and the stones, "everyone."

"You buried my brother?" He was relieved he wouldn't have to take her hand again.

She qualified, "I set his stone." She bent and tried to move his brother's marble headstone back and forth with both hands. "And I did a good job, too. Two winters of heaving ground, and it's still steady."

When she stood, her blouse gaped open at the collar, not far, but enough so Simon saw a line of collarbone from her throat to where it disappeared behind white cotton. He pretended to ignore it. "Your family runs the cemetery?"

"My father carves the stones. My brothers dig the graves and manage the grounds, and my mother manages the business."

"And you?"

"I bring in the people."

"Bring in the people?" He balked. "That sounds sinister."

She laughed, revealing small white teeth. Simon imagined their smoothness against his tongue. He bit it, chasing the feeling away. He felt his pocket and retrieved his cigarettes.

"I assure you, it's not. I talk with the dying, arrange how they'd like things, once they realize they have no other choice."

"What happens when they arrive to you unannounced?" The cigarette bobbed between his lips, and he struck a match and lit the end before she could say something to prevent him.

"They do that, too." She shrugged again. "Then I meet whomever they've left behind."

"Like me." He blew out the words in a line of smoke.

"Like you."

He focused on the figure before him. She had height. She was tall, even. He'd noticed her hair. It was a silvery blond. So white he knew where she came from. Norway or Sweden. Someplace Nordic.

Her clothing was well-made. He knew fabrics and appreciated hers, at once clean white and colorful. And her mouth. He wished he hadn't looked. Her lips were full and pink. He liked looking. He liked the color and feel of her lips.

Damn it to hell. He rolled the cigarette between his thumb and finger. How did he know the feel? The connection he'd felt to his brother had been mental, emotional. It had never been palpable, had never affected his skin this way.

"You surprise me."

He flinched. Could she read his thoughts? It was a queer question, but one worth asking.

"It's been two years since I planted that stone, but I've never seen you."

He inhaled on his cigarette and pinched a piece of tobacco from the tip of his tongue. "That surprises you?"

"I've seen people stay away. That's no surprise. But why have you come? Why now?" She seemed to ask the question of the world in general. She moved the lock of hair from her face and tucked it again behind her ear. "That's what surprises me. I wasn't expecting you today."

"Any other day?" She had blue eyes. He filed the fact away.

She regarded him and shook her head with deliberation. "I suppose not then either."

"Why not?"

Chloe gestured to the grave in explanation. "It's empty."

It was just the stone, an empty idol, really. His brother's body wasn't buried there.

Michael's stone. It had become ritual to avoid it.

He hadn't attended his brother's funeral. The possibility had been outside consideration. Simon had been loath to accept his brother was never coming back, but now it was time to accept it, to move past the denial that Michael had deserted him, this time for good.

The situation called for an off-hand remark, or the flash of a grin. Simon tried to smile, but failed. "Are there other empty graves?"

She regarded the cemetery at large with squinty eyes. "You know," she tapped her lip with a finger, "I'm not sure that there are. This is the only grave that's been left empty since I've been here."

"How long have you worked at the graveyard?"

"It's a cemetery. Graveyard sounds eerie, and it lacks dignity."

Simon arched a brow. "The word graveyard lacks *gravitas*?"

Chloe lifted a shoulder. "It makes a difference if your family is engaged in the cemetery business."

"I'll bet it was difficult for a girl of..." he asked the question again.

"I was six years old when we moved to Riverside."

A girl of six having to see the bodies of the dead? Simon studied his cigarette. This woman must have seen things he only knew from detective stories.

"I know what you're thinking, but the dead arrive here in coffins from the undertakers. We don't prepare the bodies."

Bodies.

He heard her tongue tap the roof of her mouth and land on the backs of her teeth. Simon's gaze fell without warning to her breasts. He snapped his eyes up again to a point over her shoulder and guffawed. She'd been talking about dead bodies, and he'd stolen a look at her breasts.

"You think dead bodies are funny?"

He inhaled on his cigarette and blew it out over his shoulder. He pressed his lips together and grimaced. He hoped it looked like a smile. "My apologies. I laugh when I'm nervous."

She nodded. "The Millers prepare the bodies of those being buried at Riverside, although I know many of them before they arrive. When they're alive, that is."

"You're accustomed to people dying then?" That fact tugged at him.

She bent and pulled a weed from between the tall stalks of grass at the edge of Michael's stone. "I suppose I am." Her hair fell and covered her face. She found more weeds and dropped to her knees. Her head tilted up as she regarded him with narrowed eyes. "Are you?"

He crushed the last of his cigarette beneath the toe of his shoe. "I've had some trouble getting used to it." It was all he could say. He couldn't explain the truth: he believed Michael was still alive. He felt it, and the feeling was sometimes so strong, he believed it. He'd heard laments of civil war veterans, amputees' complaints of the phantom pains of lost limbs. Simon recognized the feeling. He'd lost his twin, and the ache of his absence could be described just like that.

His brother dead?

Yes, he'd had some trouble getting used to it.

4

"I was at Michael's grave." Simon was seated in the Wolfe Castle library. Meredith Wells, soon to be the wife of the castle's owner, sat beside him, the long cushioned sofa upholstered in deep green velvet.

She looked up from her sketchbook. "What were you doing there?"

"I believe they call it visiting." Though there was no one there to visit. The absence of Michael's body should have been profound.

"What prompted that?"

"You. Wolfe. You and Wolfe together." After years of living on neighboring islands, and years more of living apart, Meredith and Wolfe had reunited. Simon had extended his summer season at the river for a fall wedding.

Meredith teased, "We drove you to visit with the dead?" His answering smile was slight, and she reached over and grabbed his hand. "I'm sorry, Simon. I shouldn't have joked."

Simon had done all that he could to bring Wolfe and Meredith together. The small exception was his offer of marriage, which Meredith had declined so promptly, the rejection had not even stung. Much.

He squeezed her hand and tossed it back to her skirts. "I'm fine." At her dubious glance, he repeated, "I've avoided saying good-bye for two years. It's time to move on." He flipped a page in the book resting in his lap, a handbook for travellers. He wasn't really looking at the maps. "I met a girl there."

"That would've been Chloe."

Simon pretended to study the lines intersecting the streets of Moscow. He dipped his face and brought the text closer. "You know her?"

"I know her well. My mother's buried there. I see Chloe sometimes when I *visit*." She grimaced at the word. "We were in school together for about a year, before she left to help her family with the grounds. We saw each other often when Michael..." Her voice trailed off. "They needed details for Michael's stone."

"I saw the boat." It was Michael's boat carved into the stone. The *Dreadnought*.

"You and I never discussed it, but your mother agreed that his boat was fitting."

He flipped a page. "You drew it." It wasn't a question.

"Her father's carving is exact."

"It is." He thumbed through the pages of the book until he found another map. He traced his finger over the coast of the Baltic Sea. "What's she like?"

Meredith's brow rose. "Chloe?" She didn't wait for his nod. "It's difficult to put into words. She is..." She hesitated.

"She's what?"

"Vague."

Simon's eyebrows lifted in humor. "You mean *vogue*?"

Meredith frowned, "I know the difference." She shook her head. "I mean vague."

Simon wanted to hear more, so he feigned interest in his book.

Meredith ran her hand over the fabric of the sofa, making a pattern in the pile. "I think we're good friends." She emphasized the word 'think,' her head tilting so that her braid lost its purchase on her shoulder and swung between them. "But we've never planned a thing, not a picnic, not a swim, not a walk in the woods. It's as though whenever we happen to spend time together, that's what we have." Meredith's brow furrowed. "There are no tomorrows with Chloe." Her palm ceased its play upon the velvet, then she grinned. "But when our paths do cross, we have *fun*."

Meredith's tone held indelicate promise, Simon's favorite kind. No tomorrows? He knew exactly the fun that could be had by ignoring consequence. Simon's mouth was open to press for details when the master of the house entered the room.

Wolfe was tall and dark. His ice blue eyes blazed at Simon. "Still trying to steal yourself a wife?" Wolfe's inflection, affected by his father's strong Russian accent, contained more than its usual menace. Wolfe and Simon had been friends since they were in short pants, and their houses while growing up shared the same block of Manhattan brownstones.

Simon extended his arm across the back of the sofa and angled toward Meredith. "My time's running out. I only have a week."

"Ten days." Meredith's smile was broad.

"Counting are you?"

"She's always counting something." Wolfe took the book from Simon's hand. "Get up." Simon unfolded himself and stood.

Wolfe sat on the sofa and drew Meredith onto his lap. He removed the sketchbook from her hands and tossed it to the seat beside them. "Your eyes are velvet green."

"Velvet is not green."

"This velvet then." His mouth chased hers for a kiss, pulling her red braid to lift her chin, but she drew back.

"Simon visited Michael today."

Simon browsed the book bindings at eye-level on a shelf, seeing none of them. After two years of avoiding Michael's grave, it was time. His friends' happily-ever-after gave him a hunger for his own ending, the desire to move on. The cemetery had been the place to start. He'd needed to see his brother's name set in stone.

Although he'd wanted closure, he hadn't realized that once he'd made up his mind, it would come so quickly. The obsessive focus on his absent brother had been diffused in an instant. He didn't care where the bastard was anymore.

The desire to know had been chased from him by something – someone – unexpected.

"I think I'll go back tomorrow."

Meredith and Wolfe exchanged glances. Wolfe nodded. "I haven't paid my respects. I'll go with you."

"Not necessary." Simon shook his head

"People miss him, Simon." Her voice was soft. "You're not alone in that."

Simon disagreed. It would've been difficult to feel more alone. At least, that's what it had been like, yesterday. Today, his mind nagged something new. He thought again about revisiting Riverside. "Perhaps I'll come by after."

"We'll be here." Meredith grimaced. "We can't go far, or Van Ogden will blow up the place." Meredith's home, Mosquito Island, a small island a tenth of a mile from where they now were, was scheduled for detonation in just over one week's time. It was to be the first of many islands removed from the river channel for an international seaway.

Simon's answering smile came fast, a quick flash. "Can't have that."

Wolfe's temper flared. "What kind of man blows up someone's home as though it were a firework?" Van Ogden needed a spectacle to launch the seaway project.

Meredith tapped his wrist. "I believe that was your idea."

Wolfe glared at the room in general. Although he'd built a bridge from his island – Wolfe Island – to Mosquito Island, Van Ogden still intended to blow it up, bridge and all.

Meredith stood from Wolfe's lap and approached the bookcase beside Simon. "Are you bringing anyone to the wedding?"

Wolfe shook his head and leaned back against the sofa. His hand rubbed the velvet. "Simon goes everywhere stag."

Meredith wrinkled her nose in confusion. "Stag?"

Simon shrugged. "Why bring a partner? It would be like shopping at a museum. If I saw something I liked, I wouldn't be able to carry it home."

She pinched his arm. "Please don't compare women to merchandise." To soften her words, Meredith lifted onto her toes and kissed his cheek. "If you see Chloe again, tell her hello for me."

5

"Now you're happy."

In the early morning, Harriet Blount crooned while she pinched her baby's toe between her thumb and forefinger. Her black hair was held back by a fetching pink ribbon but her brown eyes were rimmed dark with circles. They sunk too far into her face. She repeated the words as though the infant's full comprehension simply required repetition. "Now you're happy."

White curtains billowed into the room, pushed out from the screens by the breeze. It was a short walk to the shore of the lake. It used to be a short walk, that is. They used to take it often, until Chloe's arm was not enough to hold Hattie up. For the last several weeks, Chloe had to wheel Hattie over the grass, but she wouldn't be able to push the chair through the snow when it came. They'd have to find another way. Two thoughts came unbidden: snow in winter was inevitable, but Hattie's survival was not. Chloe tamped down dread and climbed onto her friend's bed.

She curled on her side, mirroring Hattie, with the baby nestled between them. The black flannel of Chloe's dress mingled with Hattie's pink dressing gown. Hattie always wore pink, refused in fact to wear any other color. When she was young, she had thrown fits until her mother had been obliged to make an entire wardrobe of the same hue. Triumphant, Hattie had never given the color up. This was agreeable to Chloe, because she never wore pink. With her white blond hair and fair skin, she would look like a ghost if she tried.

Chloe took hold of the baby's other foot and kissed his toes. "You were just hungry." Their croons held the same tone, and Chloe laughed. "I sound just like you."

"Just wait until you have your own."

Hattie had uttered the same words a hundred times, yet Chloe never offered a reply. What could she say? Hattie loved being a mother. It was clear motherhood brought her joy, but for Chloe, life was like walking on the edge of a knife.

On the one side was life in all its glory. Each morning, the wide river spoke with light and hundreds of islands, each with its own character. She walked amidst thick trees that blossomed beet red and pumpkin orange each year. Moss softened pink granite outcroppings in the center of deep woods, perfect for picnics and sun-warmed naps.

On the other side of that sharp blade was the certainty that life offered no promises. The cemetery included a sufficient number of tiny stones. It was a terrible truth, one Chloe would never share with a new mother.

Hattie filled Chloe's silence. "Thank you for bringing the goat's milk."

Chloe pressed the baby's foot to her cheek. "He loved it."

Hattie leaned back against her pillows. "He's the first I haven't been able to nurse."

Chloe returned the baby's foot to the mattress, and cupped her palm over his stomach, feeling the rise and fall of his breath. "Goat's milk is delicious. Eliza Preble's babies have only ever had goat's milk."

"She didn't want to nurse."

Chloe hedged, "Some women don't." The baby blinked slow eyes at Chloe. Chloe blinked back.

Hattie's face against the pillow looked tired. Of course new mothers were always tired, especially when they had other children, but Hattie hadn't looked this tired after the first two, or this pale. Dr. Reed said she wasn't bleeding, but it looked like Hattie had lost all the blood in her body.

"Have you heard from Daniel?" Daniel was on a freighter, a part of the ship's crew. He'd not been home since before baby Daniel's birth.

Hattie smiled. "Yesterday morning. His letter's beneath my pillow."

"If you keep hiding his letters there, you'll get a crick in your neck."

Hattie's smile left by degrees. "I worry about what the children will do without me. You're the only person I can talk to about this."

Chloe wanted to say aloud, *Don't make me.*

"It's a relief to have someone to talk to." Hattie traced the baby's eyebrow with the side of her thumb. "My mother can hardly look at me, and I have to pretend for the children." She moved to the arch of the second brow. "I'm glad I can be honest with you."

Chloe was tired, too. In fact, she was exhausted. She was tired of helping people say good-bye. She never wanted to do it again. The situation required a distraction.

"Did you know Michael had a brother?"

Hattie hummed her assent. "He's supposed to be the handsomest man in Manhattan."

Chloe laughed, although the rumor didn't stretch the truth overmuch. "I met him at the cemetery yesterday. He was visiting his brother's stone."

"Is he as good looking as they say he is?

"I never thought Michael was handsome."

Hattie poked Chloe's leg. "That's not what I asked."

Chloe shrugged. "They're supposed to be identical twins, but they don't look identical to me. For one thing, Michael's hair was long, but his brother's hair is cut close. Do you remember the color? It matches the shade of the grasses that grow beside the stones, the color of wheat."

Hattie's forehead smoothed as her eyebrows rose. "Is that right?"

"You can't imagine how awkward he is, in spite of his good looks. He threw a cigarette right onto Mrs. Vanderbelt's grave. Then he tried to be charming, but that only put me more on edge." Her entire body had tingled, and the tingling had been distracting.

"Did you tell him you knew Michael?"

"I mentioned it, but I didn't say outright that we were friends."

"He must know. You and Michael had been friends for years."

Chloe had first met Michael through her brother, Eric. About two years before he'd died, Chloe had seen Michael outside Eric's atelier. From the porch where she snapped peas, Chloe took in the lines of his denim trousers, and the blue knit of his cap. His shirt had metal buttons that glinted in the sun. He'd noticed her attention, but didn't smile. Eric continued to carve a stone inside while Michael had watched, unspeaking, against the door jamb.

Chloe shook her head. "He and his brother are summer people. You know they don't mix with us socially. Sometimes, I'd watch him play baseball on the green with Eric, but there was never much chance to talk when we were away from Riverside."

One day, he'd found her at the cemetery, and he'd brought her lunch: a yellow apple, bread, and a piece of chicken wrapped in paper, sent by Chloe's mother. Her mother sent him often after that. Chloe wasn't wont to chatter, so they'd practiced hitting squirrels with walnuts, and he helped her reset fallen stones. By the time he left with his family at the end of the season, she'd missed him. The last time she saw him, he'd brought her a metal button stamped with an anchor, pulled it out of his pocket as though he'd never seen it before in his life. She asked to see it, and he didn't ask for it back. At his funeral, she'd tossed it into his empty grave. She'd wanted something of him to be there.

Hattie pressed, "Simon hadn't heard of you?"

Chloe laughed. "I can't imagine Michael chattered about me to his brother. I'm sure they had other things to talk about."

"We do, too."

Chloe sobered. She knew what Hattie meant. She'd wanted to decide her epitaph since the doctor's last visit, but it was the last thing Chloe wanted to do. There were no words to describe Hattie Blount to the world if she wasn't in it. Chloe pushed herself up, careful not to roll the baby into the slope of the mattress, and rested her hands on both knees. "I propose we say something wicked."

Hattie's eyes twinkled through her fatigue. "You mean, instead of Wife, Mother, Daughter…"

Chloe bobbed her blond head once for emphasis. A lock fell forward into her face, and she tucked it behind her ear. "Harlot, Strumpet, Shrew." It was silly and macabre and absurd, and exactly what Hattie needed. Chloe's giddiness increased, too. She laughed in spite of herself. "I'm afraid, Hattie, that I'm longing to do something feckless." She'd denied herself *tomorrow* for so long, why not also shuck the responsibility of it?

"Feckless?" Hattie laughed.

Wouldn't it be luxurious to abandon consequence? "Irresponsible."

"Do it." Hattie's voice was stronger than it had been all morning.

The baby, who had just begun to doze, twitched, his arms and legs straightening and pulsing before falling again to the mattress. "Do it," she whispered again.

Chloe laughed. "Da won't carve *shrew* on your headstone."

"Let a man have his way with you."

Chloe's laughter turned into a cackle.

Hattie's voice was grave. "I'm not joking."

Chloe frowned to oblige.

"I thought perhaps with Michael…?" Hattie worked her finger into the baby's fist, then glanced to Chloe's face. "Now would be the time to tell me."

Chloe sat back onto the mattress and collected her legs in a knot. She watched little Daniel's lips purse as air passed between them. He'd already fallen asleep.

"It wasn't like that." She shook her head. "He helped me kill squirrels." At Hattie's laugh, Chloe laughed, too. "We'd wait for an hour to peg just one. He taught me to track them. I'd choose one and watch it, everywhere it went from tree to tree, until I was so attuned to it, I could feel the moment right before it came down. Then he'd peg it with a nut."

"That sounds like fun." Hattie closed her eyes, and a smile tickled the sides of her mouth. "I didn't think Michael Low could have fun."

Hattie wasn't being unkind. Michael hadn't made a habit of smiling; instead, he'd scowled, hunched and guarded. He'd been as hard as marble. But Chloe appreciated marble. She'd broken the stone often enough to know it was as vulnerable as anything else. She shrugged. "I suppose I got used to it."

Chloe listened to the sound of breathing and the tick-tick-tick of the clock. She thought Hattie had fallen asleep, until her weak voice broke the silence. "This time, do more than get used to it."

The tingling that Chloe had felt with Simon returned, a distracting tension that teased her. She whispered, "That sounds like a terrible idea."

Hattie's eyes didn't open. Without looking, she found Chloe's hand where it rested and worked her fingers into Chloe's fist just as she had with the baby's. She squeezed. "Do it."

6

"Damn. Damn damn *damn*."

The bicycle was too large for her. It looked like a hand-me-down from her brothers. Her skirts pooled over the frame, hands raised high on the handlebars. She stood on her tiptoes to avoid being divided in two by the crossbar. Rosamund LeFevre's gravestone lay in two pieces at her feet on the bike path.

"Problem?"

Her look was the picture of regret as she regarded him over her shoulder. She skipped out her foot, bouncing on the grass until she could swing a leg out over the large leather seat. She let the bicycle rest on its side in the grass and approached the white stone. She knelt beside it, picking up each flat slab until the two sides reunited, but with a hapless gap of landscape between them. "I broke another. Da is going to toss me in the river with marble strapped to each leg. "

Simon had spied her from the twin tree. When he'd approached it earlier, he'd realized that the two trees shared a single trunk. Fitting. He'd been leaning against it for an hour and a half. Now, he was pulling the fabric of his trousers away from his thighs before he realized he'd even gotten close. He crouched beside her. The toe of his shoe intruded on the hem of her skirt. "This isn't your first?"

"Not even my first this month."

He read the stone. "Miss LeFevre will not fault you."

"Mrs. She was seventy-seven."

He looked again. "That's a one. I thought it was a seven."

"It was a one." The crack was down the number's center.

"At least there isn't a string of biblical verse to be recarved."

Her eyes widened. "That's exactly what I was thinking. Though last time my father wasn't so lucky." She recited, "I am the first and the last. I am he that liveth, and was dead. Behold, I am alive for evermore. Amen."

"Even the Amen?"

"It took him three days. Each time."

"And this one?" He lifted one side off the ground.

She sighed. "A few hours."

"What happened?"

"I didn't balance it properly."

He'd seen her on her bike, lugging the enormous rock. He'd watched the bike bounce and waver, had witnessed her load falling to the ground. "Was it resting on your head?"

She laughed. "Across the handlebars."

"Don't most girls have baskets on their bicycles? For collecting flowers and baguettes?"

"Baguettes and flowers? You have a funny idea of how women spend their days."

He'd read too many magazines, chock full of advertisements. It was at one time a standard lament. His mother used to tease him over it, the stacks of popular magazines that towered beside his assigned chair in the sitting room, but it was a requirement of the job. Department store tycoon. He liked to call himself a tycoon, and he was, actually. Three department stores, his flagship in Manhattan set in the middle of the Ladies' Mile. It took up an entire block.

Flagship. It had been the name of his boat, but he wasn't a sailor anymore. He'd not gone in the water since the day he'd lost Michael in the storm.

"You need a basket. Or a wagon." He hefted up one of the broken halves, stifling a grunt. It was heavy. "How can you steer properly carrying stones across your handlebars?" A rhetorical question, as it was clear that she couldn't.

"Brute strength. I'm strong for a girl. My brother Eric tells me so all the time. Look." She lifted her arm and grabbed her cuff. She tugged it up a slender length of arm, then over her elbow. She flexed, and a small bicep swelled in a tight bunch. "Feel it."

Simon stilled. It was a pretty arm. Her skin was smooth and translucent. He thought of the silks on display across the floors of his fashion departments. *Diaphanous.*

She flexed again. "Go ahead. Touch it."

He shifted the marble to his hip. He didn't want to touch it, but he'd been compelled. His hand reached, hovered in the air between them. His fingers settled on the small, pale swell.

White. The connection was instantaneous. The feel of her skin was secondary to that brilliant, invading shock of awareness within him. He allowed her to course through him while his hand encircled her arm, bonding them together. The stone dropped from his hand and broke in half again.

"Oh, dear." Her voice was resigned.

He dropped his hand, and his gaze followed the path of marble that hit the ground at his feet.

Chloe readjusted her sleeve.

"I'll help you carry it." She couldn't balance three pieces on her handlebars now.

"Thank you. I'd leave it here and return later, but it would be…"

"Disrespectful."

"And sacrilegious." She smiled her apology.

He dipped to a crouch again and collected the three pieces of marble in his arms, piling the smaller two atop the half. The task gave him a few seconds to reflect.

He hadn't imagined it yesterday. It hadn't been a product of his melancholy mood, or nostalgia, or a heartfelt desire to commune with his brother. It had been her. He regarded the toe of her boot where it appeared from beneath the hem of her skirt. If he touched her there…?

"Can you carry it?"

"If you can, I can." He lifted himself from the ground, holding the slabs against his abdomen. They were heavy. "How far are we going?"

"To the Lake." She righted her bicycle.

The Lake of the Isles. He'd been there many times. Though the channel was better for sailing, the lake was a magical place. He shifted the stones to rest more comfortably against him.

Less than a half mile, the path to the Lake was worn. Grass was matted and rutted as though a carriage had passed innumerable times.

Simon realized why. "The dead are brought this way?"

"Everyone comes this way." Chloe's nose scrunched in question. "Do you think it's gruesome?"

"Everybody dies."

"But not everyone is tasked with what's left behind when they do."

A breeze blew her hair to one side. Bright blond strands tickled his knuckles. He took a single step away, outside the reach of the wind, avoided the whip of her hair as though it were a lashing. She stopped, and he was compelled to stop, too. He felt a quick stab of dread. Did she know that the touch of her hair left him without breath, shocked the air from his lungs in a whoosh?

He risked a look. She wasn't paying attention to him at all. He followed her gaze. A female mallard duck had approached the lane and was preparing to cross. A brood of ducklings formed a neat row behind her. Their quacks overlapped like echoes. Chloe explained, "Her first hatchlings died."

The mother reached the middle of the lane, and two small brown ducklings waddled behind, over and down the matted grass. Two more ducklings followed, separating themselves with an exacting distance. It was a slow crossing. The mother hen was not in any hurry, and the ducklings followed her lead.

There was no place for Simon to be. Judah, his man of business, was in charge of the stores while Simon placed orders from his room at the Hotel Columbian. He had no social engagements. Most of his set had returned to the city and weren't coming back until Wolfe's wedding. Simon could watch ducks too, all day if it pleased him, and something about it pleased him. She pleased him. "What happened to the ducklings?"

"I don't know. One day, she had seven. The next day, they were gone." The ducklings made their way across the path. The light breeze played with their downy feathers and the straight blond locks of her hair. A vehement gust blew Simon's own, then let it settle.

She looked at him sideways, kept half her attention on the ducklings. "I confess, you gave me a thrill yesterday when I saw you."

"You thought I was Michael." It wasn't a question.

Chloe offered Simon a self-deprecating smile. "Just for a minute. Although I wouldn't have been surprised. He was the type to haunt a cemetery."

"You knew him well?" There was so much of his brother's life he didn't know.

Her head tilted, "Not that well. At least, I'd never thought I knew him well, when he was alive. Once he'd gone, honestly, I stopped myself from thinking of him at all." She met Simon's eyes for the briefest moment before she returned her gaze to the ducklings. "It would've been nice to see him again, to tell him how sorry I've been that he's gone."

Simon grinned, unsettled by the idea that she might prefer Michael. "I'm sorry to have disappointed you."

"You know, you two look nothing alike."

His incredulity dislodged the smile. Whenever Simon had looked at his brother, he'd seen himself.

"And it's not just your hair."

Michael's hair had been wont to cover his forehead and fall into his eyes. He'd allowed a longer time between shearings. Simon kept his more closely cropped.

Chloe continued, "You're far from identical."

They both had square jaws, defined cheeks, and noses that angled down with hawk-like slants.

"Michael was severe, masculine." She curved her arms and tightened her chest like a strongman at a circus. Then she smiled at him in a way that was designed for nothing but her own amusement. "But, you, you're so handsome, you're almost pretty."

Simon let his mind ferment her words. He almost liked the sound of them. He didn't remember a time when he'd just held his tongue and listened. He relied on his wit, banter that skipped like a stone, but now he kept silent, wanted to watch the stone sink. He wanted to hear every word she said, even if it was to call him pretty.

She teased him further. "And Michael would never have worn that." She waved a hand that took in his clothes, a light-colored suit, a shade darker than his hair, and a white collared shirt without a tie. His trousers had a grass stain at the knee. He was missing a waistcoat. He'd shunned that layer because high society had already abandoned the island for the season. Even without the waistcoat, his dress was impeccable, but she was right, of course. Michael would never have been found, alive or dead, in Simon's clothes. His brother's wardrobe had tended toward sailors' trousers of dark, riveted denim and heavy cotton shirts. Michael wasn't seen without his wool cap, either atop his head or spinning in his hands. He looked like the men who unloaded the freighters at the docks in Denton.

"Would you tell me what happened? Do you mind that I ask?" Her tone was no longer teasing.

He sat longer with her words this time. Michael's loss was not a story he told. He moved the stones again to his hip. His eyes remained trained on the ducks, their brown feathers and tiny beaks, the small webbed feet that lifted and fell on the grass. He spoke before he'd decided what he wanted to say. "The annual islands skiff race had been the day before. It was close, but I took second." For two years, he'd felt the regret of that loss. "Michael won."

"You were competitors."

"We were good sailors." They'd sailed the skiff race on the river every summer for years, one of the few things they'd done together. He wished he could pull a cigarette from his pocket, but the stones prevented him. "The next day, the wind was strong, so I challenged him to a rematch. We left Grindstone at ten, right after breakfast."

"Your home was on Grindstone."

Whether Chloe had known where his family had summered or not, he couldn't tell, but her sentence was a lure. He nodded. It was one of the largest islands in the region. They didn't own it, like Wolfe did, but they owned one of its several houses. His mother still lived there, although Simon hadn't been back for two years. He preferred to spend time with his mother on Grandview than to revisit his home. "No one was on the river. Not a sail, not a soul. It was so odd." Even that morning he'd noted the strange emptiness of the water. Only now, after, did he recognize it as foreboding. "The wind took us far and fast. We'd circled Three Sisters Island and were halfway back when the wind stopped. But it was more than just a loss of wind. It was a loss of air. Suddenly it was hard to breathe." He remembered how he'd struggled to catch breath in his lungs. "I heard Michael laugh. Then he said my name." It had carried over the water, sharp and clear. The laugh haunted him now.

"The sky turned, out of nowhere." He'd never before seen a green he could call black. "The squall came down from the sky." Down. Not from any other direction. "We fought it. A few minutes at most. It broke Michael's mast in half. Then it broke mine. We were both tipped in under a minute." The water was white-capped, but swimmable. He hadn't been scared; they'd been in sight of land. Then everything went black.

"The next thing I remember is being pulled to shore. It was Meredith Wells. She'd been caught on Bloody Point. She says she saw me bobbing, then watched me go down. She never saw Michael. Says she never even saw him." It was as though the River cast a dark spell, turned enemy on Simon, her most devout.

The last duckling had reached and scaled the shore of the lane. Simon began walking again. Chloe followed, and caught up. Her skirts billowed around her legs.

"It bothers you that you didn't see him go under."

He hadn't seen his brother go down, hadn't been aware that he was going anywhere at all. It was the thought that chased him every day. Chloe had put her finger on it, on the very image his mind lacked, required, but could not obtain.

They walked in silence for a quarter mile. He was glad she didn't question him further. He'd given her every answer he had about that day. The only knowledge he'd withheld was that the moment he'd blacked out, that was the moment his brother had gone, the moment they'd been separated. He knew it but could not explain to her why without explaining…everything. He wasn't prepared. He didn't expect that he ever would be.

A cottage appeared in the distance. It was simple slats of wood, unpainted and weathered to a watery grey. After a few minutes more, she slowed and gestured to a thick tree.

"Just put them here." She smiled. "I'll break it to my Da gently."

"No pun intended." They spoke the words together.

Damn, he liked her smile. And damn if it didn't feel good to be close to her, even in the face of what she'd asked, and what he'd shared.

There was no graver topic than his brother's absence, that storm, yet he wanted to kiss her with a ferocity that surprised him. All he could do was watch the wind whip her hair and tease her lips until she pulled the strands and tucked them away.

He set the slabs against the trunk and stood, brushing grit from the marble against the fabric of his thighs.

"Well. Goodbye, then." His hand wavered before lifting, extending. He leaned from where he stood, a few feet away, his body at an angle that made the gesture awkward.

She had to let her bike drop a foot toward the ground to shake his offered hand without letting it go. "You could come to the house for lunch. Or tea. Do you drink tea?"

He was prepared this time, no longer doubtful that the feeling would return. And it did. Sexual desire pulsed through him, reached his loins in the span of a heartbeat. Fuck. He released her hand, and she tipped. Her bike fell.

Simon murmured an apology, turned and left, willing himself not to run.

7

"How many bulbs have you got there?"

Chloe started with a palm to her heart. She laughed when she saw who it was. "You have quiet feet."

Meredith rested a hand on Chloe's shoulder. "I would've thought you'd be used to people sneaking up on you." Her long red braid swung between her shoulder and the pail. "I start to hush and tiptoe the minute I walk through the gate. Doesn't everyone?"

Chloe recalled the shock of seeing Simon as he wandered through the stones. "I don't know what people sound like before they get here. They might be really loud." She yelled the last word to make her point carry.

"I see your point."

Chloe laughed and patted the grass beside her. "I haven't seen you here in awhile."

Meredith sat, turning her skirts into a blanket. She wore a blue dress the color of a robin's egg. Her brown leather boots shone with polish.

"I've been busy."

Meredith and Chloe exchanged a smile. Meredith's was sheepish. "Wolfe has returned." Wolfe had disappeared from the River five years before.

Chloe's smile was full of mischief. "I gather he remembered you." Chloe squeezed Meredith around the shoulders. "I promise I won't press for details."

"You must be busy, too. I haven't seen you at the water in ages." Meredith leaned in and lowered her voice. "Not since the time we ended up in Wolfe's library and found that book."

Chloe made a sound and covered her face. Chloe visited Meredith on Wolfe Island in the winter when the ice froze the river and she could walk across. Wolfe's library with a fire raging was their favorite haunt. One day, they found evidence that young Wolfe liked to spend time there, too. "Did Tristan ever tell you whose book that was?" The picture book they'd uncovered had been more than suggestive.

"I haven't asked, but I'm sure it was his."

"Beneath the sofa cushion is not the best hiding place."

Meredith smirked. "It might have been, had there not been two girls in the room."

Chloe laughed. "My brothers get nothing past me, either."

Their laughter faded. Chloe traced the dirt with her trowel. Meredith turned over the bulbs in Chloe's pail. "You've got at least two hundred in here."

Chloe used the back of her wrist to scratch an itch on her forehead. "Once I finish this lot, I have another two hundred to go."

Meredith scanned the cemetery lawn, her gaze moving from patch to patch of turned up dirt. "How many have you planted so far?"

Chloe held up her hands. Her slender fingers were caked with dirt. "Six hundred. Give or take."

Meredith rooted through the bucket and chose a tight smooth bulb. "Did you know that in some climates, tulips aren't perennials?" She rolled it between her palms, rubbed its smoothness against her cheek, then sniffed at the root.

Chloe blanched. "But they are here? Meredith, don't tell me I've planted hundreds of bulbs, and they won't come back."

Meredith squeezed her friend's dirty hand. "Here, they'll come back, every year."

"Until the first June frost," Chloe qualified.

Meredith laughed. "That those words can even be spoken together makes me shudder." She bounded the bulb in her palm, distracted for several moments, until she ventured, "You've met Simon."

Not only had she met him, but for the last two days, Chloe had noted Simon's absence. She wouldn't say she'd missed him, but the days had seemed emptier without him. She admitted, "He reminds me of Michael."

Meredith smiled. "They were twins."

"They're identical, but they also seem altogether different." Chloe explained, "Michael's face guarded his feelings. He was such a stoic, but the emotion on Simon's face has full play."

Meredith tugged at Chloe's skirt. "It sounds like you have a preference."

Chloe batted Meredith's hand away in a teasing gesture. "He is handsome. I'll give you that." Chloe preferred Simon's looks to Michael's, but she refused to admit that to her friend. Instead she hedged, "I dropped Mrs. Lefevre's stone because of him. I noticed him watching me, and the marble hit the ground. Handsome men fluster me." She turned up a fresh pile of dirt.

Meredith laughed. "Let's hope so." She threw the bulb in an awkward pitch over her head and hit the trunk of a nearby tree. "It seems odd that you hadn't met before, odd that none of us had met Simon before..."

She trailed off, meaning *before Michael had died*, but not knowing how to say the words. Everyone had trouble saying the words. The actual word – *died* – everyone avoided. Chloe shared, "He told me about the day we lost Michael. I wasn't sure I wanted to hear, but I asked anyway."

"He told you? That surprises me. We've never talked about it, and it's been two years." Meredith narrowed her eyes. "I remember parts of it so vividly, and parts of it none at all. I know that when I reached him, he didn't want to come back, not at first, but he knew it was useless. He would've killed me, too. I couldn't have left him out there. I wouldn't have swum back alone.

Chloe dropped a bulb into a low hole, heaped in earth and pressed the mound of dirt flat.

Meredith continued, "I'll never forget the look in his eyes. There was nothing there. He was looking for Michael, but expecting nothing." Meredith shrugged. "He already knew Michael was gone."

Chloe felt the familiar ache. It was impossible for her to imagine someone else's grief and not have the feeling stick, become a part of her. She remembered how he told the story of the storm, his discomfort laid bare. "He still doesn't believe it's true."

Meredith leaned back on her hands. "I remember when my mother died." The clouds traveled past. "I expected her to come back, out of habit, to come to my room and tuck me in.

Sometimes the expectation turned into something more real, like I was waiting for something that could actually happen."

"It would make the cemetery a much more interesting place if it did."

Meredith tossed her bulb into Chloe's skirts with a laugh. "How is that funny?"

Chloe shrugged, smiling, too.

"You always make me smile, so I've come to ask you to the wedding. Our wedding. Mine and Wolfe's."

Chloe considered it. She'd decided before that the people she met here, at Riverside, would be enough for her. They were already dying, and she knew it. She was prepared for their absence. It was her job to prepare them.

The living were a different matter.

At Chloe's dubious glance, Meredith encouraged, "There will be fireworks, and I need you at the ceremony. It's going to be small. I want a few more people there to remind me it's really happening."

Meredith phrased her invitation in just the right way. Meredith needed Chloe because her mother had died. Chloe couldn't turn her back on that kind of need. Her decision was made before she realized it.

"Of course I'll come." Her brother Eric could bring her, though he'd harangue her about it. His suit was the one he wore to burials when he served as a pallbearer. He hated to put it on outside of that. Hated to put it on, period.

Meredith read her mind. "You can bring a guest. I wouldn't expect you to arrive alone with so many of Wolfe's friends there. City people can be daunting. I'm sorry I didn't invite you sooner." She made a face. "I've been a bit scattered."

Chloe took Meredith's hand, in spite of the dirt. "I'm glad you've asked me."

Meredith stood. "I'm glad you've agreed to come."

Chloe looked up. "Where will it be?"

"Come to the main Pavilion dock. Wolfe has promised a surprise."

Chloe watched Meredith leave by the route that would walk her past her mother's grave.

Meredith's mother was one of the first people to be buried after the Swanns had taken over management of the cemetery.

Chloe's mother had warned her that mothers die. She'd said this as Chloe had complained about having her braids brushed out. Whether it was the yanks in her hair or the sight of Meredith with her father by the grave, it was a lesson Chloe remembered.

Sometimes it felt like her entire life was linked with one grieving person or another. Everyone Chloe knew had lost someone, or was in the process. She couldn't imagine taking the risk that Meredith and Wolfe did now. Really, it wasn't a risk at all. Risk meant some hope of winning, but there was no hope of that. No matter how much you loved someone, they'd be taken away soon enough. And the more you loved them, the worse off you'd be. She'd witnessed the wreckage of the people who were left behind. She would've preferred to prepare the bodies.

She plucked a piece of grass and set it between the edges of her thumbs, wetting the blade with her tongue before blowing hard enough to make a tortured sound. She wasn't sure if it was a squeak or a quack. Whatever it was, it chased away the squirrels. Two scurried up a red oak.

A wedding. Although her instincts had told her to say 'no', it was impossible now not to be excited by the prospect.

Chloe eyed the tree where the squirrels now sat. One held a plump bulb between its paws.

She'd promised Hattie she'd do something dramatic, something stimulating, a story she'd tell to distract them both. Well, here it was: a single day to forget about worrying who would or wouldn't be around tomorrow.

She let her chin rest on her hand, an elbow propped on her thigh. She couldn't bring Eric. Her brother would be a constant reminder of everything she wanted to forget. The image of Simon's face floated through her mind like a ghost. She straightened her spine and blew hard into her cupped hands. The grass squawked, chasing the image away.

8

He felt like a fool, must have looked like a fool, his hands in his trouser pockets, shifting from one foot to another, unable to stand still as she approached.

He'd spent two days away. Building her a damned bicycle cart was the only effective distraction to keep him from Riverside. He'd enlisted the help of the men at Wolfe's yacht house, given them pictures of what he thought might work. It had turned out better than he'd expected. He was proud of the engineering, even when they'd explained that his drawing wouldn't allow the bicycle to turn right or left. They'd adjusted his design, and there'd been a wood-worker in the bunch who'd carved flowers across the sides. A hinged door on the rear opened and would hold longer stones. He'd asked the man to carve her name in the side. *Chloe.* It was idiocy. He felt like an idiot.

She stopped in front of him, a few feet away, her eyes moving from the cart to him, twice without speaking.

"You can strap it to a bicycle. Any bicycle, really. It will work on any bicycle."

She wore a hard woven basket strapped to her back. "It has my name on it."

"Your bicycle," he faltered, "you can strap it to your bicycle. If you like." His art of conversation had left him. Utterly.

"Are those impatiens?"

Impatience? That sounded right.

She knelt by the cart and traced the petals of one flower. "Or daisies?"

He was ignorant of the type of flower the man had carved. The type with petals.

"I like them both." She looked up at him from her knees, tucking her hair behind one ear. The gesture had already grown familiar to him. Her bicycle lay in the grass. She swung the basket from her back and placed it on the ground at her feet. She withdrew a headstone, smaller than the one she'd broken a few days before. She placed it in the cart. It lay in the center, with plenty of room to spare on each side.

It looked ridiculous.

He felt his face grow hot. For the love of God, he was blushing.

Her smile was wide. She liked it. He hoped that she liked it and was not laughing at him. Although he might have respected her more had she indeed been laughing at him.

"Will you show me how it works?"

She righted her bicycle and positioned it in front of the cart while he strapped the leather to the frame. "It should be a metal frame that connects them, but I couldn't find a welder."

She pulled the bicycle along the grass, and the carved wooden box followed. He rubbed the back of his neck, then gestured toward the cart, mute.

"Shall I see how fast it'll go?"

"Please don't."

She laughed. "You lack confidence."

"I lack quite a lot of things, but I've never before been told that confidence is one of them."

"I mean you lack confidence in the cart. Come on."

"Fine." He relented. "But I don't want to be the cause of another broken headstone." He removed the stone from where it mocked him.

She kicked her skirts over the frame. "Tell me when."

"On your mark."

She pushed off the grass and started pedaling.

He called after her, "I suppose that was *when*." After a wobble, she gained speed. The fabric of her skirt was pulled tight beneath her seat, and Simon's gaze followed that point while she bumped across the lawn, off the path, between the markers, the cart at a clip behind her, bouncing too.

Her twists and turns between the headstones were designed to test its limits. Each time she cleared a stone without incident brought a small shriek of delight, and each squeal was followed by laughter, more and more laughter. Her laughter was infectious. It bubbled up within him, impossible to control.

The sound of his own laughter had become foreign to him. Was it funny? He wasn't sure, but it felt good to watch her bicycle weave in and out of headstones like a child around the trees, good enough to laugh.

A sharp turn caught the cart. Simon felt the foreboding before he saw her fall. In that moment between the suspicion that the bicycle would topple and the surety that she would, his legs moved. He snaked the stones, jumped over them, knowing as he did so that she was all right. She was all right. She hadn't hurt herself. She was fine.

"My skirt is just caught." She looked up from the ground.

He pushed her fingers aside with the back of his hand, and worked the fabric from between the chain and the sprocket. The skirt came free with a smear of grease. He pulled a handkerchief from his coat and worked the stain.

"Don't rub. Dab." She leaned over his hand. "That will never come out without water."

He dabbed, pretending to give a damn about the stain he was fast making worse, unable to release his grip on her skirt.

"Leave it. I'll soak it tonight." She peered over his shoulder at the toppled cart. "I hope I didn't break it." She watched his efforts for a moment longer before she leaned on her arms, then back fully on the lawn. "I haven't done that in ages."

He still held her skirt, felt the thick, soft fabric between his fingers. It was cotton flannel. He recognized it from the clothing he sold at the store. Warm, easy to launder. Soft to the touch. "You've done this before?" He kept his eyes on her skirt, finding purple flecks in the heathered gray.

"My brother taught me to ride here. He made me go in and out of the stones, faster and faster." She closed her eyes to the sun. "I loved it."

Her hair was a bright halo around her head against the grass. "Why did you stop?"

"Why do we stop doing anything that we love?"

It was a good question. Now that her eyes were closed, he could take a full inventory. Until now, he'd been afraid, as though a look head-on would blind him. Like looking into the sun.

Her lips curved, contented. Her eyebrows, only a bit darker than her hair, relaxed high on her forehead. He tracked the lines of her cheekbones where they dipped beneath full eyelashes, to the small slope of her nose and the square lines of her chin, softened by a shallow dimple. He followed her jawline to where it curved into her neck. He spent an additional moment regarding her lovely neck. The short standing collar of her white cotton blouse had fallen open at the sides. He wondered at her name. Swann. Perhaps all the women in her family had long, graceful, exceptionally lovely necks.

His gaze travelled lower to where the fitted bodice of her blouse swelled across her breasts. Round and firm, he imagined them in his hands as he fingered soft flannel. Her chest rose and fell with her breathing. He watched the rise and fall. He dragged his knuckles across her skirt, pretended it was across her breasts, right at their peaks where he would find her nipples. His mouth was dry. He wet his lips with his tongue.

Move your eyes, Simon. Move them.

They wouldn't move. It took a half-minute more before he returned his gaze to her face. Damn. Her eyes were open. He'd been caught red-handed. Red-faced was more apt. He was blushing again. How was it possible that he was blushing? He was the rogue. In truth, he was an utter scoundrel. A scandal. And she was...not.

She should at least understand that when a man's gaze remains trained on your breasts that he is thinking untoward thoughts. She clearly didn't understand the direction of untoward.

He had to say something.

"You remind me of a woman I saw in a magazine once."

She sat up, curious. Her skirt pulled from Simon's fingers. It draped across her knees. Only the toes of her boots showed beneath the hem.

It was Botticelli's Venus, and he'd seen the painting at the Uffizi in Florence, but he couldn't very well tell her that. Not after she'd caught him staring at her breasts. She'd think he was trying to seduce her. The idea gave him a thrill of pleasure and dread. But she did remind him of that painting. She looked like the Goddess of Love, minus the clamshell and the red hair. "I think it was a soap advertisement." She blinked, and he held up her skirt. "I was thinking about soap." She lay back in the grass, and her eyes shut again. Before he could stop them, the words were out. "Do you have a beau?" Damn, he winced. He'd just told her outright that he'd not been thinking about soap.

Chloe opened one eye against the sun. "You don't spend much time with the locals, do you?"

Simon shook his head.

She continued in explanation, "I have a reputation."

Simon snorted. So did he.

Her other eye opened at the sound. "Men are put off by the idea of…" She lifted her arm from the ground beside her and waved her hand above her. She trailed off and shut her eyes again.

Simon had an idea what she meant. Her brother was a colossus, and an unfriendly one at that. Any man who showed a bit of interest in Chloe would've been risking his life. He looked over his shoulder.

A sigh lifted her chest, strained it against the cotton. "I suppose I've not gone looking."

Simon's ears pricked. "You don't want a beau?"

"What's the point?"

He studied her lips, full and smooth and pink. "Marriage? A family?"

Chloe's face wrinkled like a prune. She shook her head once in the grass. "Love is a nightmare."

Simon laughed at her face and her words, peculiar for the women he'd known. "You're more cynical than I am."

"Are you cynical?"

He'd been cynical, but he wasn't anymore.

When he didn't answer, she continued, made an argument against her closed lids. "I'm practical. Why start something guaranteed to end?"

He nodded, straight-faced. She was teasing. All women wanted love affairs. The conversation was mere banter. "No love for you." He played along.

"Not if I can help it." She opened one eye and surveyed him. "Can I tell you a story?"

"Please."

Her eye closed again. "I never met my grandfather. He died before I was born. He died before even my mother was born. Mamere, my grandmother, never remarried." The one eye opened again. "We spent a lot of time at the cemetery in Oostend where we lived before." The eye closed.

Simon stopped caring that each time her eye opened, she found his gaze on her face, her neck, everywhere.

"I still remember his headstone. It's the first headstone I remember reading, and it haunts me."

"What did it say?"

"It said, *You inside me, me inside you.* I was never sure what it meant." Her head cocked in the grass. Both eyes opened. "Do you think it's dirty?"

Simon blinked. "I don't think your grandparents…"

Chloe laughed, "I was never sure. They were close. She lost him so young, almost her entire life was spent missing him." She shrugged. "That's no way to live."

Simon was taken aback. She didn't want a beau. She wasn't teasing him at all. It should have been refreshing to meet a woman who wasn't trying to marry him. He'd spent the entirety of his adult life avoiding the kind of woman who wanted marriage, but he found the news unsettling. The minutes ticked by in silence. Simon wondered if she'd fallen asleep.

Finally, she said, "You know Meredith."

He wasn't sure if it was a statement or a question. He waited again, but when she said nothing more, he offered, "Meredith and I met after Michael..." He struggled with the next word. "Left."

She pushed herself up to sit beside him. With her legs crossed, the tips of their knees touched. Chloe took his hand before he could prevent it. He felt the energy pulse between their fingers and made his hand be still in hers.

"Everybody dies, Simon."

He studied the point where their fingers twined, surprised that the electricity he felt wasn't visible, like the path of lightning to a key. "I'll take your word for it."

"Can I ask you something?"

Simon nodded.

"Did you get along with your brother?"

He could tell her the truth. In fact, he already had, in a way; but he could be clearer. He could clarify. Here was an opening. Simon loosened his grip on her fingers. The muscles in his hand twitched from the undertaking.

"You don't have to tell me." Chloe released his hand and tucked her skirt around her legs. She rested her chin on her raised knees.

He exhaled in resignation. "Did we get along? Sometimes. If we shared a goal, we worked well together." That his brother had vanished was ample evidence that, in fact, they shared very little, least of all a goal. His brother's disappearance was just another way Michael had proven the distance between them.

What was there to say? He wracked his brain for any goal he and his brother had shared. "We shared a room when we summered on Grindstone. My mother would make us clean it before we could go sailing. We would clean it quickly." And silently, Simon omitted.

"Did you ever argue?"

Simon played with the hem of her skirt, lost in the memory of the last time he spoke to Michael, the morning of the storm. "No." They didn't argue. It wasn't a lie, outright, nor was it the truth.

She encouraged, "You were close, allies."

"I'm afraid it wasn't like that at all." Simon would never say they were close. "Michael wanted very little to do with me." Simon was never sure why.

"You can't believe your brother didn't love you."

Simon blinked. "I don't know that my brother loves anyone." Simon wasn't sure Michael was capable of it.

Chloe studied him. A squirrel nosed out from behind a stone, and she scoured the ground for a nut. She gave up her search and returned her attention to Simon. He tried to hide his frown but wasn't quick enough.

She leaned forward and covered his hand where it rested on his knee. He studied the slender length of her fingers, absorbed until she spoke. "It sounds like you didn't know him very well."

The words were meant to be comforting, but they were far from it. They confirmed what he'd always known. He didn't know his brother at all.

9

Chloe carried the ironstone bowl to the table and set it in the center. The stew was hot and tomato-based, which meant it would stain. A skirt was already soaking.

"Careful, careful!" Her mother tapped the hands of her brothers away, and took up the ladle. Her eyes fixed on the bowl, she asked, "Chloe, did you look in on Harriet Blount?"

Chloe winced. She knew what was coming next. "We have plans to see one another first thing tomorrow."

"You should've done it today. She doesn't have much time left."

Her mother wasn't deliberately being unkind, but the words pinched a place in Chloe's chest. She shook her head. "Hattie's fine. She looked better when I saw her yesterday."

Her mother gestured with the ladle, and drops of stew landed on the linen table runner. "I heard that the Dooleys have been visiting her. They don't waste time on healthy people."

The Dooleys managed the cemetery in Denton, the closest mainland town. Chloe removed the runner from beneath the serving bowl and folded it onto her lap.

Her brother Josef agreed. "The Dooleys had a load of pink marble delivered last week. *Pink marble.* Until we have cash in hand, the Dooleys can scoop her up."

Chloe bit her tongue. She had an uncommon knack for attracting the friendship of the sick and the dying up and down the river. Her friendship was often all that was required to secure commitment for a headstone at Riverside Cemetery. Chloe remembered with shame that she'd told Simon she *brought in the people.* Oh, of all things, why had she said it like that? It did sound sinister. In fact, it sounded like her mother. *Bring them in, Chloe.*

Chloe brought them in. But Hattie Blount was her oldest friend and the mother of three young children, and she was not dying.

Her father saved her from a conversation she didn't want to have. "You should see what Eric carved today. He's already better than I'll ever be."

Her eldest brother shook his head. "Not true."

After ladling stew in her father's bowl, her mother started down the family line. Her oldest brother was next. Relieved for the distraction, Chloe asked, "What were you working on?"

"The Frederik stone."

It was to be a twenty-foot tall obelisk, with each family member's plot fanning out in a cross. None had passed yet, but the stone would be set where they wanted to be buried when it happened, and her mother would wait with anticipation until that time came.

Chloe hated talk of business. To her, they were people, friends. She felt a connection to each and every one.

Josef teased her. "Don't worry. We won't ask you to carry it."

Jude agreed. "From now on you should stick to the little stones. Marble is too heavy for a girl."

Her mother nodded. "I agree. We could use another man around." She looked across the table at her eldest brother. "Eric."

Chloe's mother said her brother's name in a tone that let Chloe know what was coming next

"Why don't you bring your friends to the house anymore?"

It had been two years since Eric had introduced a friend to the family. Not since Michael had they met any of Eric's friends. Their mother had done her best to direct Michael's pursuit, but it hadn't ended well. In spite of past misfortune, according to her mother, it was time Chloe had a beau. So, dinner had, of late, begun with her mother's supplication to Chloe's eldest brother.

"Baseball has started up again," her mother continued. Two teams of men converged on the green where the Grandview Island Hotel used to be, and where a new hotel – The Columbian – had just been erected. "That means *dozens of men*!" Her mother's words were a high-pitched lament. "If you brought more young men around, one might court Chloe." She swept the butter across a hard roll with a long, blunt knife. "Death is good business, but it could be better." Her last words were punctuated with thrusts of her blade.

Eric remained silent throughout his mother's exhortation. He seemed reluctant to engage his friends in romantic pursuit of his only sister.

Chloe's younger brothers snickered. Her mother turned to them, each in turn. "Why are you laughing? What is it?"

Chloe waited for their explanation with not a small amount of dread.

Jude looked at Josef, his eyebrows raising and lowering in encouragement, and Josef grinned, almost embarrassed, but not enough to hold back the words. "They're frightened of her."

Josef nodded. His lips curled with mischief. "They're spooked."

Eric shook his head with a scowl. "They're not frightened of her."

Her mother's knife jabbed across the table, a yellow dollop of butter threatening the cloth beneath. "Who's frightened?"

Chloe was, a bit, while she watched her mother's knife jab. Linen steeped in butter meant three consecutive afternoons of soaking.

Jude's chin jerked at his sister. He spoke through the dinner in his mouth. "They say she's the Angel of Death."

Josef's fingers waggled in mock terror. He echoed Jude's words with a sing-song warble, "Angel of Death."

Silence ensued. Superstition and reality collided at the dinner table, and that, as they say, was the end of that.

Chloe had at first been astonished by the revelation, and more than a little vexed. It wasn't her fault that most people she met died soon after. They were dying *before* she met them. That was the point.

The sick on the island all asked for her now. The minute they had a hint of their own demise, they asked for Chloe, as though she were a gatekeeper of heaven itself.

Angel of Death. Chloe didn't feel comfortable referring to herself in such a grandiose way, but she was reminded of her nickname when the situation fit. When, for example, she was planning the murder of hungry squirrels. Or when she was accused of sounding sinister.

She hadn't wanted to tell this to Simon Low, not at their introduction. He was the first man she'd been alone with since Michael had gone. Whatever the reason, she didn't want to chase him away, but it was only the first of two things she was glad she'd been able to keep to herself.

The second? The second was worse.

Yes, she'd known Simon's brother. Known Michael Low well enough to like him. He'd been one of the only people she'd befriended without death hanging between them.

Then he'd died.

Chloe bit her lip. "I actually had some help today. Eric, you might know him." He raised his eyebrows at her, inviting her to continue. His hands rested on either side of his bowl. "Simon Low." When he didn't respond, she continued. "Michael's brother."

Jude and Josef were already eating when Chloe returned her full plate to the space before her. At the name, they stopped. "Simon Low?" Jude asked, his eyes fixed on hers.

"*The* Simon Low?" Josef had the words out before Jude had even finished.

"Yes, Michael's twin."

Eric shook his head. "That's not what they mean, Chloe."

Her mother held her spoon above her plate. "He's rich, isn't he?"

"I don't know." Chloe looked from her mother to her eldest brother beside her. "Is he?"

Eric nodded, solemn. "Very."

Across the table, Jude exchanged a glance with Josef. "He's not just rich. He's notorious."

"Notorious?" Chloe frowned. "What's that supposed to mean?"

It was her father who answered. "He's a man of ill repute." The words were formed to fit the space of time between the bowl and his mouth.

"I know what 'notorious' means, Da. But why?"

"He loves women." Jude grinned.

Josef nodded. "And women love him back."

Chloe was incredulous. "Simon Low is a *ladies' man*?" She felt another inexplicable pinch in her chest.

Eric regarded her. "You sound surprised."

Surprised was not the word. She was dumbfounded. "He's the most awkward man I've ever met."

"So you've met a lot of men, have you?" Jude teased.

"Don't be coarse," Eric admonished. Her elder brother by five years, Eric ruled her brothers with an iron fist. Their father hadn't the knack for discipline. He turned to Chloe. "Simon Low has a reputation."

"Whispers and titters."

"What?" She turned back to her brothers, close enough in age and appearance that they could have been twins.

"His name is passed around New York City on whispers and titters. That's what they say."

They must have Simon confused with someone else. "He's hardly the type. He's sweet. Shy. He made me a wooden cart."

"A wooden cart?"

"To carry headstones. It has my name on it. And little flowers." Her voice trailed off.

There was a beat of silence. Jude and Josef's spoons hovered in perfect alignment beneath mouths that hung open. Laughter overtook them. Great guffaws that rattled the table as each hit it alternately with his palm, a syncopated beat. Her father lifted his plate to prevent it from spilling, while her mother looked from one to the other with wide eyes.

"He's a smart one."

"He should write a book."

"A cart to carry headstones."

"With tiny flowers."

"Weren't there any tiny hearts?"

Their laughter turned hysterical, and tears ran down their cheeks.

Eric continued eating, his eyes focused on the center of his bowl.

Chloe looked at her brothers, each in turn. "You don't know what you're talking about."

"But he's rich, isn't that right, Eric?" Her mother's spoon now rested in her plate, her hands clasped on her lap beneath the table.

"He's rich, all right. He's making a mint from those department stores." Eric looked at her. "Watch yourself, Chloe."

She shook her head. Watch herself? As if Simon were dangerous?

They weren't talking about the same man.

But Eric continued, "He's in the business of making women," he hesitated and appeared to be searching for the right words, "want things."

Her father returned his plate to the table with a thump and a rattle. His spoon renewed its slow, rhythmic trips between his dinner and his mouth.

Her nose scrunched. "Whatever in the world could he make me want?"

Jude and Josef spit stew in concurrent bursts. Chloe was glad she'd removed the table runner.

Men were ridiculous.

She would want what she chose to want. Wasn't that the way it worked?

10

"*At last,*" Simon read aloud.

"His wife died," she gestured to an adjacent stone, "more than twenty years ago. Now he gets to be with her again. At last."

Simon teased, "Are you sure he didn't mean *alone at last?*" Chloe pushed against Simon's arm in protest at his laughter, and the tingle coursed through him. "Widows and spinsters likely hounded him for twenty years. Brought him cakes and puddings wanting to chat, when all he wanted was some peace and quiet. It would have been maddening."

"No, that wasn't it."

"Are you sure? That's how a man's mind works."

Chloe nodded once. "I'm quite sure. He told me himself."

"The late Mr. Holden explained his epitaph to you? I repeat, that sounds rather sinister."

"He was not 'late' at the time. He told me the story of how he lost his wife. How he longed to be with her again. So we decided together what his headstone would say."

Simon finished the deep, blunt trench and tossed the shovel to the grass. It was his third trench of the morning. When Chloe had found him hours earlier smoking against the twin tree, she hadn't seemed surprised to see him. Within minutes, she'd enlisted his help with the three stones she was tasked with setting. He'd been pleased to see she used the cart.

He lifted the last stone and hefted it into the channel. Energy pulsed through him, and he twitched.

There. She'd touched him again. Her fingers lingered at his waist as she peered around him to watch his progress. The touch was fleeting, but he noticed. It could have been a mistake the first time, maybe the second, but not this time.

It was no mistake. She was touching him on purpose. Each time she touched him, it was a focused point of light. He felt her stomach against his bottom. He willed himself not to lean back. With any other woman, he'd lean back all right. They'd be frolicking in the grass here and now, visitors of the dead be damned. But this woman was off limits. He wasn't allowed to get involved with a local girl. He'd be throwing away ten plus years of caution, of knowing the right women to entertain, and the women he absolutely should not. He felt her again where she pressed against him, the softness of her stomach against the hard curve of his backside, and his vision blurred.

Fucking hell.

He extricated himself from between Chloe and the stone, and his knees bent of their own volition. He pretended to check the stone at its base. She dropped beside him and repacked the dirt. Their hands touched. His fast retreat failed to deaden the tremor of connection.

"*Low*. You say your name means the water?" She renewed the conversation they'd begun while setting their second stone.

"L'eau. The water, really." His family was of French descent, and they had changed their name, Americanized it to a phonetic spelling when his grandfather had arrived.

"And you named your stores *Atwater & Low*?"

"That's right." Atwater & Low. The name was supposed to be witty, a wink between he and anyone who knew his love for the water, anyone who knew him at all.

She sat in the grass and looked up at him. "You're named for the water. You move between here and Manhattan, two islands, yet you're determined to shun open water. You won't even touch it?"

Not if he could help it, not since the storm that took Michael. "The irony is not lost on me." That it was not lost on her either made his heart somehow lighter. She recognized the significance of his loss, and the insignificance. For the first time, he wanted to laugh, to joke about what was, he was sure, The Tragedy of his life.

Their tasks complete, they replaced the shovel in the cart, and in silence they walked to rest on a swell of grass beneath a nearby tree. Across the hillside stood small towers of stone.

He shook out a cigarette.

"Why do you do that?

He wanted badly to touch her again. Maybe she would do it for him. He answered without thinking. "I need something to do with my hands." And his mouth. But he was of enough mind not to say that. "Would you rather I didn't?"

"What else would you do with your hands?" She tilted her head, regarding him. When he did not reply, she continued, "I could read them."

"Read my hands? Like the gypsies do?"

"I suppose you think I wouldn't be as good at it."

He replaced the cigarette in the pouch, and the pack to his jacket pocket. She was angling to touch him again. He knew this for a fact. He knew women, and she wanted to touch him. The knowledge thrilled him, made his heart pound with apprehension and anticipation. He extended a hand, palm up. "I didn't say that."

She grabbed his hand before he could finish, and he was jolted, at first by the feel of her fingers at the backs of his hand, at the center between his wrist and knuckles, then by something more visceral. He inhaled.

"Are you scared I might see your future? The universe is telling you something. What do you think it will say?"

Words. He forced himself to focus on her words. She was right. The universe was telling him something. What would she say? Curiosity and that something else held his hand in hers.

"This line here is your lifeline. It splits here," she traced her finger from the outside of his palm to its hollow, "into three separate lines." She looked at him. "I don't know what that means. But, here. This one is your money line. No wait. That's just a crease."

He peered with her into his palm. "I think the creases are the lines." It was difficult not to simply let it happen, to allow the wash of feeling to overcome him. He followed its path with his mind. It started in his hand, skipped his arm and went right to his brain, and to his cock. Holy hell. He felt her. She was inside him.

With his brother, the connection had been different. It was his brother. With her, with her...Well, she was a woman, and to be this intimate and not want to enter her, too, was unthinkable.

"Let me see your other hand."

He found it balled in his lap. He offered it to her before she could reach for it. Had she done so, her hand would have been his to hold, tight and firm against him. It would have been unavoidable, compulsory.

"The creases are different in each of your hands. If the lines are the creases, then you have two different sets of lifelines." She released him, but her eyes smiled. "I wish I knew a gypsy."

He feared he would expire from the effort of holding his breath, making his inhale even and silent. He reached again for his cigarettes. It took him three matches before one struck a flame.

"What does that taste like?"

He looked at the cigarette, confused by the sudden change of topic. "Like tobacco." He offered it to her without thinking. "Would you like to try it?"

She shook her head and laughed. "I've never seen a woman smoke." She wrapped a length of straight blond hair behind her ear. Her blue gaze met his. "If I'm to taste it, I'd have to try it without smoking."

His heart hammered in his chest.

She continued, "I might...." Her head tilted as she considered it. He knew without her saying the words what she meant.

When he did not respond, she smiled. "You'll have to stick out your tongue if I'm to taste it."

When her eyes found his mouth, he felt his lips part. His tongue touched between them, disappeared again inside his mouth.

It was an eternity while she moved herself across the grass, carrying her skirts with her as they caught between the ground and her legs.

He remained still as a stone. She placed her hand on the earth and pressed to kneel before him. Her mouth hovered over his. "Are you going to hide it from me?"

He could hear his answer outside his head.

No. He would not hide his tongue from her

11

Simon had been to visit three times that week. He'd built her a cart carved with tiny flowers and her name on it, but he couldn't bring himself to look at her, let alone be touched by her. Whispers and titters? The idea was ludicrous. He was practically distraught. Chloe had been testing him all day. She'd taken every opportunity to touch him and gauge his response. He'd jumped each time she laid a hand on him. This from a man who made women want things. Ha!

In spite of it, she had to admit that he was handsome. She couldn't argue with that. He had a sly sense of humor. He made her laugh, and she wasn't sure he even tried. She liked his company. The only thing she didn't like was that he seemed to be averse to the idea of kissing her, and, for the first time in her life, she wanted to be kissed, very badly indeed.

Hattie's dare had provoked her. It was time to take a risk. What was more, the words of her brothers the night before had made her curious, more curious than she'd ever been before about what a kiss from a man might be like. A kiss was not life or death. It was a trivial thing, really. Yet the desire to kiss this man was blocking out all else, the sound of the wind in the trees, the smell of the blossoms weighing down the boughs.

She pressed her lips against his, and he started as though by electric shock. She thought he'd stop her, but he let her kiss him, seemed to wait patiently for her to finish.

Their eyes remained open, close. She blinked.

Her brothers didn't know a thing.

She wouldn't have minded dangerous, but there was nothing dangerous about it. No risk at all. She felt not a small amount of defeat.

When she tried to withdraw, his hand on the back of her head stopped her. The separation between them became energized as he paused, then closed it again with a steady pressure, pulling her back. His lips brushed hers, not pressing as she had done, not fully closed, parted. She felt his breath against her mouth.

In spite of her teasing, she was not prepared for the feel of his tongue. When it licked along her lower lip, they parted in surprise. He held her still while his tongue caressed her lips. He shifted closer. His hand found the side of her neck, and his thumb touched her chin, opened her mouth wider for him. His tongue entered her, at once smooth and rough. The pressure of his lips increased, and pressure built inside of her. His hands held her head in place while he feasted on her mouth. His lips captured hers, tugging, taking, again and again.

He was making her want him, want exactly what he was doing to her, and making her want more.

Chloe's head tilted to the side to allow him her neck. His lips grazed it, from the bottom of her ear to the top of her shoulder. She shivered. He made his way back and found her mouth again, felt that each pass of his mouth and tongue created desire in her. He had not considered that possibility, that her response would be so clear in his mind, spurring him on, making it damn difficult to check his hands, leave them on her neck, in her hair, and refuse their travel to her breasts, where he felt her aching for him. He separated from her in a hasty retreat, a sound of regret in the back of his throat.

He'd not given her the chance to look into his eyes for more than a few distracted seconds since they'd first met. He was always moving, looking elsewhere, avoiding her eyes, but he looked at her now. Her eyes were a mixture of blue and gold. She touched her lips with the tips of her fingers. He wiped his with the pad of his thumb.

She had said the universe was telling him something. Well, he was listening. It was a roaring in his ears.

Her tone was accusing. "You've done that before."

Hundreds of times, and never. "There's something you should know…"

"My brothers said you could make women want things. I didn't believe them."

"I feel…" He could not fail to tell her.

"Was it your goal to make me want to kiss you?"

"...a connection." Simon blinked. She wasn't listening.

"Tell me the truth. You've been playing a part to woo me. The awkward, attentive man…?"

Not only was she not listening, she'd called him awkward. *Awkward?* Now there was a fresh affront.

"But you aren't awkward at all. You know how to kiss. You know how to kiss very well."

Of course he knew how to kiss. He'd written the book on it. He'd had to recite his own instruction manual line by line in his head to keep himself from throwing her down and eating her alive. It had been absolutely out of his control since the moment he'd met her.

I have not been playing a part. It was the only thing he could think to say.

But it would have been a lie. He had been hiding himself from her. Point in fact: She thought he was trying to seduce her. *Trying to seduce her.* Irony, it seemed, was the order of the day. To her, he was a cautionary tale. In reality, he was a Brontë novel, gravestones and all. "Kissing has not been my goal, I promise you."

If she regretted his pronouncement, she didn't show it. She didn't take his words as a dismissal. She did not retreat. Instead, she picked at the grass beside her skirt. "Meredith is getting married on Sunday. She says there will be fireworks."

Simon nodded. It was going to take more than fireworks to stop the train headed toward Mosquito Island. The conflict with Van Ogden was coming to a head. The man wanted to blow up Meredith's home, and he would, unless Wolfe could somehow prevent it.

"I've been invited."

Her words were the flash of an image. *White silk.*

She asked, "Will you take me?"

He saw the reason behind it, why the universe would see fit to place her there, with him. Meredith could use the company of another woman. Her maid of honor, Virginia, wasn't the nurturing type. To Simon, it suddenly made sense that she would attend the event that was the only thing he cared about, the only thing, outside of being with this woman.

He rejected the thought as soon as it arrived. He didn't care for her, not in that way, not in any way that mattered. He wanted her, just like the other women he'd wanted and could not have. Caring for women wasn't an option. Certainly not for this woman, with whom there were no options at all.

"Take me. Or bring me," she corrected herself quickly. Her head dipped as she rubbed a smudge of dirt from the toe of her boot. "You don't have to answer. I shouldn't have asked."

A waft of perfume accompanied the fall of her hair. He'd never been asked by a woman to a wedding. It was rare to be asked by a woman to any event, unless it was to one in a bedroom. If it was the type of woman to extend such an invitation, then it was the type of invitation he could accept. He shouldn't accept this one, but he hadn't a choice. He couldn't reject her. He didn't want to reject her. "Allow me to escort you." His head spun. "Your hair smells sweet."

"Sweet?" She tilted her head and crinkled her nose, doubting him. They'd been burying marble in the hot sun for hours. She looked upwards and again at him. She pointed. "The Japanese hydrangea are in bloom."

Although the branches were not high above them and their perfume was fragrant, his senses allowed entry to nothing but her. Simon followed her gaze up and back. His eyes landed on the sweep of her neck. His lips still felt the softness of her skin, right below her ear.

12

"I kissed a man." Chloe peered into the bassinet where Hattie's baby slept.

"You did it." Hattie's hands on the cradle tightened in excitement. "You kissed a man. Who?"

Chloe affected calm. "Michael's brother." Her voice was matter of fact. Hattie's was not.

"You kissed *Simon Low*?" Hattie laughed as she reached into the bassinet.

Chloe stopped her. "Sit." She pulled a rocker close to the bassinet, settled Harriet into it, and retrieved the baby herself. He was getting heavier by the day. All his weight was in his cheeks, both sets. Deep creases lined the juncture of his joints: wrists, thighs and ankles. Chloe placed the baby in Hattie's arms, pulled another chair up close to the rocker and sat.

"I never met him, but I told you I'd heard of him. Before Daniel and I married, I spent a winter in the city. Do you remember? Simon Low was all any of the women could talk about. What a *reputation*. At least one woman I knew was ready to let him have his way with her. And you kissed him." She hugged herself with a dramatic shiver. "What was it like?"

It had been awkward. Then it had been anything but. "It was nice."

"Nice?" Hattie winced. "You kissed Simon Low." The syllables were *forte* downbeats. "I wouldn't be surprised if you told me you'd swooned."

Chloe traced the creases in the little boy's thighs. She hadn't swooned. She thought for a moment he might, but he hadn't either. Instead, he'd done something else. He'd kissed her thoroughly. She asked, "Did you swoon when Daniel first kissed you?"

Hattie made a face. "Daniel and I'd known each other for too long for that." Her eyebrows rose and sunk. Her head tilted. "There was that time he apprenticed at the harbor in the city. I visited my aunt so I could be near him."

Chloe remembered. "I have your letters."

The wood of the rocking chair's legs rolled against the floorboards. "I'd been so sure of him, but then the setting changed. Suddenly, I wasn't sure anymore. His clothes were a little more formal, his smile a little less forthcoming. He was the same man he'd always been, but, with that little distance, I loved him more. Not for the frowns or the clothes, but it was there that I realized he wasn't mine. I didn't own him." Hattie rubbed her cheek against the baby's soft skin.

"You can't own another person." The words were out of Chloe's mouth before she could stop them. She knew too well that people were taken away, whether they were yours or not.

Harriet nuzzled little Daniel's bare feet and regarded the small body in her arms. "I know that now, but you can love them, be hungry for them in their absence, feel whole only when they're near."

To Chloe, it sounded terrible, like disaster waiting to happen. She was a whole person, all by herself. If loving another person broke you into pieces, then she wanted none of it.

The rocker stopped. Chloe listened to the silence. The press of the baby's tiny foot against her palm reassured her, until Hattie spoke into the quiet.

"Your mother paid me a visit this morning."

Chloe knew why her mother had visited. Her heart pressed low against her stomach. "Did she bring you a pastry? She loves showing them off."

Hattie smiled, "It had chocolate inside."

Chloe forced an answering smile. She and Hattie sat at the precipice between hope and resignation. Chloe's job was to encourage the dying to topple over the edge, to lose hope. It was a sorry job, but Chloe refused to watch people, one after another, surrender their last days, blind.

But this was not her job. This was her friend, and Hattie had been failing since baby Daniel's birth. Chloe knew it, and Hattie knew it, but the words had never been spoken aloud. Silence wasn't good for business, but the alternative was to admit that she'd lose them all, everyone she loved, one by one.

What could she say in the face of it? There was only one answer. The truth, but a different one, a distracting one. "I want to kiss him again." In fact, Chloe hadn't wanted to stop kissing him the first time, and the wanting had yet to go away. She'd gone to sleep with it last night, and had woken up with it again this morning. The last thing she wanted with Simon was to feel whole only when he was near, but she was already falling to pieces.

"I knew it!" Hattie almost shrieked. Little Daniel's arms lifted from his sides in a twitch of surprise, then settled.

Chloe whispered, "Hush. Or I'll make that your epitaph." She squeezed little Daniel's toes, softly, one at a time.

Hattie giggled, "*I knew it.* I like that one. Very mysterious."

Chloe was torn between the conversation they faced, or distraction. They both preferred a discussion of kisses to headstones, so Chloe leaned back in her chair, then forward, her arms on her knees. "I want to kiss him again, but I'm not sure I should." She wondered if she would even have the opportunity. Her forehead dropped into her hands. "I'm not sure he wants me to."

"Of course he wants you to." Hattie was adamant. "You just have to learn to read the signs."

"What signs?" There were no signs, unless his nervous twitch whenever she got close was a sign.

"If he kissed you once, you can get him to do it again. There will be signs." Hattie's tone was resolute.

Chloe's head lifted. She could desire a man and not love him, couldn't she? She could kiss him again, again and again, if she wanted, and never swoon. She pledged, then and there. She would not like Simon anymore than she already did, but she'd kiss him again. It was a sound plan, and safe enough. Kissing was not love. Wanting was not love. She was no closer to being in love with Simon than before she'd kissed him. That was certain proof that all her pieces would stay stuck together. She ran a finger along the baby's fat thigh. "He's taking me to Meredith's wedding."

Hattie's chair rocked forward. This time her voice remained a whisper, albeit a loud one. The baby slept on in her lap. "When?"

"Tomorrow."

"Tomorrow!" This time the baby twitched. "Tomorrow?" she asked again more quietly. "What are you wearing?"

It didn't matter what she wore. It was not the thing foremost in her mind. In any case, she hadn't enough time to make anything. "The dress Mamere sent me. I've never worn it."

Hattie's eyes grew big. "You've had it since we were sixteen."

Chloe shrugged, "It's still new."

"Have you tried it on? Our bodies have changed, if you haven't noticed."

Chloe laughed. "Yours has."

Hattie pinched Chloe's arm as she reached out again to touch the baby in her lap. "Yours has, too. You'd better make sure it fits. I wish I had something to lend you, but you're too tall."

Chloe tweaked her back. "You're too short."

"Watch it. I'm unwell," Hattie teased and rubbed her arm.

Chloe smiled, but it was for show. Hattie was unwell. Her energy had waned while they'd talked. Chloe's talk of kissing had kept Hattie upright, but it was late morning and time she returned to bed. Chloe took the baby from Hattie's lap and set him in the crib. When she helped Hattie from the chair, she could have lifted her friend's body into her arms. Chloe pulled back the blankets and readjusted them after Hattie crawled beneath.

"I can't wait to hear about it." Hattie's eyes were closed, but her smile was wide-awake. "Don't hold anything back. Try it all. You'll have to tell me everything. You're my Scheherazade."

Chloe needed no further encouragement.

13

The morning of the wedding, Simon compelled his legs not to run from the hotel to the Swann cottage. His shoes were hard, shiny leather. It helped that they were not made for running.

Her brothers were out for a burial. Her father was in his atelier carving. It was her mother who stayed home to send Chloe off. Simon learned all this while standing on the steps outside the cottage before Mrs. Swann bustled him in through a narrow wood door. The kitchen served at once every function, foyer, parlor and dining room. A longhouse table ran the length of its center.

"Do you drink tea?"

Simon's attention was recalled from where he searched for Chloe in the corners of the room. "No, thank you." He wasn't fond of tea.

"I'll make you a cup." She gestured with her chin for him to sit, already lifting an iron kettle from the stove. She poured water into a porcelain teapot decorated in royal blue and gold, with magenta flowers. She placed the pot in the center of the table with ceremony. A matching sugar bowl and creamer followed. A miniature cup and saucer were set before him, the pair smaller than his hand.

"I've been to Manhattan. Several times, in fact." She sat across from him on a four-legged stool, the seat carved to accept a curved bottom. "And I've been inside Atwater & Low. I have one of your hats."

Give it back. It's the only thing he thought to say, so he kept silent and lifted his empty cup.

Mrs. Swann poured his tea. "Tell me about this season's hats. Are they as large as last season's? Will you have anything other than purple? Why was everyone wearing purple last winter? Purple, purple, purple. I'm sick to death of purple."

Chloe emerged from a hallway that disappeared into the depth of the house. Simon stood, and the stool fell behind him with a loud clap. He chased where it rolled across the floor. His face grew warm. For the love of God, had she seen him drink tea from that ridiculous cup?

She smiled as though reading his mind. "Isn't my mother's tea set pretty?"

She stressed the word pretty, and he almost took a step toward her. He wanted to grab her and swoop her up, carry her back down the hall from wherever she came and make wild love to her, so he lifted the stool off the ground and set it with another loud clap on the floor. With two strides, his hand found the door pull, and his other arm lifted to encourage Chloe along. He turned to her mother. "Thank you for the tea. Purple is banned this season, outright."

Chloe laughed when they made it outside, but after that first burst of fellowship, their mile walk to the river was mute. He listened to the swish of her skirts and remembered the dress now hidden beneath her cape. The black silk was high quality noil, nubbed and heavy weight. It cinched her waist and pulled tight across her chest, so tight in fact, he'd struggled not to stare. The white cotton blouson that puffed from beneath was embroidered white against white. Where the neckline scooped low, the white blouson teased. He was relieved she'd donned her cape.

He stole glances at her feet. With each step they kicked from beneath the hem of her skirt. They were covered in white tights and black satin slippers.

The next time he looked, as they ticked off the mile in short, fast steps, he concentrated on her hair. He'd seen it down, had grown familiar with the battle she waged to keep it out of her eyes. Today, a truce had been arranged. She'd wound it in a braided coil at each ear. He'd never seen anything like it. Each time he risked a look, she caught him, and her smile made his heart hammer in his chest. He was relieved when they reached the water. A thick haze of desire clouded his reason, made it difficult to remember that he would take nothing from this girl.

At the main dock, the river lapped against the pilings. Five hundred feet away was the *Onoko*, long and lean and larger than life. Wolfe must have pulled a half dozen strings, and pulled them hard to get this mammoth iron freighter to reset its course for Mosquito Island.

Chloe was thunderstruck. "It's the biggest boat I've ever seen."

Simon nodded. "It's a ship."

As if invoked, Wolfe's head appeared over the side. Gripping the rails, he leaned forward and called out across the wide expanse of water. "Come aboard!"

Simon balked. "Do we have to?" The ship would take them more than forty feet up.

Wolfe's laughter reached them, carried by the wind. "The wedding is aboard ship, and you are best man. You have to."

Chloe's eyes widened. "You're best man?"

"It's not a claim often made, but today, yes."

They boarded a tender captained by one of the Wolfe yacht house crew and after only a minute of strong strokes through the water were brought to marry with the freighter. The man roped off and gestured to Chloe. "Ladies first."

She looked askance at Simon as she peered up the black hull. There was no docking plank as with passenger ferries and ocean liners. The *Onoko* was anchored between Wolfe and Mosquito Islands. The only way aboard was up.

Simon turned to Chloe and said, "Give me your shoes."

She lifted her skirt to peer at her slippers. They might not fare well on the metal rungs of the ladder. He placed each in a jacket pocket and stood, his hand grasping hers while she positioned herself at the bow. Her skirt whipped at his face as he held her waist, waited for her to gain her footing, then hoisted his body behind her, close and tight so she would not fall.

The climb was treacherous, not for the height nor the wind nor the slip of the metal under his patent leather shoes. His hand hovered behind her where it absolutely should not as they climbed. It made him woozy.

A gust of wind blew out her cape. It was the same nubby silk of her dress, and it trapped him beneath. For a another ten steps up the ladder his breath filled the tent of fabric, his face pressed close against the back of her skirts. He moved in tighter and climbed three rungs in quick succession. The silk slid over his head and returned to her back when he leaned out far to let it fall.

"You aren't scared." Her breath carried the words.

He wouldn't have heard her had he not already swung himself in again, been pressed up tight. In point of fact, he was terrified, but he wasn't afraid of heights. He'd climbed riggings two times as tall as the hull, and that was on a narrow stick. But Chloe was thrilled, as though this was a great adventure, and she vibrated with it. Her vibrations made his skin tingle, numbed his fingers on the rail. His loss of control scared him to death. He could not tell her that.

His face was level with the back of her head, the collar of her hood brushed his neck and chin. He leaned in until he felt the rough silk against his cheek. "Are you alright?"

She didn't look up or down. She smiled as she looked out past his shoulder, her avoidance of the water below was deliberate. "How far have we come?"

Simon regarded the water. "About twenty feet."

"How much higher?"

He glanced up. "Twenty rungs more." They were halfway there. "Are your feet cold?"

She shook her head.

He was glad of that. Cold, stockinged feet were not ideal for climbing the hull of a freighter.

"Just don't let me fall."

He wasn't planning on it.

They took ten more steps. A gust of wind blew her skirts and they caught beneath her foot. She stumbled, and for a moment, it was only her arms that held her, her arms and his. He bent his knee beneath her, catching her as her body, unplanned, sat against him.

"See? You can take a rest anytime." He didn't know if the image of her falling thirty feet to the water was hers or his. He answered it with an image of his own: catching her wrist, hauling her up, and kissing her against the hull like a pirate.

He compelled the image to remain fixed in his mind, added a sweeping, musical score.

She tilted her head. "What are you thinking about?"

"How much fun this is." He smiled through the terror. "Ten more steps. Are you ready?"

She nodded, smiling back, laughing through her words. "How are we ever going to get down?"

"We can worry about that later." He bumped his leg beneath her, urging her to stand. "Up."

She kissed him before she did, a fleeting kiss across his lips.

He stared at her. "I hope that wasn't a good-bye." It felt like a good-bye.

"I'll see you at the top." She stood and pulled herself to the next rung.

When they reached the top, Wolfe and his first mate hauled Chloe on deck. Simon closed his eyes and rested his head against the ship's hull.

How would they ever get down?

He followed her over the side.

Wolfe greeted Simon with a handshake and a perfunctory bow. He brushed the shoulders of Simon's coat with his hand. "You made it."

Simon ignored the soft blows to his white jacket. "Miss Chloe Swann. Meet Master Tristan Wolfe."

Wolfe's eyes narrowed and the blows stopped. "Did Meredith tell you to call me that?" The words delivered all the force of his Russian accent, but Simon only lifted a brow. Wolfe relented, made Chloe a second short bow and accepted her hand. "Meredith has asked to see you."

"This ship is her wedding gift, I presume?" Simon tried to light a match and failed. The wind blew each one out until he had none.

Wolfe grinned, white teeth in contrast to his black curls. "The keel is almost three hundred feet long. She has a breadth of beam of nearly forty feet, and a twenty-five foot depth of hold."

Chloe laughed. "I didn't understand a word you just said."

"She's big."

"That I understood."

Simon handed over her slippers. Her fingers held his shoulder as she replaced each one.

Wolfe's grin widened. "Captain Minch has agreed to keep her anchored for as long as necessary. Hundreds of dollars a day will be lost if Van Ogden doesn't back down. There's iron in the hull. A thousand tons."

Simon was relieved. It meant a stay of execution for Mosquito Island. "And what for Minch?"

Wolfe snuck his hands in his trouser pockets, warming them. "I'm chair of the Seaway Commission. I've means to give him whatever he asks."

Simon laughed. "It's a coup." As head of the board that would make the river an international seaway, Tristan had the power to fill Minch's coffers with silver, if that's what the Captain desired.

Chloe interrupted. Her shoulder brushed Simon's chest as she inserted herself between them. "Master Wolfe, where can I find the bride?"

Wolfe's eyes snapped, and Simon held up his hands. "I didn't tell her to call you that."

Wolfe regarded Simon with suspicion before offering Chloe his arm. "Call me Tristan."

It was a tight fit in the bride's quarters. Meredith sat with her father and her maid of honor, a woman Chloe had seen for years on the streets of Denton, the closest mainland town. The three sat together on low chairs. Their knees touched in the center. Chloe had met Meredith when they were children at a terrible moment in her life. This moment, although it pulsed with joy, was just as intimate. Chloe was on untrodden ground. She was more familiar with grief than happiness. The door closed behind her with a snap.

Meredith stood and held out her hands. "Did Tristan tell you? Mosquito Island will be flanked by this great old ship. The *Onoko*. A military defense!"

Chloe took Meredith's hands and kissed her cheeks before retreating to her place at the door. "Is that legal?"

Meredith's father shook his head, stood as Meredith sat, and bowed. "I don't believe anyone but you has asked." He spun his hat in his hands. The black suit he wore was from another time. He ran his hand over the top of his head, but his hair would not sit down.

Meredith's hands splayed on her lap, and she nodded at a woman seated beside her with practiced formality. "Virginia Waterstone, this is Chloe Swann." Virginia's chin dipped and rose in a nod. Meredith gestured with an open palm. "Chloe, this is Virginia. She's my maid of honor, so you should call her Ginny."

Meredith's maid of honor held a monstrously large hat in her lap. Her dress was a rich shade of midnight blue. The neckline was high, and the sleeves covered most of her arms. Yellow gems sparked in her ears and at each wrist. Chloe knew of Virginia Waterstone. The Waterstones were the richest family in Denton. Chloe's knees dipped. It was like looking at a queen.

"Look." Meredith stood again from the hassock and twisted her shoulders to show off the back of her head. "Ginny did my hair."

Virginia had spun Meredith's hair like gold. Each curl wrapped around the next. The curls hung or bounced; some floated. Woven through was a strand of seed pearls connected with fishing wire. Chloe could not fail to be impressed.

Meredith's father continued standing. He looked at his hat as though he ached to put it on. "I'll see if they're ready."

Chloe moved to let him pass, the poor man. How long had he been made to sit with two women on his daughter's wedding day? Grief and celebration had this much in common, at least. No one would have said what they wanted to say.

Meredith tapped the seat next to her. "Sit with me while we wait. You'll stay after for the fireworks?"

Chloe would've been able to see the fireworks from home, but she'd stay. She was more exhilarated than she'd ever been in her life, and it wasn't out of fear. It was exactly the opposite of fear. "We climbed up the side of the ship."

Meredith wrinkled her nose. "We have to go down the side again, but there's to be a party on the green at The Hotel Columbian. That'll give us pluck"

Lake of the Isles was a twenty-minute walk from the hotel green. She could return home directly after the ceremony. She should. She wondered if she would. She doubted it, if Simon wanted her to stay. She wanted him to want her to stay.

Virginia regarded her in the silence. Her curious assessment took long enough that Chloe was relieved when Virginia finally spoke. "I've never seen hair done like that before. Is it an immigrant style?"

Chloe fingered the braids wound into circles at each ear. It was an old country style that she relied on when she attended any formal occasion, like church. She'd been wearing it since she was a child and had never discovered another. She was taken aback, but not at the question. Virginia's voice was the loveliest Chloe had ever heard, tenor with a touch of vibrato. Chloe unfastened her cape collar and before she could respond, either to the question or to the sound that made it, Virginia interrupted, "Is your dress from there, too?" The melody of her voice was a foil for the rough examination.

Two halves of thick black fabric were decorated with brightly colored embroidery and hooked tightly across her chest. The neckline was cut from shoulder to shoulder, a parallel line beneath her collarbones. The sleeves were white linen. Her breasts pushed out over the top of the bodice.

Chloe fidgeted with the tense fastenings at her chest. "I've had it for ages. I didn't have time to make another."

Virginia waved with a flourish. "You've a lovely..."

They fell silent again. Meredith drew with her finger on the silk of her skirt. Her hair glowed red against ivory. She looked around the room, pinched and pulled at the lobe of her ear, smiled at Chloe, then at the ceiling. She brought her hands together in her lap. A black curl bobbed alongside Virginia's high cheekbone as she gave her head a curt shake. It was a look of warning directed at Meredith, but Meredith took no heed. She gave up the pretense of interest in the wood patterns above her head and rested her forearms on her skirt. "You came with Simon."

"Meredith." Virginia shook her head and pressed her lips together.

Meredith unbent and sat upright again. "There's no time for decorum, Ginny."

Virginia pursed her lips then nodded. She turned to Chloe. "What do you think of him?"

Virginia's good breeding was something she could shed on demand. Chloe liked her even more for it, so she answered with the truth. "He's sweet."

Meredith and Virginia exchanged a look.

Meredith asked, "He's been sweet to you?"

"Simon is rarely sweet," Virginia challenged. Her back was straight as an arrow. "He's more satire in him than Jonathan Swift."

Meredith shrugged at Chloe, only half in disagreement.

These women knew firsthand of the man beyond the gossip. Curiosity compelled Chloe to ask, "How long have you known him?"

"Two years. Since the storm." Meredith frowned, twin lines appearing between her green eyes. "It feels like a longer."

Virginia swept a hand across her skirt. "I've known him forever."

"I asked him to escort me." Chloe said. It felt like a confession.

Meredith explained to Virginia, "I invited her. Simon didn't."

"What did he say?" Ginny's words were each singularly punctuated with a want to know.

Chloe frowned. "He said he liked the smell of my hair."

Virginia and Meredith exchanged another look.

The dam of etiquette broke with a rush. Chloe looked to both women, each in turn. "What's he really like?" She leaned forward on her elbows. "My brothers say he's a rake." She had more than an offhand interest.

Virginia nodded. "He's a heart-breaker."

Meredith affirmed it. "He breaks women's hearts."

Chloe leaned back in disbelief. "It's true?"

Virginia frowned in consideration. "Although I don't think he's ever passed time with a native girl."

Meredith raised a phantom glass. "To the native girls." She pretended to drink and regarded Chloe over the rim. "I think they're supposed to call us the *local residents*."

Virginia's head shook again in a curt negative. "No. I'm sure of it. He never has."

Chloe's hands rested in her lap. She pretended to hold a champagne flute. She shouldn't care, but the news gave her diaphragm a pinch. It was just curiosity, born of her brothers' gossip. She tamped down the worry that it was something more. She didn't care who Simon spent time with, not one bit. A knock made her jump.

Professor Wells stuck his head in the door and the jamb knocked his hat awry. "The captain is ready."

They stood all at once. None moved toward the cabin door.

Here it was moments before a wedding, and she was talking about a silly crush. Chloe's head bent. It wasn't a crush. She didn't know why she even thought the word. A crush implied something that hurt. This didn't hurt, and it wouldn't. It was just curiosity, nothing more. And today was not about her. She was here for Meredith, who'd asked that she attend her. Chloe loved her siblings, her large family. Meredith had only her father. Chloe touched her friend's skirt. "You must wish your mother were here."

Meredith hugged her in reply, capturing Chloe's hand in the crisp fabric between them. "She's here all the time. I'm wearing her dress. Watch it spin." She tried to turn in place, but there wasn't enough room to lift the skirt. The newspaper would report the color as ivory, but the lustre could not be seen in print.

Virginia stayed Chloe with a hand on her shoulder as they were going out. "I made you self-conscious. I'm a fool."

"We're all fools at one time or another."

Virginia's tone was dry. "Can you make that my epitaph?"

We're all fools. It was a good one. Chloe nodded, reminded for a moment who she was. "I promise."

14

The bridge was at the prow. Windows hugged her captain's back in two curved sweeps. Wood screens along the front and sides of the narrow room slid open to the breeze, high above the water. Behind them, in the direction of the captain's gaze, was the long hull of the ship. Before them, the length of the river.

Captain Minch had sandy blond hair and a drooping mustache. He removed a piece of paper from his navy jacket and unfolded it with the slowness of ritual.

Wolfe leaned across the short expanse between the bride and groom. "I took the liberty of providing him with our vows."

Meredith met him halfway. "Aren't there standard vows for getting married on a ship?" Their whispers were heard by everyone in the room.

"I found these in the library. They seemed suitable."

They returned to their upright positions, and the captain turned to Meredith.

"Repeat after me. Tristan Adolfo Wolfe." Meredith mouthed his middle name before repeating it aloud. "I pledge that I will take you to be my husband and master." Meredith smiled as she repeated the words, though her smile faltered more than once during the remaining vows. She seemed to find the words difficult. One or two caught in her throat.

Then it was Wolfe's turn. When the captain started to recite the vows, Wolfe interrupted. "I remember it." He positioned himself before her. "Meredith Margaret Wells." His eyebrows rose, and she tried to laugh. "I take you to be my wife and my spouse. I pledge I will be faithful to you and loyal with my body and my goods. I will keep you in sickness and in health, in whatever condition it will please God to place you, and I shall not exchange you for better or worse, until the end."

He took the ring from his pocket. Meredith hid her face. A bouquet of green dianthus made her sobs pretty. "With this ring I honor you, with my body I wed you, and I endow you with the dowry agreed upon by my friends and yours." There was a pause. "I'm sorry. I didn't mean to remember that last part." He stepped forward to claim her. He pushed the flowers down. "I honor you." He wrapped an arm around her back, and pulled. "With my body I wed you."

Simon was glad Virginia was there. Her fierce resolve stayed any tears that threatened. He didn't hear what the captain said next, what he said to marry them. He turned around and found Chloe. It was easy enough. There was no one else there. There were no chairs. Meredith's father had joined them at the prow, so Chloe was the last in attendance, her back pressed against the cabin door. Simon didn't even have to look past a steward.

He'd already taken in the strained bust of her dress and the guileless twists of her hair. Her cape was elsewhere. Now Simon noted her eyes. He'd somehow forgotten they were blue, a light, aching cornflower blue. The eyes were windows to the soul, but he had other avenues of entry. He would have to remember to remember her eyes.

The general commotion brought them close. Their heads came together and brought their voices above the din.

"Have you recovered from the climb?" Simon wished he remembered how to wink.

"I wouldn't have made it without you."

The echo of solemn vows played tricks with her words, filled them with meaning. Sound and movement blurred, brought her face into focus.

They were the only ones in the room.

He should tell her now. He really should tell her.

You touch me from the inside out.

But they were in the way of passage to the captain's quarters, and everyone wanted a toast. He couldn't say two words to her amidst the deluge of people. Five, there were only five other people, but it felt like a wave.

They all pressed together, and he stiffened so as not to flatten her against the door. "We'll toast to the way down."

He needed a drink to slacken the pace of his heart.

The captain's quarters were spare. In the center of the room, a spray of white flowers with black centers like poppies sat atop a round table bolted to the floor.

Meredith cupped the base of a flower with her fingers and turned to her father. "Papa, how did you grow windflower this time of year without my seeing them?"

Wolfe answered for him. "I've had the devil of a time keeping you out of the greenhouse." He took Meredith's hand and secreted it between them. Chloe noted the connection.

Simon placed his empty glass beside the vase.

Chloe was surprised. "Are we leaving?" She'd been prepared for a lecture on hothouse flowers. Meredith's father was prone to lectures.

Simon nodded. "Wolfe has more in store for us at Grandview."

Wolfe extended his hand, and Simon shook it. "We'll follow soon. See that the champagne is chilled."

"The best man's most important responsibility." He turned to Chloe. "That and returning Miss Swann to shore."

Chloe felt a chill of fear and smiled in the face of it. She hadn't felt this excited in her life. "Can't we just jump?"

Meredith's hands pressed Chloe's shoulders in a hug that brought her close. "If you can get Simon in the water, we'd all thank you for it." She kissed Chloe's cheek. "I'll thank you in advance, just in case."

Simon gestured toward the exit. "On that note, we start our descent." A steward opened the door with a short bow before Chloe and Simon were ushered through.

On deck, Chloe looked over the side, and the wind whipped at her cape. The noonday air wouldn't numb her fingers or toes on the way down, but Simon's heat against her back would be welcome. She cast a sidelong glance in his direction. He'd been quiet since the ceremony.

Chloe had felt its gravity, too. Descending the side of the freighter was nothing compared to the risk Meredith and Wolfe had just taken. It frightened Chloe to think of it. Anything could happen to take love from them in an instant. The bond between them was palpable, visible in the way that Wolfe did not let her out of his sight, the way that, whenever they were in arms length of one another, his arm extended and claimed her. Wolfe positioned himself beside his bride at every opportunity, as though it was the most natural thing in the world that she should be beside him, as though of course she would welcome his hand claiming hers. Meredith's instinctive response to Wolfe's presence was to make room, to lean in. Chloe had been surprised today to see them together that way.

Simon had been less awed by Wolfe and Meredith. Each time Chloe had found him in the captain's quarters after the ceremony, during the toast and the chatter after, his eyes had been on her. They were on her again now. One hand clutched the side rail, the other he held out to her.

"Shoes on or off?"

Chloe curled her toes in her low heeled shoes. "On."

"Come on then." He pirouetted his finger, indicating she should turn around. "Climb on."

Chloe spun and clutched the curve of the ladder where it jutted above the ship's side. She felt behind with her foot. One steward stood on her either side. Lowering herself by a rung, then another, she unbent and nestled against the side of the ship with Simon behind her. After another step down, the stewards' faces disappeared. They were too well-trained to gawk over the side at them as they descended. Chloe lifted her chin over her shoulder to Simon behind her. "How will they know when we've gotten down all right?" She leaned back into his chest when she felt the hint of his shrug.

"When they don't hear a splash."

He stepped down once and waited. It became a rhythm. Each step down he took down was followed by a pause, when he waited for her to follow. She slowed her pace, pretended to hesitate with each step. She didn't want to reach the bottom, not yet. They stood close enough together that Chloe was warmed by the heat of him. Each instinctive glance she took behind her before stepping backwards, she caught sight of his hair, tousled by the wind and the brush of her cape.

"I've got you." He mistook her hesitation for fear.

She studied the iron side of the ship's hull. The paint was glossy black. Not a chip of rust marred its smoothness. She wasn't worried about falling. She was worried about the opposite. She'd been holding on dearly, all her life. What would it be like to let go? On the next rung down, she eased her fingers open so they weren't clutching the metal bars as tightly. Her backside brushed against his waist. He took his next step more quickly.

It would be so nice to let someone else take care of everything, to let someone else be in charge of the fall, what came after. "Can we take a rest?"

He returned to a higher rung until his body protected her head to toe from the wind.

"My hands have cramped."

His body was a cage around her when he covered her hand, then removed her fingers from the ladder. His voice was in her ear. "Your hands are frigid." He massaged her fingers, pressing first his thumb into her palm, then folded her fingers inside his hands, warming them. Had she been given the choice of remaining on the side of the ship with her hand buried in his, or returning to dry land and never touching him again, she would have taken up residence here in a nest.

He returned her hand to the ladder, released it, and mimicked the same action with her other hand. Her heart pumped. He was so strong behind her, she didn't even need to hold on. If she balanced just right on the round iron under the balls of her feet, she could let go and still stand, let the frame of his body keep her upright against him.

"Simon?"

He held both rails tight on either side of her. Her hands lifted from the ladder, one at a time, each finding and wrapping her fingers as best she could around each of his wrists. Her fingertips felt the pulse at the base of each palm. She held on to nothing but him.

"What is it?" His voice made vibrations through his shirt. The linen smelled of lavender, and his skin smelled the way skin does after being outside in the cold. She half-turned and her jaw brushed against his chin, still smooth from his morning shave.

"Thank you."

His brow wrinkled. "For what?"

The balance of her feet shifted to her heels. "For taking me. Bringing me."

"What are you doing?" He tightened his arms as she spun in an awkward circle. He didn't relinquish his purchase but her position forced him to loosen his frame to make room for her. You're going to fall through." He released the ladder and grasped her around the waist.

"You won't let me." He wouldn't let her fall. Chloe smiled. It wasn't an actual sign, but it was good to know, nonetheless.

He didn't smile back. His soft lips were a grim line that drew Chloe's attention. His eyes trained on the pulse of her throat, just beneath her ear.

His eyes left her neck and met her gaze in agitation. "What are you doing now?"

Still balanced and stable against him, she extended her arms across his shoulders, and her hands met behind his neck.

"Chloe," he reproached her, "hold on."

"I am holding on."

"Not to me." His breath was a plea.

His chin lowered, knowing what she wanted, but withholding it. She dipped her head too, kissed his cheekbones, his temple, the space high on his jaw that was smooth, the base of his ear. She baited his mouth to follow hers. When his face lifted, she kissed him, and the arm around her waist tightened. She felt the same surge of electricity she'd felt the first time she kissed him, the first time he'd kissed her in return. He returned her kiss now. His lips were soft, tentative. His mouth grew deliberate and curious.

He brought her closer with an arm that also held her up, then pulled his mouth away by slow degrees until their foreheads levered them apart. He looked up the side of the hull. "We have an audience." When Chloe followed his glance, two stewards' faces disappeared over the topside. Simon continued their descent before she was aware he would. Her entire body pressed against his. He held her up with a single arm while the other negotiated the ladder.

"You'll stay through supper." He wasn't asking.

Chloe's eyes glowed. She was in no position to deny him.

"And after." He took another two steps down. His breathing was ragged from the weight of her and something else. "There will be fireworks."

Chloe let herself be carried down the side of the freighter. For the moment, she let go of everything but him.

Fireworks. She felt them already.

15

The lobby of the Columbian Hotel surrounded its guests from all sides with the grain of dark wood. Midday light shone white through the windows, and electric sconces shone yellow along a back wall. The entirety of the hotel's dining staff was on hand in formal whites. Two rooms beyond the lobby were laid out for an early supper. White cloth contrasted with walnut. Large Persian carpets lay plush across shining wood floors. Chloe's neck craned up at the repeating balconies that swooped overhead, up four floors. The hotel had opened for the first time earlier in the summer, and she'd not yet had time to sneak a look. The extravagance was breathtaking, and Wolfe had supervised its construction.

"Simon."

The voice was a woman's, and it indicated knowledge of the man that Chloe herself did not have. Chloe spun around. Beside her, Simon smiled and took the woman's hands in his and kissed her on the cheek. Chloe watched where his lips pressed smooth flesh.

The woman continued, "Where have you been? Last year, you spent all summer in the city. I absolutely depended on you. But here you've gone and spent the entire season, and half the fall, Upstate." She said the final word with added remorse.

Simon turned to Chloe and propelled her forward with a hand that hovered at the small of her back. She felt it only because the wool of her cape twitched. "Rita, this is Chloe Swann. Chloe, Rita Smythe."

Chloe accepted her hand. "You have ancestors here?"

Rita gestured with her hand once it was released. "The Smythe family is huge. Do you know someone?"

"Robert Smythe." She recited the verse from Revelations in her head. Her father had carved that stone twice.

Rita's head tilted. "I believe that branch of the family moved north for religious purpose."

Chloe nodded. That would make sense.

Rita turned back toward Simon and pulled him from where he stood behind Chloe. His pants took Chloe's skirt for several inches before letting it go. Rita leaned in, as though with a secret, "I've arranged to have us seated next to one another." The words were meant to carry under her breath, but they travelled directly to Chloe's ear. Simon straightened and looked at Chloe, then bent again. Chloe didn't hear the rest. She didn't have to. *Whispers and titters*. It was true. Other women wanted him. This woman wanted him.

She understood now what Hattie had meant, how a change of scene can make the light fall differently. He'd done nothing differently, nothing whatsoever, yet there was a change, a shift beneath her. He'd gone and done it, just like her brothers had warned. He made women want things. He'd made Chloe want things.

Simon returned. "They'd like everyone to sit." Chloe hadn't noticed how his conversation with Rita had ended, but she was glad it had. She removed her cape, and it disappeared with the help of a steward.

As they entered one of the dining rooms, Simon explained, "Rita Smythe's father is on the Seaway Commission with Wolfe."

She nodded. Chloe didn't ask how Simon knew her. The details were unimportant.

He pulled out her chair, then pushed it into her skirts as she sat. She expected he would sit down beside her, but he walked around the head of the table and seated himself across from her. Wolfe strode up and sat himself at the head. Chloe looked from the groom to Simon. They were at the very head of the table. She never would've dreamed that she'd be seated here, beside one of the wealthiest men in the islands. She searched for Meredith. The bride was seated down the long narrow table at the other end, flanked by her father and Virginia.

Simon lifted his chin to Wolfe. "A bit far away, don't you think?"

Wolfe unfolded his napkin and placed it on his lap. "It's better this way."

Simon comprehended his meaning. "Don't want to get distracted from your soup?"

Wolfe muttered under his breath, his eye drawn down the table. "What is she…?" He rose an inch from his seat, his eyes fixed on his bride as though ready to put a stop to imminent misadventure. He hovered above his chair, lifted a single eyebrow, then sat again, a corner of his mouth turned up, apparently relieved by the outcome of whatever scene had unfolded. Chloe's eyes did not make their way down to Meredith, fixed as they were on Rita Smythe's approach.

Simon stood as Rita was seated beside him.

Wolfe greeted her. "What a surprise. I expected your mother."

She teased him with an easy smile as she arranged the napkin across her skirt. "I hope I'm not a disappointment." Then Rita leaned over to Simon, and her arm extended at an angle indicating her hand was no longer in her own lap.

Chloe dropped her napkin, and before anyone could retrieve it, she ducked beneath the table. The linen tablecloth pulled at the coiled braids of hair as she went under. There was her napkin, and she was correct. There was Miss Smythe's hand, on the inside of Simon's thigh.

Chloe returned upright, extricating herself from the table linen.

By the time she had resettled in her seat, Miss Smythe's arm was at the proper angle, and Simon was eyeing Chloe with interest. Specifically, her bosom, with interest. Chloe realized Rita's gaze had landed there too.

She felt the bust of her dress, finding the hook and eye that had been accidentally released by her descent. She had to refold the metal with her thumb before she could slip it through the threads again. Her chin tipped in a subtle nod to glance at her progress, but she focused her eyes elsewhere.

Beside her, at the head of the table was Master Wolfe. He was trying not to laugh, his elbow propped on the table, fingers rolling on his lips, but he was not looking at Chloe as she refastened her dress. His eyes were at the far end of the table, where Meredith was drawing something in the air with her hands.

"That's an unusual dress." Rita directed her attention to Chloe.

"Thank you." She leaned forward. "I apologize. I didn't have time to make another, and I haven't had it on since before…" She looked down. They weren't even that large. Chloe checked with Simon, not knowing whether or not she might have crossed the bounds of etiquette, but he gave her no indication that anything untoward had happened at all. His gaze was in the empty plate in front of him. In spite of the woman beside him, her hand in his lap, and his risqué reputation, she wondered if he even knew the direction of untoward.

Rita dismissed her with a polite reply and turned to Simon again. "I hope there's dancing later. I can't wait to dance with you again."

Chloe leaned forward again. "Do you waltz?"

Simon reached for his glass, and Rita placed a hand over her heart, and her head tilted back. "Does he waltz?"

She asked the question as though it was rhetorical, and Chloe understood. *He could dance.*

Simon stood. Chloe realized with a start that he was really, very tall. She was used to men shorter than she was, so she'd stopped paying much attention to height.

He clinked his flute, and the room fell quiet. "On behalf of the groom, and his bride," he lifted his crystal in every direction, "I welcome you to the Hotel Columbian." His voice was loud enough to reach down and out to the second dining room, "And to these thousand islands. For some of you, I know this is outside your usual hunting grounds."

Laughter ran up and down the tables.

"Now that you're here, tell me that you ever want to leave." The general consensus was that they did not. "In spite of the fishing...and the boating...and the swimming…" A smile followed each phrase's pause. "Not to mention the magic of the water itself...Today, there is only one reason we are here."

He gestured to Wolfe and to Meredith, each in turn. "To the master and mistress of Wolfe Island, steadfast friends to others and to themselves, who waited, by my estimation, too long to wed…" He lifted his glass higher. "At last." Crystal clinked in agreement.

Chloe's glass was tapped, and she felt a flutter in her tightly bound breast. Oh, dear. How could she have thought him awkward? She sipped her champagne. He wasn't awkward at all.

16

Oak trees with trunks thick enough to hug lined the outside edges of Grandview Island's community lawn, a central green that surrounded the Hotel Columbian. The green sloped up to the woods and down to the water. Wolfe had ordered lit torches to surround a perimeter of green between the hotel and the River. Their fires added light to the setting sun and kept the mosquitoes at bay. Chairs had been arranged around rings of stones so guests and locals, too, could sit and overlook the water while a fire burned between them. The chairs around each ring were large and made especially for the hotel's numerous balconies. Wolfe had one hundred delivered to the lawn for the night's celebration.

Simon found a ring of stones at the center of the green, equidistant from the river and the hotel. Dropping to one knee, he arranged branches in a neat upward sweep. Once the campfire was ablaze, he pressed his knee into the grass and stood, scanned the hundreds of people strewn across the green. Through the dim light of dusk, he found Chloe. She'd been an irresistible flame for him all morning, and all day. He'd been forced to watch his plate for the entirely of their dinner to keep his eyes from the bust of her dress.

The green teemed with people. Shouts of laughter carried from the Pavilion. It was a grand party. Everyone was celebrating, but to him, the magic of the evening was more than the wedding, more than the titanic ship guarding Mosquito Island.

Her head was tipped back as though to look at the stars, but the sky was still too bright to see them, a midnight blue in the orange-pink of sunset. Her white sleeves and yellow hair glowed in the settling darkness. Sensing his eyes on her, she caught him watching and beckoned to him, as though he'd any intention of going elsewhere.

He wiped his hands on the back of his pants, hoping the black of the fabric would hide whatever dirt he put there. He took the shortest path across the green, but it still took him a full half-minute to arrive. While he walked, she studied his approach. He straightened his collar and tried not to stumble. He looked away. Oh for Pete's sake. Now he was shy? He forced himself to meet her eyes and smile.

One side of her head dipped toward the grass. She pointed at the sky. The clouds caressed a slivered almond slice of moon. "It was a new moon only a day ago, and look what we have now." Then she pointed at the water where the gorgeous shadow of *Onoko*'s riggings included three tall masts visible beyond Wolfe Island. "And look at that. The ship doesn't look as big from shore." Chloe raised herself up on her toes in a step that closed the gap between them with a bounce. "Everything feels new as that moon, don't you think?"

Simon could not have withheld his own smile had he tried. There was no reason to try. "You're drunk." The light was just going out of the day. It set off to the west, upriver. The red skipped pink over the water, and cast an otherworldly glow over the blond of her hair.

She stood straighter and checked the bust of her dress. "I am not."

He laughed. "That's right. You're a friend of Meredith's. You know how to hold your champagne."

His eyes abandoned her face and dropped again. Chloe's breasts were pulled together tight, forming white half circles over the neckline. The memory of the broken clasp teased him. Her hooks and eyes were handmade, and apparently prone to straighten. Not quite 'at the will of the wearer,' they had not been mass-produced. There were eight handmade fastenings, all fit to burst, and the only thing holding them together was the grace of God.

Simon opened his mouth, then shut it again. It was the right time to tell her. He had to try. He didn't even bother to reach for a cigarette. She stood beside him. Her cape was open, hood lowered. Her blue eyes glinted, although the catch light from the torches was yards away. "You have something," he touched his face just below his eye, "right here."

Her finger rose to her cheek to brush it away. She checked his face. "Did I get it?"

"No. It's..." His hand hovered above her cheek, then returned to his own, "...here."

She swept her cheek again.

Simon lied. There was nothing on her face. He just wanted to touch her, as though it would be easier to tell her if he were touching her, as though touching her would be enough. A part of him believed that she would understand now, if he touched her. *With my body I wed you.* The pledge would not leave the stream of his consciousness. His hand rose again.

She lifted her chin, offering her face to him. His fingers felt her jaw, the space between her ear and her cheekbone. He felt the tendrils of her hair. His thumb ran across the delicate bone beneath her eye. "There." He said, "There." But he thought, kiss me. You've done it before. Do it again. Right here beside this old oak. He willed the words through her. *Kiss me.*

"Your secret is safe with me."

Her lips cast a spell on him, and he couldn't look away until she spoke again, startling him.

"I've gotten an earful about your reputation."

He straightened, but his thumb remained on the curve beneath her eye. "Have you, now."

"I have. Even your friends say you're a heartbreaker, but you needn't worry about me. I'm immune."

"Immune?" He let the center of his palm find her cheek.

"It means resistant to disease."

"I know what it means." His eyes narrowed. "How do you?"

"I read the medical journals in Dr. Reed's office."

Dr. Reed was the physician who lived on Grandview Island. The locals all used him. Simon couldn't imagine why she'd be reading his medical journals, except that her experience tended toward the morbid. Perhaps the physic was a step in the right direction. "So, you're immune to *me*."

"You're dubious, I can tell. But it's the truth."

She was flirting with him. For some reason, it came as a shock. It shouldn't have shocked him at all. Women flirted with him. That's what they did.

She was close against him, her face tilted up to his. In any other situation, had it been any other woman making so little space between them, he'd have been kissing her by now, even with an audience. He'd been too busy begging her in silence to see it was just what she was looking for. His fingertips pressed the back of her hair. The base of his palm rested on the line of her jaw.

"My friend wants me to do something reckless, and since I'm immune to falling in love..."

The words hung in the air. Simon waited to hear what she would say next. The silence grew between them while she watched his mouth and waited. He held his breath until he could hold it no longer.

Her eyes twinkled in the dark, lifted to his. "I'm considering it. Just for fun."

He blinked. She was neither in earnest nor in jest. He had no inkling what she thought, what she felt. It was a hard task to tell her the truth while she teased him about not falling in love. His hand fell from her face. "There." Simon rubbed his fingers together and pretended to look for an eyelash or a speck of dirt. "Got it."

His lips hadn't formed a word he'd planned. He was a coward. He pinched a cigarette from the pack and checked his pockets for a match. He was looking for someone to ask for a light when the fiddle started, and the air crackled with something new. Before he could give it a name, his attention was pulled to the source.

It was Chloe. She'd vibrated when aloft the *Onoko*, but it was nothing compared to her response to the strings.

Chloe whispered the word in the hush between them. "Dancing." Then she picked up her skirts and pulled his arm. "Eric plays the fiddle and, when family comes, we all dance." She laughed at his surprise when she pinched the cigarette he held between his lips and tossed it over her shoulder. "Come on." She tugged on his arm and didn't relinquish her hold until they were halfway across the green.

Her hand abandoned his forearm to clap. He flexed his arm twice before his hand swiped across his sleeve, wiping the feeling away. On the fringe of mayhem, her smile was wide and infectious. She pressed against the bodies that formed a circle around the dancers. Simon stopped a few paces behind her, beyond the catch light of the torches. Every few minutes, she checked on him over her shoulder.

Without warning, a man in need of a partner dragged her into the press of bodies. Simon took an unthinking step forward when Chloe was swallowed by the mass. He held his breath until they all portioned out again, and he relocated her form. The dancers fell together and apart, time after time, a pattern: sometimes squared and sometimes round. Pairs of dancers wove inside other couples, collapsed to the center and returned out.

She moved through all other partners, circled around before returning to the first man who'd claimed her.

Simon chewed the outside of his thumb and studied the steps. Chloe already knew them. Sometimes she stumbled, but that too seemed part of the dance, catching her a part of the rhythm. Each man's arm wrapped around her waist. Each man's hands held hers. Turn after turn until she was dizzy. He frowned.

He wanted to be the one to make her dizzy.

Simon waited for the set to end, then took his place beside her, a hand on each side of her waist. She looked up at him in surprise. Her face was bright with joy. He didn't even care that it was for the dancing and not for him. The fiddle strings started again. He led her around the dancers and wove her through. Circling, weaving, touching her first at her waist, then holding her hands. Swinging until he felt the pull of her weight away from him.

Until suddenly she was gone, and he held a new partner. He watched her swing through. They passed close during a weave and a circle. He took her hands and pulled them high above her head, spun her once, twice. Then she was gone again. It pleased him to see other men could spin her only one time each.

Simon tracked her progress, focused on the step that would bring her close on another's arm, waited until it made her all the way through. The chaos and speed of the steps prevented speech. When they came together, they couldn't talk. He anticipated each return with an anxious thrill.

He was glad for the chance to watch her, and to grab her when he could, but letting go drove him nutty. Her fingers grasped his hand on a pass, and her thumb found his palm. He felt her deliberate caress. Then, like that, she was gone.

He made his face the picture of smiling nonchalance. By all accounts, he was having fun, dancing. It was grand. It was celebratory.

It was torture.

He should never have made the attempt.

She drew closer. This time, her hand touched the small of his back before it snaked around his waist. He looked down to remind himself of the length of his jacket. Was it long or short? Her fingers on his back made him hard as a rock, and the torch light made everything bright. He missed a step, and her arm tightened around him, the pressure of her hand increased as she guided them both through the final turn.

He swung her from the circle as soon as the bow fell on a last high note. She laughed as he propelled her from the rush, ushering her to the edge of the green, beyond the torchlight.

They reached the edge of the crowd, and Chloe caught her breath. "You can dance!"

He cut her a look, unable to suppress a grin. "Awkward men can't dance."

She blushed, or perhaps she was just flush from dancing. Either way, he liked it.

Chloe stretched her legs toward the fire, and lifted her skirt at the ankles. She ran her hands along the wooden flats of the lawn chair.

When she'd been pulled to the center of the group, she'd regarded Simon over her shoulder, thinking perhaps he might care. A small smile had lifted the corner of his mouth, his face aflame in torch light. Pleased. He'd seemed pleased enough to watch her dance with another man.

What should prevent him from being pleased? She asked herself the question, expecting it to give rise to an answer, but no answer arrived.

She wasn't the jealous type. She'd never before had the chance. She'd known Simon for less than a week, and in that time, he'd been the perfect gentleman. She'd been the one to tease him with her touch, a kiss. She'd been the reason they were here together. She'd asked him to bring her here. What right had she to feel jealous? Until now, she'd never even understood the word. Hattie had confessed to her, once, that she was jealous of the women her husband might meet in ports along the coast. It had seemed to Chloe at the time absurd to worry about something that was probably not even real, let alone a certain truth. Not like death.

She squeezed her fingers around the square edges of the wood and remembered the feel of her fingers along his side, around his waist while they danced on the green. She was surprised by how quickly he'd learned the steps. By the way he'd studied the dancers' feet, it was clear he'd been unfamiliar with the dance before now, but he'd picked up the steps quickly, as though he'd been dancing all his life. Perhaps he'd even studied the waltz. Isn't that what rich men did in the city? Study the waltz until they could perform the dance with beautiful women who danced just as well? An image flashed of Simon in a ballroom, twirling refined ladies across a shining floor.

Or perhaps he'd never danced at all before now, and Rita had been teasing.

No. She didn't believe it. He was a rake. He'd managed the woman's flirtations during dinner, before dinner, and after, she reminded herself. Not just managed them. No, he'd done more than that. Simon had gathered Rita's flirtations and played with them, like a cat, before sending them back, returning them, warmed and full of promise.

"Where's Tremont?" Virginia's soft voice interrupted Chloe's reverie.

There was a pause in the low conversation between Meredith and Wolfe. Loud calls from the green came in fitful bursts, and the fiddle played on. Virginia stroked a feather plucked from the hat that sat atop her head.

Wolfe broke the silence with a single raised brow. "I thought you didn't like him."

"I don't like him." Virginia shifted in her chair. "He couldn't delay his departure until after the wedding?" She shrugged. "Not exactly a show of friendship."

Chloe felt like a fish out of water. She'd stumbled into a story already halfway through. She leaned closer to Meredith, who sat beside her. The wood slat of the arm pressed into her stomach. "Who is Tremont?"

Meredith leaned in, too. "A friend of Wolfe's. They met during one of his trips abroad. He manages warehouses."

Simon arrived with more kindling for the fire. "Import and export."

Meredith leaned closer and smiled at Virginia across the fire. "He's very handsome, and a very good swimmer. Apparently he seduced a German princess."

Wolfe shook his head. "That story has not been verified."

Simon sat down in his chair. "I won't accept a retraction. The story is too good."

Wolfe shrugged. "I wasn't there, and Tremont knows how to tell a story."

"Then what of Mrs. Glynn?" Simon remained dubious.

Wolfe shook his head. "Also not verified."

Again, it was Chloe's turn to feel awkward. During dinner at the hotel, she'd felt out of place at the head of the table. Rita's friendship with Simon made Chloe feel even more wary of how far she'd strayed from Riverside. Now, they were talking about a man who had seduced a German princess, a friend of Wolfe's. Simon was also a friend of Wolfe's. Neither seemed much taken aback by the seduction of a foreign royal.

Simon sat across the fire from her, the other end of a semi-circle that opened to the water. Chloe grew hungry for his attention. If she lifted her skirt higher, he would see a flash of something white. He was a rake. He appreciated women's ankles, didn't he? She was tempted to do it. She'd never been tempted to do anything in her life. Now everything was a temptation. Chloe's heart beat against her chest. She willed her gaze from his neck, his hands, his jaw.

She shouldn't have come. The warning was a tinkling bell. Her feelings of physical desire and temptation were stronger than she'd expected. She thought it would be easier to control them, that like everything else in her life, the experience of them would be tempered by what came after, what always would come after, but the present was overwhelming her thoughts of the future. She had to get control, when all she wanted to do was let go.

Meredith tapped her arm. "Come swimming with me."

"Swimming?" Chloe looked around the green. The wedding party was in full swing. "You really would?"

Meredith looked across the fire. "Come with us, Ginny?"

"It's too cold to swim."

Meredith scowled. "Bite your tongue. It's only September."

Virginia hesitated, then relented. "For you, I'll put my feet in."

Chloe turned to Meredith, "I know just the place."

"Where the lilacs hide the rocks?"

Chloe nodded. "There." She cast a glance at Simon across the fire. If he had an opinion, he bit his tongue. He saluted her with a carefree finger to his brow and a half smile. Her own smile faltered.

Hattie had been dead wrong. He wasn't thinking about kissing her at all.

Wolfe passed Simon a cigar. The music was reduced to a single fiddle, playing a slow, sweet tune. They watched the water and smoked without speaking for several minutes.

Wolfe regarded the glowing orange tip of his cheroot. "I buried my father in the city. I've never been to Riverside."

Simon nodded, waiting. He and Wolfe had known one another a long time.

Wolfe, usually reticent, spoke again. "She's not your usual sort."

The fireworks started, a single hiss announcing the launch of the display. They watched the sky for more.

Simon leaned forward in his chair. "Do you think she likes me?"

Wolfe blew out a long trail of smoke. It was almost a laugh. "Why don't you ask her?"

Simon fell back again. "That's ridiculous. I'm not going to ask her."

This time, Wolfe did sound a rare bark of laughter. "God forbid."

Simon drummed the arm of the chair with his fingers, then ran a hand through his hair. He leaned forward once more, unable to sit still. "Have you ever had a moment of reinvention? Where you become suddenly someone else so completely you don't recognize who you used to be any longer?"

Wolfe frowned at the question. "I don't think I'd like it."

Simon kicked wayward embers toward the circle of rocks, then grabbed a few sticks near his chair. He broke each one in half before tossing them into the fire. "I've got an itch to try something new."

"If you're considering *someone* new, be careful."

"You're warning me away from a local girl?" Simon scoffed. "Coming from you, it's a bit hypocritical."

"I've known Meredith since she was as high as my hip."

"How long I've known her is not the only difference."

Wolfe tossed his cheroot into the fire and looked sidelong at Simon. "If you don't love her, stay away from her."

It was not love he felt for Chloe. The feeling, their connection, was too physical for love. He recognized desire, simple and pure, and he enjoyed it, everything about it. That is, he used to enjoy it. He used to love the discovery, the kindling, the build-up and release. But this, this was something new. Every feeling was wrapped up in ball, every moment of desire all at once, beginning to end. Simon fell back in his chair again and kicked at the dirt with the heel of his boot. There was no release, and, fucking hell, Wolfe was right. There wouldn't be.

Chloe rested the back of her head in the water. The Lake of the Isles was gentle, but the channel robbed control. Loud chops of water muffled sound, except her breathing and the hiss and bang of fireworks. She kicked and pumped her legs to stay afloat, swept her arms across the water. Cool water slapped against her cheeks and chin. The river was empty. Meredith and Virginia had left her at the shore to return to the campfire. Not a boat was in sight, save the *Onoko*. The fireworks launched from Wolfe Island crackled light across the water. She heard another hiss, then a booming pop.

That one she'd felt.

She thought of Simon. She liked him, enough so that it made her happy and frightened her at the same time. She'd wanted to kiss him when he brushed soot from her cheek. She'd never wanted anything so much in her life. It felt good, finally, to want something. She'd always held the feeling at bay.

A new round of fireworks were launched, and they lit up the sky, bounced off the water in reds and blues and greens. Everything about the day had been just this beautiful, the apex of what a day could be. But as beautiful and exciting as life was, it could be taken away in an instant. It was important to remember that nothing was forever, that death came for all, including her. Someday. She listened to the fizzle and sparks.

Not today.

She'd swum in the nude countless times, but she'd never before felt the water in quite this way. It pushed against her, everywhere. She let it push, let the waves move her from every direction. She closed her eyes and felt it. She thought of Simon, saw his face in her mind, pictured his hands on her neck, felt his hands move their way down her body, over her breasts, to her belly and thighs, between them. She watched her arms as they swept the water, watched the surface, the sudden color. Her legs scissored in a slow rhythm, her mind filled with Simon's face, his hands.

Simon shifted uncomfortably in his chair. Virginia and Meredith weaved toward them through the crowd. Chloe wasn't with them. It took the women a few minutes more to reach them, and he willed himself to remain seated, not to meet them as they approached.

They arrived and stood close to the fire, warming themselves. Meredith's hair was dry, but fallen tendrils were damp and curling. She had not gone under. Virginia still wore her hat. She had not gone in.

"Chloe?" Simon forced himself to remain seated.

"Still swimming." Meredith sat beside Wolfe. "The fireworks look like magic from the water."

Simon tossed his cigar, overtaken by a sense of foreboding. Chloe in the river. He shifted again in his chair, loosened the fabric of the tuxedo bow, and undid the top button of his collar. It was difficult to breathe.

He straightened to allow air more easily into his lungs. His hand jerked to his chest. He could get none, no air at all. He knew with a certainty he couldn't explain. Chloe was under water.

Getting out of his camp chair was slow. It clung to him like a child. Then it released him and he was upright and running. It was difficult to run without breath. He forced himself to inhale. He sprinted across the green, hearing noises of surprise as he passed. His legs pumped, and he bumped into bodies. He made a beeline ten marks south of the willow, then veered to the lilacs by the rocks, took the steep wooden steps three at a time out onto the adjacent dock, shedding his jacket and shoes. He heard the tuning pluck of a fiddle, the pop and crackle of fireworks. He tensed his thighs, jackknifed and straightened, angled to go deep.

In the dark water, her skin glowed like a beacon. She hung suspended, and her hands... His stroke shifted, and he pushed the water back, reversing directions, but not taking his eyes from her. Her hand pushed the water up, keeping herself down. Her other hand was at the juncture between her thighs. For the love of all that was holy. She wasn't drowning. His heart raced. He watched for one moment more, before lack of oxygen became a problem. He cut through the water again until he reached her. His hands found the spread of ribs beneath her breasts, and he launched her up to the surface. He followed her up with a stroke and broke the surface beside her.

She spun in a circle, her eyes on the water, her arms beating the river as she searched the surface.

"Chloe!" He called above the riot of sound – the fireworks, the splash of water, the chop of the waves in the channel. Her arms stilled, and in the pause of the firework display, he heard her breath, a cross between a gasp and a gulp of air. The fiddle strings from shore traveled the span of water.

"Simon." She gave a last glance behind her back, her head twitching over her shoulder. Then she cut the distance between them, seeming not to believe that it hadn't been the Loch Ness monster that had launched her to the surface. Her arms circled his neck before he could stop her. "What was it? Did you see it?"

Her bare legs kicked against his and he felt the warmth of her skin beneath his trousers. His shirt was thin, and her bare breasts pressed against his chest as though the cotton was not there at all. He remembered what she had been doing just the moment before. Had he stopped her before…? His hands spanned her bare waist to steady her.

She was frightened by what might be in the water with them, but she should have been frightened of him. Without her clothing between them, her skin pulsed with electricity, beyond any surge of energy Simon had felt from her before. The connection was primordial. Sparks must have flashed from his eyes, because her gaze shifted from fear to something else. It was his cue to release her. His eyes directed her to shore.

He swam close behind her. She was a fast swimmer. Her long arms pulled her through the water at a clip, and it was a challenge to keep up. He used to be able to sprint for a quarter mile, hell bent and without thought of breath, but he'd been too long away from the water.

Her eyes met his time and again over her shoulder. Reassured that he was still there, she swam faster. When they arrived to land, she scrambled up the rocks. Her body shone white in the darkness. Her skin glistened with it in running sheets. Her circles of braids were laden with water, yet still their luster was silver. The sprint had made him woozy, and the lack of oxygen had made him batty. It was clear he'd lost his mind, because he'd swear she was raining.

He tripped with his first step, caught himself and took two more while her eyes raked over him. He saw the question on her face as though she'd spoken the words. *How did you find me?* If she'd asked out loud, he would've told her, finally, what he'd been trying to tell her for days. They were connected. From the first moment they'd touched, they'd been fused together inside him as though invisible, inviolable filament extended between them. The connection was wholly sexual, and it was beyond sexual. It was as though if he ever… The shock of thought was interrupted by his shudder of breath. If they ever came together, he would dissolve.

She scanned the wet rock at her feet as though whatever creature had found her underwater might have chased her to shore. In her confusion, she had no idea that the only creature out there had been Simon.

He found his coat, stumbled to her. "They're coming." The words were a whisper for lack of air. Urgency compelled him. "Put on my coat." He covered her and fell away, putting as much distance between himself and her naked body as he could.

Everyone else arrived at once.

She shouted up at them, though her eyes never left his face. "There's a shark!" She brought the sides of Simon's jacket close together and tried to lose herself within it. Meredith descended to Chloe in a sweep of ivory silk. "The freighter brought a shark. Carried in the hull!"

It was mayhem. Everyone spoke at once. Gathered at the top of the slope, they peered down to the dripping couple below. Someone asked the crowd in general, "Shark in the hull?"

Meredith closed herself more tightly beside her. "Chloe, it's an iron clad hull. It carries one thousand tons of ore, dry as can be.

It could not have carried a shark." She whispered the next words in a patient hush. "That's not how ships work."

"Then a large school of fish. I was nearly drowned by something that swam into me."

A disembodied voice from the crowd suggested, "Muskie?"

Chloe shuddered. A muskie could swallow a person's head.

Simon leaned at a right angle, his hands grasping his knees. He'd nearly caught his breath. A finger pointed toward heaven. "It was me."

Chloe took a single step forward. Her bare foot pressed against the rocks. "You?"

He stared at her, then stood in a new struggle for control. Gasping became just great inhales of breath. His clothes were sodden. "There was nothing in the water. Only me." He'd tried to save her. Maybe she would think him heroic. "I thought you were drowning."

She flushed and clutched the sides of his jacket together more tightly.

There was a pause in the general tumult above them. Then, silence. The spectacle that had drawn them was given meaning. The men took in Chloe's nakedness, clad only in Simon's jacket. The women took in everything at once.

Wolfe descended and stood between Chloe, his wife, and the gathering throng. He leaned forward, so only the two women could hear him. "Shark in the hull." He enunciated each word. It wasn't a question. Although it was difficult with his Russian accent to hear inflection, he did not seem pleased.

Meredith took another look at Chloe and then at Virginia, who gave a whistle. Her wave rustled everyone from view of the shoreline. Meredith helped Chloe ascend the bank and guided her to the willow where she'd discarded her clothes.

Virginia tucked her arm through Simon's. "You're practically wheezing." She pulled him up the slope to the green. "I didn't know you were asthmatic."

He allowed Ginny to lead him, but Simon's eyes did not leave Chloe, where the hem of his white silk coat stopped at the middle of her thighs, right below the curve.

17

Chloe stared into the fire, her back to the water. She should have felt embarrassed. She'd been seen by countless guests in the all together. She'd suggested a shark had been in the river, wanting to devour her. There was no shark. It had been only Simon.

Simon.

She'd forgotten that she had been, in the moment before he emerged from the water, terrified. His white shirt clung to him as his chest rose and fell, hugged his arms, revealing the tanned skin and muscles beneath. His pants clung too, everywhere. He was long and lean, his thighs strong and well-formed. Everything that men's trousers hid was made clear. She'd not forgotten where her imagination had taken her only moments before he'd found her. If not for being seen without her dress, or for thinking a man-eating fish had found it's way into the river, she should have been mortified for that last part at least, but she was distracted by his uncanny timing. How had he found her? Her face grew hot again. Had he seen what she'd been doing right before?

Chloe put her chilled hands to her face to cool her cheeks. When she removed them, Simon had returned. He studied her from across the warped air of the fire.

"You're not going to have another episode, are you?" It was Virginia, sitting tall in her chair.

"One can never be sure, Lady Virginia. I think it's time I took Chloe home."

He'd changed into less formal attire, out of his black tuxedo pants and white shirt into a dark suit. She realized with a pang that she'd left his tuxedo jacket beneath the willow. She'd almost left her underclothes there, she'd been in such a hurry to dress.

He'd also dressed in haste. He'd forgone the niceties of a tie, and one piece of his shirt hung outside his trousers. His hair was still wet and had not been combed.

They walked for fifteen minutes at a strenuous clip. Chloe struggled to keep up. She prided herself on her physical health, but she was out of breath by the time they entered the path to the Swann cottage through the cemetery grounds. The unspoken burdened her lungs further. They ached with the unsaid.

Finally, she could wait no longer. "Simon."

He stopped and turned, waited, mute. She sensed words ready to tumble forth and made her voice soft. "I thought you didn't swim."

It no longer mattered how he'd known, or what he thought. His brother had drowned, and tonight he thought she'd been drowning. She couldn't allow him to believe it. "I…I wanted...Since we've met…" She stammered. How could she possibly explain? "I wanted to know how it felt to be touched." She ignored his silence, pushed through the embarrassment. "How it would feel to let go."

The Frederik stone was beside her, a monument in the night. Her brothers had set it the day before, with dramatic muscle and sweat. It stood tall and white. She lifted her hand and trailed her fingers down the marble. They dipped and tracked with the words carved there.

He stepped closer. "At first I thought…But then I knew...I'm not sure which was worse."

She stepped away, closer to the stone, its weight and substance.

He stepped again, closing the distance between them. She felt the warmth of him. It contrasted with the cold marble against her side, and then her back, as he pressed himself nearer.

At last she voiced the question. "How did you find me?"

His eyes found hers. He understood her question, what she asked of him. It was the last thing she thought before his hand found the back of her head and pulled her to him.

She hadn't time to consider anything but the exhale of breath as his lips found hers, a warm respite from the questions that teased her. She'd wanted him to kiss her for hours. She was not disappointed. He lifted his mouth. "Don't do that, out there, again."

She shook her head and chased her mouth to his, but he pressed his forehead to hers. Anxiety, the fast walk, and his kiss had stolen her breath. His finger trailed down the center of her dress. It tapped a pause on each hook, pointing to the rise and fall. It stopped its descent at the bottom on the last fastener, then his thumb joined his finger. He said, "I'll find you if you do," and pulled.

The hook straightened with a pop of release. His eyes did not leave the space that it left open. His finger trailed to the next fastening, an inch above. Again he pulled, testing, focusing on the experiment of when, with how much pressure it would bend, or whether the threads would break.

Chloe held her breath until the need for air pressed her chest against his hand. She exhaled once, twice, then held it again. She didn't want to help him break open her dress, but she didn't want him to stop. She wanted to watch.

The sight made it difficult to pull air into her lungs. His fingers and the journey they made cast a spell. He raised his eyes to hers, waiting for her to put a stop to his ascent.

Instead, she touched his head. The fingers of both hands combed through the thick, sandy hair that had dried in waves. He stilled when she touched him. His hands hovered at her ribs, between her abdomen and her breasts, so close that she felt a pulse of energy between them.

The wind shifted. His head bowed over her breasts, his hands tugged the white blouse low. Found by the cool air, her nipples peaked and tightened. His shoulders tensed, then his mouth was on her breast. At the feel of his tongue, her shoulders and hips pressed against the stone. The bowed arch of her back brought him closer. His hands found the curve of her back, pulled her tighter, then pushed her back. He found her wrists and lifted them above her head, transferred her arms to one of his hands. He reached down and pulled at her skirts, grasping the fabric in handfuls. She moaned when his finger teased her, and her knees buckled. His thighs between her legs held her up.

With my body I wed you. He pushed inside her and was overcome. It was that simple. The hand that had held her wrists released them, and his palm flattened against the stone. His face pressed against her neck. He breathed in the scent of her hair. He finished while her cry was still in his ear. His face fell into her neck. An adulthood of study and application into what pleased a woman, and nothing to show for it. Not that it mattered. He wished that it could.

It took him a moment to come to himself, place himself where he was. Focus his attention on any point outside of her, any point at all.

It was her fingertips finally that roused him. They pushed the hair from his forehead, traced the bones beneath his eyes. The sky was dark, but the white of her sleeves and the white of the stone found their way through the darkness.

He felt every muscle in his back. He was still hard. "I'm sorry I hurt you."

She shook her head.

He pulled himself from her, pushing away from the stone with the hand that had held her wrist. She lowered onto her heels from her toes. Her dress was open to the waist, the metal teeth gnarled. The coils of braids on each side of her head were lopsided, and her eyes gave off a preternatural glow. He couldn't imagine what she thought. There was only one way to fix the situation, but there was no time to do it again, properly. He had to get her home. Simon buttoned his pants. She watched his hands as they retucked the tails of his shirt.

"I left your tuxedo jacket on the green." She met his eyes, then they dropped again. "Would you fetch it?"

The green was a twenty-minute walk, fifteen minutes each way, if he ran. He reached for her dress, prepared to fix the fasteners. "I have to get you home."

"You should go." His hands hovered before dropping to his sides. She qualified, "To get it."

He took one last look at the gnarled metal hooks, each hem at the bust falling open off-center, turned, and ran.

Chloe dipped her head and started re-bending the wires, looping them through each eye. She'd gone and done it. She'd put up no fight at all. No hesitation. Not a word of resistance. Had she done any of those things, he would have stopped. She knew it in her bones. He would've let her go. She was safe with him. She bit her lip as she moved to the second hook. But she didn't feel safe at all. She liked him much, much more than she should. She'd wanted just a taste of what it meant to be close to a man. She'd wanted a taste, and now she had it. It was time to go home and forget the whole thing.

She refastened her dress, worked up from her waist the way he had done not five minutes before. Her skin prickled, tingled at the thought. Forget the whole thing? How in the world would she do that? Every single thought, static images and the motions of strung-together pictures, whatever remained in her mind now made her tingle. Her body responded to the memories of its own accord. The memory of a sound, his voice in her ear, shocked the muscles in her abdomen, pushed out her breath in an involuntary rush. Her hand covered her mouth, forgetting for a moment the perverted wire. It had been the most thrilling moment of her life.

She tried to focus on the next hook. She still had three more to go, but her attention was drawn to beneath her skirts. She bit her lip again. The lake was close. The point formed a small bay, where it was easy entrance for swimming. Less than a quarter mile away, she might not make it back before Simon returned. He might believe she'd fled without saying good-bye. The thought arrived with another in tandem. What if he wasn't coming back?

18

Damn. He hadn't seen that coming. He wasn't sure he would've been able to prevent it if he had. Damn, damn, *damn*. The word kept time with his steps. He walked, then ran, walked again, his gait picking up speed until again he ran. Running or walking, either choice felt ridiculous. There had to be another option, an alternative where his feet didn't have to touch the ground.

He should've seen it coming, should've stopped it outright. What was the good of being a rake if he couldn't control himself? He'd taken her without any thought of her pleasure, or her safety. What if he gave her the clap? His pace slowed. No, he didn't have the clap. He ran again. It had been a month since he'd been inside a woman. He would've known in less than a week if he'd been sick. Anyway, he'd always worn a sheath.

He tripped on a something, spun in a circle looking for an offending branch and found nothing.

Wolfe had been right. She wasn't like the women in the city. He'd avoided women who wanted marriage, avoided their fortunes and their families and whatever lived beneath their skirts, but he'd not avoided this one.

He didn't want to get married.

The declaration in his head, once familiar, held now no resonance.

She might say no. His steps slowed again. What if she said no? His pace increased. She wasn't allowed to say no. Neither of them were allowed, not after tonight. They'd be married, whether she wanted to or not. He'd make the case to her family. They'd see reason. The memory of her brother, Eric, stopped Simon in his tracks, almost threw him backwards. He hoped he wouldn't have to make a case to Eric.

He arrived at the green. The party still raged. The fiddler hadn't stopped playing. The torch lights hadn't stopped burning. He saw Meredith and Wolfe at the edge of the water boarding a boat that Simon presumed would return them to Wolfe Island, or to Mosquito Island. He wasn't sure. They hadn't shared where they'd spend their honeymoon. Their intimacy left no space between them, no space at all.

The willow beckoned him from the far edge of the green, close to the water. His jacket winked bright in the dim moonlight. It was bundled neat and tight. The lapels had been smoothed, and the silk white handkerchief in the front pocket tucked and pulled out again in a perfect triangle. He picked it up from the grass with a swoop of his arm and started the run back. He didn't fool himself with walking. He chanted again in time with his steps, ran through Italian verb conjugations in his head, the way he used to do when he swam distances to keep his mind occupied. Io sciogliere. Tu sciogli. Noi sciogliamo.

I dissolve. You dissolve. We dissolve.

He ran through the cemetery, pushed his way through thick hedges, and slid down an embankment. The breaking of twigs made a racket. Simon heard his fall echo back from the lake across twinkling light on rippled glass. The tops of her thighs crested above the waterline, her skirts collected in her arms. When she noticed him on shore, she waded back faster, sheepish, her skirts held high against her chest. Gathered about her, her petticoats looked like a bird floating in the bay. A graceful, white swan, sleek and silent.

She dropped her skirts, and she followed them to the ground. Sitting, she lifted her toe into her stocking and rolled it up. "You found me again."

He sat beside her and, brushing her fingers away, pushed her back against the grass. He lifted her skirt higher and found her garters, clipped them on with an easy snap, one on the inside and one on the outside of her thigh. "I told you I would."

"How did you find the path?"

"There was a path?"

Chloe pushed herself up from the grass and touched the stain of mud at his knee where it was clear he'd fallen down the bank. "If you didn't find the path, I'm surprised you're not covered in mud. It's a ten-foot drop. Why did you bother?"

"You were here."

"How did you know that?"

He ignored that a simple answer would be the perfect way to tell her. They were connected, whatever the word meant, for good or ill, in sickness and in health, whether she was up for the task or not. Instead he said, "The water's here. I'm fated to follow you to it tonight."

"I wasn't drowning." Her fingers rested against his leg, even after they'd brushed the dirt away.

Simon's smile wavered. "I know what you were doing. Tell me what you were doing this time."

She shook out her skirt. "I was uncomfortable."

"I made you uncomfortable."

She shook her head. "You've never made me uncomfortable. Not so far."

He forced his next smile. "I'll have to try harder."

She sat up again and reached for her second stocking, mimicking the actions of the first. When they were rolled on, he pushed her down again, again took charge of the garter snaps. He let his fingers trail over her inner thigh, feeling the pull again to be inside her.

She tilted her head along the grass. "I thought you were in a rush."

He was, and he wasn't. He had been in a rush. He would still be in a rush. He knew it. "I never...I've never…" He did not know which never to list first.

She looked at him with a peculiar expression, a mingling of confusion and surprise. "I meant in a rush to get me home." She sat up and slipped on her shoes. She shook out her skirt, then paused. She edged to the shoreline and asked over her shoulder. "Do you have a handkerchief?" He handed one to her, and she wet it with lake water.

He edged closer, seeing what she was about. A weight dropped in his stomach. Her dress was blood-stained. The white underskirt was streaked with red at the hem. Her chin hovered above her bent legs as she leaned forward to clean it.

She tilted her head, and a cheek rested for a moment at the peak of her knees. "It was my first time, too."

Simon thought his heart would break. He took the handkerchief from her. "Don't rub. Dab."

* * *

It was midnight. He'd promised to have her home by ten.

"I should discuss the hour with your father."

"You won't be discussing it with my father. It will be Eric." She whispered as they entered the lane to the cottage. "Da's in bed."

Simon slowed. Her brother, Eric was a tall man, large and blond. He would have been brutish, but he carried his height with a long, lean frame and a shock of white blond hair. Eric was a Viking, and he would pummel Simon into the ground.

He gestured with his hand to her hair. The braids at her ears were still crooked. She grasped each side at once, and pulled them into alignment, straightened them like a hat. Simon covered his mouth in a laugh. It had helped. He stopped laughing when she stepped against him, and brushed his cheek with her lips.

"Goodbye, Simon." Then she was in the shadows, and the darkness swallowed her cape.

Eric greeted him outside a shed that glowed with orange light. His greeting was a drawn-out "Hey." The syllable ended with an upward lilt, like a question. Another man might have thought the word a sign of welcome, casual and unguarded. Simon knew better. It was the only word Simon had ever heard him speak. He'd said it before in passing. It was his way of saying 'hello.' It had never been partnered with a smile, had never been anything more than an acknowledgement of sharing the same space. True to form, Eric was not smiling now.

Simon didn't bother with small talk. He approached without speaking until he stood a few feet away. Eric straightened from where he leaned against the jamb, and tossed whatever had been in his hands back into the shed. Simon heard wood and metal land together. Then Eric's attention was on him, waiting, expectant. His arms rested at his sides. One of his hands twitched.

"We should be married."

Eric's face grew fierce. He took a step forward. "I should knock you down."

"Do it."

Eric took another step and hit him solid and fast in the jaw. Simon took it, but did not go down. Without question, Eric had held something back. Had he used the full force of his fist, Simon would have hit the dirt in a senseless heap. He was glad it had been his jaw and not his nose. Those punches hurt more and looked worse.

Eric pushed his body against Simon's, using his chest to rush him again. "You think we'll just let her go?"

Simon pressed his shoes into the dirt. Eric struck him again with his body. This time Simon's feet traveled two steps backward before he caught himself.

Eric's fists were in balls at his hips. His body threatened Simon again with a jerk, but he retreated before they clashed. "She even want to marry you?" His tone suggested that he didn't believe it.

Simon studied the man's face, tense with restraint. He chose his next words carefully, though there were few options. "You could persuade her."

Eric fell back a step, for the first time giving Simon space between them. "Persuade her?" His laugh was a harsh syllable in the dark. "What would she gain from a marriage to you?"

Simon considered the question. He had no answer that didn't include an inventory list from his store.

Eric did not relent. "You're not the man for her."

Simon shook his head, not having to consider his next words. "I am the only man for her." He would allow no others. It was just a matter of how to stop them. In one fell swoop, as he now proposed, or one by one, until he died chasing them off.

Eric's fists released slowly. The set of his jaw showed his determination against the idea. He was well aware of Simon's reputation, that trusting him placed Chloe's happiness in a precarious position, but his words were a capitulation. "Mass is at eight tomorrow morning. The priest will be at the chapel by seven."

Simon's shoulders fell with relief. He hadn't realized they'd been approaching his ears, waiting for a physical blow. Instead, Eric would simply send him away to stew in the urgency that flooded his veins. "Where is she from?"

Eric was taken aback by the question. "From?"

He should turn on his heel and run before Eric reconsidered and beat him to a bloody pulp. "Your family isn't from here."

His lip curled in contempt. "Is yours?"

Simon was treading on dangerous ground. To suggest that a person was from elsewhere implied that they did not belong. Immigrants. Simon shook his head. "My grandparents came over on a boat. So did yours. But from where?"

Eric still eyed him with a wary frown, but he answered. "My mother's family is from Belgium. Chloe has a grandmother there, in Oostend."

People spoke French in Belgium. There must have been some exchange between the two countries. A small part of him had wondered if he and Chloe might be related. If he'd felt what he felt with his twin, and now with Chloe, perhaps…

Eric continued, "My father is a Swede."

That explained the blond hair. Simon had been right to think her Nordic. So perhaps they were only distant cousins. The idea was absurd, but the most absurd ideas had been traveling through his mind at the speed of sound. He didn't believe they could be cousins, however much he liked the thought of sharing her blood, but he wanted to know where she'd come from. He wanted to know everything about her, find the source of this thing that was feeding his soul.

19

Chloe sat in the middle of her bed, legs crossed. Her braids were still coiled, but she had shed her cape and her dress. Her nightgown was thick and white against her, tucked beneath. Her heart pounded. She wondered if her brother would ask her for details. She had, until now, never given him a reason to question her.

Eric appeared in her doorway and began as he always did, without preamble. "Do you like him?"

The words sounded foreign on Eric's lips. Until now, there'd never been a man to ask about. Chloe fumbled for a reply.

He pressed his question. "Do you like him?"

Simon was likeable. Likeable. Chloe repeated the word in her head. He was that. "Yes."

Eric frowned at her answer. "Good. You're getting married before mass tomorrow."

She stood from the bed. The goose down blanket sagged where she'd sat.

Married? She knew she'd looked disheveled, and that Eric had seen her from the entrance to the atelier. He'd been leaning up against a jamb, waiting, a whittling knife and a stick making rhythmic noises in the dark. She'd slowed down to greet him but had not stopped. With that, he'd known, and now he was going to make Simon marry her.

"He doesn't want to marry me."

"He does. He's proposed it."

"Well, he didn't propose it to me." Her chest tightened. She felt the old suffocation. One night she could manage. The memory she could handle. A marriage? She gulped a breath of air and blew it out in a whisper. "Why would he do that?"

"Why do you think?"

She'd seduced him, and he'd been a virgin. How was that for a reason? She should've listened to her instincts. Everyone had talked of his reputation, but she'd seen something different than the man they'd described. Her face fell to her palms. She should've stopped it. She should've stopped everything.

Eric continued, "Simon Low has one thing in his favor as far as I'm concerned. He has the means to take you away from here. A cemetery is no place for a girl your age. Not my sister at least. Do you want to be known your whole life as the Angel of Death?"

She'd wanted a means of escape, a means of letting go of the burdens of goodbye. Here was a way out, but to a place far more dangerous. It would've been easy, simple to separate the two, desire and love, but not if she had to spend every day with him. How would she protect herself against him then?

Eric stepped into her room and closed the door behind him. His stillness spoke. "Could there be a baby?"

Chloe hadn't thought that far ahead, had not thought beyond the moment that replayed now in her head, came in waves that washed over her. No, she had not considered repercussions. "I don't know," she lied. Eric swore, and made to punch the thick oak door behind him, but held his fist back. The sound would have woken the household.

"When was the last time you bled?"

She hid her face in her hands. "Oh, God."

"That has something to do with it. It's how they know to breed the cows."

Exasperated, Chloe spoke through her fingers, "We're not farmers, Eric."

"No, we're ditch diggers, but you should know something about the process. Anyway, I thought you were reading those doctor books."

Her hands dropped. "I don't have to learn about making babies from a medical journal." She wasn't a complete idiot. She knew how babies were made. Hattie had made three already, but Eric never thought of that.

"You and Meredith Wells plundered Wolfe's library of every lurid book you could get your hands on. You might've learned something about it from there." He continued, "What about Meredith's pictures?"

Meredith had illustrated an anatomy manual for women. Chloe had an advance copy. "What pictures?"

You don't have to lie to me. I've seen them." He rubbed the back of his head until his hair stood on end from behind. His arm extended to her like an entreaty. "You could've learned a thing or two from them."

Chloe sank onto the mattress. Her legs would no longer support her. The memory of the Frederik stone pressed against her back. She pressed her eyes with her palms. "I don't want him to think I did this on purpose."

"This is Simon Low, Chloe." Simon's name on Eric's lips sounded dirty. "Women do what he wants. There is no purpose but his own, and right now he wants to marry you." Eric's face softened, although to anyone other than his sister, it would've looked the same. "You can't say I didn't warn you."

Oh, she'd taken his warning. Taken it and tugged at the strings of its meaning until the warning had unraveled in her hand.

When what she should have done was buried it, buried it like a stone.

Simon pushed off aboard a boat from the Grandview dock where Wolfe kept one moored. It wasn't unlike the skiffs he and his brother had been racing the day of the squall. It was still hours before dawn. The wind was up. He hoisted the small sail, moved from bow to stern as air caught in the lightweight canvas. The skiff carried him at a clip.

He'd not sailed since that day, had done his best to stay clear of boats, with the exception of a required ferry. He'd made exceptions to travel to Wolfe Castle or to see Meredith on Mosquito Island, but each trip had been maddening, strung him taut while he waited for the water to pass beneath him, waited for his shoes to touch land.

Neighbors on surrounding islands must have considered it a favor when they'd hauled the wreck of Simon's boat to shore after the storm, but the sight of it had made him sick. He'd burnt it that very night in a bonfire after breaking it into pieces with an ax. It was the first thing he'd done after losing Michael. The very first thing, after he'd told his mother her other son was gone. Somehow, by the time he'd reached her, she'd already known. Her face had told him as much. He supposed mothers always knew.

He hadn't visited his mother at their summer home in two years. It was a journey he'd been loath to take, a space of water he wouldn't cross. Now, the thirty minutes it took to reach home felt like an age. He trained his eyes on the island's tree-lined shore as soon as it came into view, found his mother's house on the eastern side, flanked by two tall pines, and fixed his vision there. He didn't glance from side to side. He was alone on the water. There was nothing to avoid. Not even a shoal. Nothing to avoid but the water itself, and it was too late for that.

He reached the shore and married the skiff to the dock, taking down the sail before he'd fully arrived. The dock had fallen into the water. Two bad winters of ice and thaw had degraded it to a mass of half-submerged boards and tilting pilings. He pushed at what remained to test its strength before hopping onto it and tying off.

At the end of the dock was a small boathouse, painted green and white to match the house. The paint was chipping, but paint this far north was always chipping. Someone would scrape it early next season and apply a fresh coat. The boathouse had pitched. Its foundation had shifted over the last two winters. Simon wasn't sure what was to be done about that. Wolfe would know.

He took steps up the rock face to the lawn before the house. He was glad to see it was not also falling down. Two white diamonds shone in the center of the painted green front. Horizontal and true, they lacked expression. They didn't deride him for having stayed away. He walked across the stout lawn and followed the rounded porch to a break in the expanse of screen. The porch floor was painted blue, and he could see even in the moonlight that it did not require repainting. It remained the color of fair-weather sky, and the floor still creaked. It was all there, all the same. All different, transformed. It wasn't his house that had changed.

He pulled the white porcelain knob and lifted the door out of the jamb before pushing into the house with a scrape of wood. The entryway opened into the main room. High ceilings vaulted with natural wood beams. They'd had to use a ladder to remove nests from the rafters, and the house always had bats.

When they were ten, their father had once locked he and Michael in a room with a bat, a sack, and a badminton racket. Simon had screamed with a high-pitched squeal of delight and terror, eyes shut, waving the racket above his bowed head, each time the bat had flown close. Michael had remained, as usual, stoic. He'd aimed his racket with more purpose. In the end, they'd had to work together to catch that bat, Michael with the racket, Simon with the sack.

Light through a window bathed the back porch in yellow. At two in the morning, it was rare for anyone to be awake. The river made people take to their beds well before their usual bedtimes in the city due to exhaustion or exhilaration, or both.

He walked through the main room to the back and found his mother upright in a wicker rocker, her lap covered with a knit cotton blanket.

She looked much the same. Even asleep, she had apples in her cheeks. Her knitting was on the table, not put away in the basket at her feet.

He pulled out a chair and sat. His knees faced her. He leaned in, taking her hand. "Maman." Her eyes opened. They rested on his face for several beats before she blinked. She worked the fingers of her second hand into Simon's, where he already held the fingers of her first.

Simon admonished her. "You were pretending I was Michael."

"It was good to see you both."

Simon indicated the oil lamp still burning at the table. "Were you expecting someone?"

"It appears I was expecting you. Have you eaten?"

"It's two o'clock in the morning." He'd eaten at two o'clock in the morning before, but it had never been a meal made by his mother.

"Eggs?" She stood. "I was about to make myself some eggs."

Simon followed her through the dark to the kitchen. She opened the gas, and the lamp beside the stove glowed. She pulled a bowl of eggs from the pantry and looked over her shoulder at him, looked him over, head to toe. Then she nodded to the table at the wall. He sat. He ran his finger along the grooves of the soft wood. His knees hit the table's edge, so he extended them beneath.

Neither said a word while butter and eggs sizzled in the iron skillet. She lay two thick pieces of bread along the edges, flipping them once after turning the eggs. Then the mass of food was on a plate and set before him. A fork and knife followed. His mother pulled out a second chair, sat, and waited.

Simon wasn't hungry, but he cut the food into pieces until the entire thing was a mass of yolk and fried butter and bread. His mother lifted the salt and pepper shakers from their place on a shelf above their heads and placed them at the top of his plate. He used both and ate while she watched. When he finished, he pushed the plate away.

"I'm getting married."

"Does she cook?"

Simon blinked. He didn't know.

"What's her name?"

"Chloe."

"She's French."

"She's from Belgium."

"She's French. That's a French name. Who's her father?"

"It's Matteus Swann." At her blank look, he reminded her, "He carved Michael's headstone."

She frowned. "That's odd." Before he could agree, she continued, "I wouldn't have thought the local women were for you."

He made a wry face. "Families have tried to keep them away."

"This one did not?"

"Not hard enough."

"Why didn't you bring her?"

"She's asleep." An image of Chloe beneath white sheets startled him. Her white blond braids resting each against the pillow. "And she hasn't yet agreed."

"When will she give you an answer?"

"Tomorrow morning at seven."

His mother's eyebrows rose. "What's the rush?"

What was the rush? It was all rush. He hadn't forgotten Meredith's words. *There are no tomorrows with Chloe.* He fidgeted with the fork against his plate until his mother took it from him and carried them both to the sink. She pressed her backside against the gleaming white cast iron and waited.

He leaned back against his chair and crossed his arms over his chest. "I want it settled."

"You've found a new toy?"

"Maman." It was a rebuke.

"You and your brother were the same that way. Every Christmas, you would take your packages and retreat to your rooms."

Simon shook his head. Michael went. He'd followed. "It's not like that at all. It's something else."

The city was filled with women who wanted him, and Simon knew what it felt like to need a woman. He'd grown used to attachments with women fueled only by sexual curiosity. This was not that. "It's…" He pressed his hands to his eyes. "Electrifying."

Her head tilted as she looked at him. She studied him for an age. Then she stood. "It's ridiculous you didn't say so in the first place."

"Say what?"

"You're in love."

Simon stood. "I'm not."

She shook her head. "Men are daft." He followed her through the main room to the stairs, which creaked as they ascended. He followed to her bedroom. A quilt covered the mattress between the four-poster bed. The room smelled fresh. Windows were open, and a breeze pushed out sheer, white curtains. A jewelry box sat atop a low wide set of drawers covered in glass. When she opened it, it spit out three layers of velvet shelving. Beneath the tiers was a small compartment, and she reached into it. "My aunt was a twin."

Simon nodded. "I remember."

"The other died at birth, so she didn't grow up with her sister. But twins are strange things." She removed a square wood box, opened it. A ring sat in the center of a tuft of cotton. "My aunt gave me this when she died," she held it up, "for you or Michael when you marry." She handed it to him. The choice of its owner had been made. "There's an inscription. I thought it might be religious." The tip of her finger stopped an inch away from the ring as Simon tilted his head to read its interior.

You inside me. Me inside you.

Simon made a noise. How had Chloe's grandfather's epitaph arrived inside his great aunt's ring? There were no calculations he could attempt to explain it. Aside from the obvious answer, that Chloe's grandfather was a rake who made his way from Belgium to France, where his great-aunt was born and buried…His train of thought was interrupted. What if he and Chloe were related? Their love story would become a Dickens novel, but what was the other possibility? How was it that Chloe's wedding ring would now have the same inscription as her grandfather's grave? There was another answer, and the door that led to the secrets of the universe banged against its frame like a screen door in the wind.

His mother looked at him in surprise. She read the words aloud. "Do you know what it means?"

Simon nodded. It wasn't religious.

20

When he reached his room at the hotel, it was half past five. The dawn and lack of sleep made everything dreamlike. He redressed in his tuxedo. He was glad now he'd retrieved the jacket. Two hotel chambermaids arrived with a portable ironing board and two flat irons. Simon answered the door without his pants. He had his shirt, buttoned to the neck. But his trousers were in shambles. He had held them aloft. "I'm getting married at seven this morning." He didn't know how else to explain it, the urgency he felt.

The uniformed women looked at one another and closed the door behind them. One bobbed a crooked finger at Simon and said, "Off with your shirt."

When he arrived at the chapel, the Swanns were there, two twinnish boys that shared Chloe's brilliant blond hair, and her mother.

Chloe and Eric were nowhere in sight.

Smooth rolling and a following thunk signaled wheels on the sidewalk, the end of one piece of slate and the beginning of another. A young woman sat upright, pushed in a wheeled chair. Her fingers hovered over the wheels while two small children stood on either side. A boy and a girl, both younger than school age, navigated the sidewalk. She carried an infant swaddled tight in her lap. Her knees were raised high so the baby wouldn't tumble off.

They were coming to the ceremony, all dressed in their Sunday best. There was nowhere else they could be going. They stopped where Simon stood at the walk that led to the chapel. He scanned the sidewalk in both directions, hoping to find Chloe and her brother approach.

Nothing.

Simon squatted next to the young mother. "May I carry you inside?"

"Yes." She extended her hand. "I'm Harriet Blount."

He accepted it. "I'm Simon Low."

"I know. You're the only groom here."

He looked to the children. "Can you help me carry your mother inside? You look together like you might be strong enough." They smiled like each had been offered a chocolate. He pushed the chair to the steps, then hefted her up.

"I'm Chloe's maid of honor." She nestled her fingers in the curl of the baby's hand, then corrected herself. "Matron."

Her face was eye level with his. She was pale and her eyes were circled in shadow. She couldn't have been any older than his bride. "Where is she? Is she coming?"

She raised her eyes to his, surprised. "Eric asked me to stand up for her. That was only an hour ago. I haven't spoken with her yet." He set her down, but her chin lifted to maintain contact with his eyes. "You don't know if she's coming?"

Simon grimaced. "I haven't asked her directly." The uncertainty of Chloe's arrival made his heart beat, made him feel it. Every blasted, blessed thump.

Harriet moved the child to her shoulder, and rubbed her cheek against the skin of the baby while she watched Simon's face. Finally, she said, "She could do a poorer job of it."

Simon hoped so. He walked to the front of the chapel and clasped his hands in front of him. He stood for a full five minutes, alternately avoiding the eyes of every person in the room.

A bell rang in the roof, and Simon stood at attention. Its mournful bong reverberated along the empty street. Someone was pulling on the rope.

An hour too early to be beckoning churchgoers, Chloe knew the bell was for her. Would she never hear a bell that didn't terrify her? Her father's feet shuffled beside her. They waited, silent, for Eric. Now would be the time for Chloe's father to impart some wisdom, to have finally some opinion on the matter of her life and its direction. His eyes were clear but unconcerned. To him, it seemed just another morning. Some mornings were for burials, others for weddings.

"Da."

His eyes rose to hers from where they'd been watching his feet, unsurprised that she had something to say.

She willed his attention. "I think we should go."

He pursed his lips and rubbed the lobe of his ear. "Your mother will be unkind." It was an understatement, but her mother's interest in Simon's money was no reason to get married. He tugged at his ear again. "And Eric will have something to say about it."

"But, Da, what do *you* have to say about it?"

He shrugged. "You'll feel better once you get used to it."

She pulled at the sides of her skirt in frustration. Used to it? She didn't want to get used to it. That was the problem. The entire problem. If she got used to it, she would miss it when it was gone. It. Him. The way he looked at her, the way he touched her, the way he took care of her. She didn't want to get used to it, or to him.

There. She made her decision. She'd tell him goodbye. She owed him that much.

She turned to go, but Eric's approach stopped her. He stood at the bottom of the steps she'd just determined to run down and looked up, divining her intentions. He wore the suit he hated. His white blond hair was too long, The shock of it had been pushed from one side of his forehead to the other, and another thick swath fell into his eyes. He used his fingers now to put back in place. "I never knew you to be scared of anything before."

She tried to memorize that blond shock of hair, the hard challenge of his eyes. Someday her brother would also be gone. Her hand gripped the metal rail that edged the chapel steps. "I'm scared of everything."

Eric entered the chapel and walked up the aisle. Chloe entered behind him, dressed in a simple yellow dress with long sleeves and a high neck. Buttons ran from collar to hem. She carried no flowers, and her hair was collected in the same, coiled braids, centered and true. Her father trailed behind her, trying to keep up. Harriet's children ran to her, a swarm of two. Her hands landed on each of their heads. She pet them as she continued toward the altar at a clip reserved for exercise. What with the bell ringing, the children tugging at her skirts, and the arrival of a dour priest, she had only time to ask him, "How did you sleep?"

Simon had been born to hear this woman ask that question every morning for the rest of his life. He wondered if he was doomed to love everything she said from now until the end of time.

He left her at the altar and approached Eric, seated in the first pew beside his mother, and bent to him. "I need a best man. Would you stand up?" With his brother dead and Wolfe on his honeymoon, Simon had only this man, who looked as though, priest or no, he wanted to belt him again.

Eric waited only long enough to let Simon know his misgivings, then stood. Together they joined Chloe at the altar.

The wedding preamble was grim. The priest's sermon during the following mass would be about lust. That was clear from his verses.

The vows were perfunctory. They carried none of the indulgence of the previous day, but it had been only yesterday Simon had heard them, and he remembered his part of the pledge. He took her hand and placed the ring on her finger. Her right hand covered her left, and she hid the ring in the cup of her palm before moving them both behind her back. Simon wouldn't have minded holding her hand a moment longer, in spite of the shocks that passed through him at their touch. He shook his head at the priest when it came time to place a ring on his hand. He'd forgotten.

There was no offer of a kiss, so he didn't take one.

Her mother approached to offer them congratulations before the priest's pronouncement was finished. In spite of the circumstances, she looked like she'd struck gold. Chloe's mother, it was clear, didn't mind what had occurred the previous night to make this morning possible. It must have been difficult to work in a cemetery and at the same time believe that propriety had anything to do with life or death.

Simon shook the men's hands when they approached the altar, and they moved *en masse* to the door.

A photographer, perhaps looking for leftover spectacle from the night before, was sitting on the chapel stairs when they emerged. He scrambled to stand and asked for a picture.

Simon looked down at his bride. Her cheeks were flushed, and her eyes were an incandescent blue. They glowed with sleeplessness and disbelief. He was sorry for that, and more. He wanted to tell her, apologize for the inelegance of his persuasion, but a mass of people flooded past, shifting them bodily apart. He found Harriet behind him and carried her chair down the steps. He returned to Chloe's side.

Before turning to the photographer, he tested her, willed her to do something that would show him how she felt, that she felt even a fraction of the current that ran through him. He thought, *kiss me*, before God and everyone. She regarded him with a curious expression, and the flash of the camera blinded him.

21

They were obliged to attend the scheduled mass that followed the ceremony. It was not a full house. Simon fidgeted like a child. His hands didn't stop moving for the duration of the service. They folded in his lap, then rose to beneath his chin where they pulled at his tie. He touched the empty ring finger, then browsed his jacket pockets. Chloe hoped he'd pull out something of interest, something that would distract her from the mortifying sermon, but they emerged empty each time.

Had Simon been a child of six, she would've set her hands atop his to quiet his fidgeting. She would've taken his hands and moved them into her own lap. A child's fidgets meant nothing. But Simon's fidgets meant he was anxious about something, and she didn't need to have finished school to understand he was anxious about her. He'd just been forced to marry her. Whether he was compelled by custom, or her brother, he'd married a woman he'd met the week before, a local woman with no society connection, and no money. True, Wolfe married a native girl, but that was different. They'd known one another since they were children.

They all emerged from the chapel for the second time, solemn and unspeaking. Chloe's family made the mile-long walk to the lake, but Chloe and Simon walked Hattie home. When they reached the Blount cottage, Simon lifted Hattie's chair up the steps. Before he could enter the house, Chloe handed him baby Daniel and shut the door behind her.

Hattie swung on Chloe, the wheels of her chair spinning beneath her fingers in a show of energy she'd not had in weeks. "What happened?"

Chloe bit the nail of her thumb. "Have I done the right thing?"

"It's too late to ask that. I'm only looking for they why of it."

Chloe grimaced. "Last night…" She hadn't the words to explain.

"You had a moment."

Chloe exhaled in a long breath. "A few moments, strung together." Her stomach jumped with the memory.

"But only one would have led to your brother knocking at my door at six in the morning."

"I'm so sorry."

Hattie waved her off. "Eric didn't seem pleased today."

"Did anyone?"

"The more important question is, are you pleased?"

"I can't say."

"Have you fallen in love with him?"

"This isn't about falling in love." Chloe tucked her chin. "It's about having a bit of fun."

"Not about falling in love? You should have seen him this morning before you arrived. He was nervous as a cat before you showed up. Take it as a good sign. That's the recommendation of an old married woman. Don't go looking for problems. There'll be enough time for that after the honeymoon."

The honeymoon. Her face grew hot. The desire for anything beyond what she had already was new. It felt as large as a fist in her stomach.

Hattie noticed her flush. "I wish I could start all over again."

"I'm not starting anything."

"Don't be ridiculous. I just attended your wedding."

"It was supposed to be one day, Hattie. A single day. One wedding." She held up a finger, "One." Chloe was finding that wanting something, once started, was hard to stop. It wouldn't be just one day. Now it would be just two days, or three. She bent down so that their cheeks rested together. "I'll come back as soon as I can."

Hattie spoke into Chloe's hair. "You have a husband. Don't talk already about coming home."

At the Swann cottage, Simon sat on a short end of the dinner table, flanked by Jude and Josef. Simon looked like he wanted to make a run for it. His fidgets had subsided to a slow roll of his thumbs, each over the other. His shoulders were broad beneath the white of his jacket. She was glad she'd made him fetch it. In spite of the dunk in the river last night, he looked pressed and more than presentable. Her father leaned against the long stone hearth. Eric guarded the door. If Chloe were the sort of person to consider forever, she'd want to look at her new husband for the rest of her life.

"What does your mother think of this, Simon? I assume you've told her." Chloe's mother turned to her Da. "That poor woman lives all alone since losing her son."

Chloe winced. From where she stood at the sink, she didn't see Simon flash straight, white teeth in a distracting smile. "Maman sends her regards and best wishes."

Undistracted, her mother pressed, "You don't have any other brothers and sisters?"

Simon rubbed his jaw. "No, it was just the one."

"Cousins?"

Simon smiled again. "Not that I'm aware of."

Chloe's mother nodded and her fingers steepled. She rested the tips of her fingers against her mouth. "So you'll be wanting children, then?"

Simon exhaled in a breath that sounded like he'd been kicked in the stomach, then coughed into his hand. Chloe fumbled a plate and juggled before dropping it. It shattered with a crash into the stone sink bottom. A squawk of wood accompanied the sound as Simon pushed back his chair. His hand reached into the sink and grabbed her wrist before she could collect the pieces.

Judah laughed a loud guffaw and spoke to the room at large. "He should get used to that. Chloe drops everything."

Josef affirmed it. "You married a butter fingers."

Simon shrugged off his jacket and tossed it to his chair. He rolled his sleeves over his wrists in the few steps it took him to return beside her. She felt the warmth of him from her hips to her shoulders. "Good timing there. A useful trait." His voice was so low she almost hadn't heard it.

Simon picked up the pieces faster than Chloe could retrieve them. She stopped trying and watched his hands. One made a cup with his palm while the other fed the broken porcelain into it. Her own fingers gripped the edge of the smooth granite rim of the sink. *Children.* She couldn't. She never would. She'd buried so many children.

Her family behind them made intimacy impossible, and the appearance of it embarrassing. Simon said, "I'm sorry Harriet couldn't join us."

Chloe continued to watch his hands work. Now that the larger pieces had been collected, what remained were only smaller shards of glass. She made no attempt to include her family in the conversation. Her voice was low. "She's been told to remain in bed, but she's got three children, and her husband has been away since June. How is she supposed to remain in bed?" Chloe stared into Simon's palm. Her voice reached only him. "Dr. Reed doesn't think she'll see the winter."

"Dr. Reed never leaves the islands. Has she visited any other physician?"

Chloe regarded him with surprise. "Why would she do that?"

Simon's gaze didn't waver. "She should seek more than one doctor's advice."

"Wouldn't all doctors say the same thing?"

He shook his head, serious. "They wouldn't."

"Why wouldn't Dr. Reed direct her to see another doctor then, if it was the right thing to do?"

"There's no answer to that, but she should. She should come down to the city, to one of the hospitals there."

Chloe shook her head. "Her husband is on a freighter halfway to Nova Scotia. She hasn't seen him since before the baby was born. Until he returns, she hasn't two pennies to rub together."

"I have more than two pennies. I can send up a doctor. Would she see one?"

"She would do anything." She has three children who need her alive. "You can do that?"

He nodded, "If you think she'd agree."

Chloe nodded, but his attention was in the sink, prowling for missed pieces of broken plate. Her heart squeezed, an odd little pulse that had her catching a breath. "Are you always this nice?" She kept her fingers on the granite so she wouldn't touch his arm.

He gave the sink a half smile as he located the trash bin and emptied his hands of glass. "Awkward and nice. You're shredding the last remnants of my reputation."

"Is your reputation still important? Now that you have a wife?"

He stood and used a linen towel borrowed from Chloe's shoulder to brush slivers from his palm. "My reputation was never important to me."

She tried again to meet his eyes. "What is important to you?"

He looked over his shoulder, embarrassed by the question. The room behind them was silent. He flashed a smile that faltered when the rest of the room continued to study him with solemn interest. He allowed another beat of silence before, to Chloe's mother, he said, "Dessert." Her mother had been boasting of a skillet-fried *beignet* since she'd learned three hours earlier that Simon's family was French. "I'm sorry to have to hurry away directly after."

Chloe's skin tingled as the blood left her face. Was that how it was to be? It hadn't occurred to her that he would leave her behind, abandon her on their wedding day. It was the perfect solution. She felt ill.

He addressed the room at large. "We have to leave on the five-o'clock train." He added, "We board a ship in two days for Belgium. I telegraphed my man of business this morning. It's all arranged."

Chloe's eyes widened. *Belgium?* She looked to her brother at the door. "Eric?" Chloe hadn't seen her grandmother for nearly twenty years.

He nodded. "She'll be expecting you."

Simon continued to address the room. "The ship lands in Antwerp. We'll continue to Oostend the next day. I didn't have a chance to tell you." He met her eyes for the first time since they'd stood on the steps of the chapel and the flash burned her eyes. "I'd like to take you home."

Chloe packed her bag in five minutes. She completed the task without thinking. She avoided thought on purpose, careful not to look ahead to her return, or to the prospect of never coming back. Her feelings were too muddled to allow a wish in either direction. She wanted to cross the ocean to see her grandmother, and she wanted a honeymoon, everything that came with it. On the other hand, she had to stop wanting anything, immediately. Immediately as possible. She'd give it another day. She'd have an adventure, see the city, spend a night with her husband, then come home. Her mother wouldn't be thrilled. She'd have to plan that part a little better.

She took from a hook on her wall a fitted blue duster. Her fingers worked the buttons. Hattie had made Chloe buy the fabric because it was the color of Chloe's eyes. She checked herself in the mottled mirror above a short bureau of drawers and wasn't surprised that although her face tingled with cold sparks, she was rosy as fever; she didn't even need to pinch her cheeks. They were leaving for the city tonight. This very evening. And she would be going with Simon. Her husband. Her mind flashed with an image of his hands separating her thighs.

Simon stood from his chair when she reentered the kitchen. She was tall, but he was taller, and he had to bend a considerable distance to whisper in her ear. "I'll have every color of that design on sale in the store by the end of the month." Chloe's face warmed, and he liked the flush of pink in her cheeks, that he was its cause.

"Chloe spent three weeks on that coat," her mother interrupted from across the room. "She sees designs in her head. Once she has an idea, she won't quit until it's done."

Simon lifted her arm and studied the buttons at her wrist. "You've a good eye. I can put you to work at the store," he teased and pulled the satchel from her hand. He scanned the room behind her for more and frowned. "Only one?" She'd packed a single bag.

"She can get anything she needs at your stores, can't she?" It was Chloe's mother, giving voice to her inner reckonings.

Simon conceded, "She'll have everything." The words sent Mrs. Swann to Chloe's arms in a flight of tears. Chloe hugged each of her family members in turn. Her father and Eric each received a kiss on the cheek.

Simon hadn't meant to make that his farewell speech, but it got them out the door.

During the walk to the green, he measured his steps to match hers, carrying both her bag and his. The comfortable silence they'd shared while at the cemetery packing dirt was no longer comfortable. Twice, Simon looked at her sidelong and smiled, his lips pressed together, just a single side of his mouth lifting. Each time, it was more a grimace than a smile. Once, she raised her eyebrows at him, as though waiting for him to say something. He ignored the invitation and trudged on. They boarded the ferry at the Grandview Park Pavilion with a small handful of other people, none of whom he recognized. He stood with his back pressed to the rail, his eyes glued to the captain. Chloe stood close to him on the boat, her hip pressed lightly against his thigh, as though sensing he hated the trip. She faced the water. The wind blew wisps of hair back from her face.

He studied the tails of her coat where they beat an irregular rhythm against the back of her legs. The blue was darker than a robin's egg, greener than the sky. It suited her, made him curious. "What's your favorite color?" The fabric whipped and settled. He'd seen that color before.

She lifted her face to his, and the wind blew wisps of hair against her lips. "Why?" She tugged the loose strands back and hooked them behind her ear.

A pit opened in his stomach. "I've been dying to know." The fabric was the color of her eyes.

"Poppy." She returned her face to the water.

He shifted until his hip leaned against the rail. "That's not a color."

"It is," she said, defiant, nodding once at the water. "It's only one color."

His laughter was lost in the wind. "All right, then." He half bent to make his voice heard. "What's your least favorite color?"

"Mud."

The thought was sobering. It was the color of an open grave, rain snaking down a mound of dirt. He leaned into the rail to see her face. "Mine is blue, if you'd like to know." He liked this game of getting to know her. It distracted him from the water, where they were, the emotions that pulsed through his veins. At the same time, it was no distraction at all. It focused his attention on the very thing. "What do you like most? What's your favorite thing to do?"

He thought she leaned closer. "Dancing." The word ended with a lilt, like a question.

"Ah, I should have guessed." He turned and faced the water, so their gazes both landed on the chop as the ferry pushed through the waves. He leaned his forearms on the rail, his hands clasped over the side. "What's your least favorite thing?" It became all at once important that he knew.

"Least favorite?" Her face puckered. "Why does anyone's least favorite thing matter?" Then she smiled again. "I know what you'd say if I asked." She nudged his hip with hers, and he lost his footing.

He straightened himself with a laugh and nodded. "You're right. Mass. Now tell me yours."

Chloe leaned further over the side until she was folded in half by the rail. She studied the hull where the water lapped against the side before unfolding again. "Unbraiding my hair."

"Unbraiding your hair?" He leaned into her, teasing. "That sounds awful."

"When I have to take it down, it's like everything has ended, whatever it was I braided it for."

Her answer made him uneasy. The ferry approached the docks of Denton, and Simon focused on the snake of the train aimed toward Manhattan.

They sat in a first-class rail car, opposite one another on matching wooden benches. An utter absence of talk impregnated the silence. Her right hand fiddled with her wedding ring in the blue folds of her skirt. She spun the wide gold band on her finger.

His hand moved to the back of his neck, and Chloe's gaze followed it. His eyes moved from the floor between them to the window. He leaned forward. "There's something I need to tell you." He met her eyes.

Chloe waited. He thumbed the soft cotton of her coat where it hung in the space between them. It could be any number of things that now as her husband, he could say to her. There were thousands of things, little and large, she didn't yet know. She'd learn this thing first.

"Last night." His hands folded together between his thighs. He met her eyes. "You weren't my first." Memory flashed to the night before, back to the Frederick's stone, to the lake. She focused on his words, rather than on the image that made her wish he'd take her hand. Her thumb pressed the inside of her palm.

"Then why did you...? Why are we…?" She stood and regarded him from her full height. The top of his head reached her breastbone. She sat again, this time beside him. "Oh Simon, it's all my fault." She interrupted his short, incredulous laugh with a hand on his sleeve. "You didn't have to marry me. You have a terrible reputation. Everyone told me."

"I never told you."

"Everyone told me but you."

"I didn't have to marry you. I..." Simon ended the attempt abruptly. "The universe was telling me it was time to settle down."

She laughed softly. "The universe must have made a compelling argument. I can see the bruise on your jaw." Her mind worked in silence. A minute passed while they sat beside one another, both staring at the opposite wall. "What have you never done?"

"Pardon?"

She faced him. "Last night. You said that you had never...?"

His brow furrowed, and then lifted in understanding. Then it furrowed again. "I don't remember."

She let him know with a look that she didn't believe him. She tried again to persuade him. "We should turn back."

"We're not turning back." He stood up. "Give me your coat."

They stood close in the small compartment, lodged between the two wood benches, and looked together down at the long row of tiny buttons she'd covered in the same egg blue fabric of the coat. She started on the button at her throat. It was cotton twill, lightweight, and her fingers released each fabric nub through its slot. The patience it took her to cover forty buttons, attach them and bind off their corresponding holes rivaled only the patience it took to reveal herself to him while he watched.

He helped her slide the sleeves from her arms, touching only the fabric. He folded it and put it away above their heads. The train swayed at the next bend and they were thrown together against the smooth glass pane of the railcar. Simon caught himself with his hands against the window at her back. When she found her balance, she released the fistfuls of fabric she'd grabbed of his jacket to keep from falling.

They were inches apart, his hands close on either side of her face. She felt the lean dip of his waist before she let go and ran her palms down the skirt of her yellow dress. The farm fields blurred by through the thick plate of glass. The train rounded another bend and his shoulders bunched to keep himself steady. Her eyes were level with his mouth.

He began, "Last night was… Well, it was…"

"Fast."

His head bowed. His lips pressed together, but her words forced a smile. "I can get nothing by you. Yes, it was fast. I'm used to going a bit more slowly."

The lift of his mouth pulled a string tight at her stomach. *Just touch me.* She felt as though everything inside her was going to spill out if he didn't touch her, and that everything would spill out if he did. His eyes were dark blue with a hint of grey, the lashes a light brown. She said, "I'm sure I will like it both ways." He exhaled in a soft burst of air that sounded like a dog's whimper. His gaze found her lips.

A loud rap on the car door bumped their heads together.

Simon rubbed both their foreheads at once, his own with his palm, and hers with his thumb as he held her cheek. "I'm sorry." Her hand replaced his when he left her standing at the window. She heard the slide of the door. Words were exchanged with a man who was hidden by the breadth of Simon's back. Chloe heard their tickets punched and the door slide shut. The train whistled twice, each time long and low. Simon turned from the railcar door and met her eyes across several feet that seemed to Chloe insurmountable. He rubbed a hand down his face. Their eyes met, and the railcar lurched.

She asked, "Why don't we have a berth?"

He shrugged and opened his palm, indicating she should sit. "I didn't want to be presumptuous."

With regret, she stopped shifting in her seat and settled into the hard wood of the bench. "It's like a pew."

"Now I know what you mean." He sat across from her and watched as she tried to get comfortable.

She pinned him with an incredulous look. "You'd never been to church before. You really aren't religious?"

"I'm really not." A furrow between his eyebrows appeared again. Finally, he asked, "Would you like to lean against my shoulder?"

She stood, turned and sat beside him. After a moment, she rested her head against his upper arm, the white silk of his jacket smooth against her cheek. He shifted, and she lifted her cheek and waited for him to settle. She settled again, too, against a shoulder that was firm and unyielding. Only the wood wall of the railcar and the glass plate window would be less rigid.

He rested his head against the back of the bench, leaned away and lifted his arm, brought it down around her again, and she nestled into his chest like a bird. She moved as close as she could against him on the hard bench while the railcar swayed.

She breathed in the scent of him, smelled the air of the river on his white jacket, lavender soap, surprisingly, and something spicy, like clove. She could press her face into that scent forever. When he'd asked her about her favorite thing, she'd wanted to say *this*.

His arm extended the length of the bench behind her. His fingers drummed the edge, then stopped. She waited for his arm to drop and circle her, but it remained along the back rise of their seat. She kept her own hands in the lap of her skirt. The sun dropped behind the trees, emerged, then dropped again. The light inside the car yellowed. She dozed against him. The coil of her hair pressed against the side of his chest. He rested his head against the rail car window and stared at the rushes, the rolled bales of hay.

22

He dreamed she wore shimmering gold. It covered her body in a tight sheath, dipping low in front. He ached to run his hands over it, feel the textured fabric of her curves against his palms. She moved closer. The skirt of the gown grew taught with each step. Her feet were bare. "Shhh. You don't want to wake them."

The wood between the rail cars was thin. She wanted him to be quiet. He wasn't sure he'd made a sound. The noise of the train on the tracks as it sped along was thunderous. A whistle punctuated the steady roar. The pale blue light of a crescent moon came through the window making her skin glow, her hair the color of angels' wings. Untied, it fell down her back in long curtains of enchanted white. He yearned to touch it. Her hands rested on his knees and she knelt between his legs.

"Marry me." His voice was a whisper.

"Shhh." Her hands ran up his thighs and down. He shifted in his seat. He couldn't remain still. He searched for the cornflower blue of her eyes.

He must have said something, because she quieted him again. Then he heard only the sound of the tracks, the low, airy whistle.

Her slender fingers worked the buttons at the front of his trousers. He wanted to stay her hands, but his own wouldn't move. He could only watch, his eyes riveted as she fit each button through its hole and moved down to the next. He waited. When she released him, he tried not to breathe, not to make a sound, not to wake up.

Chloe woke to his hand moving against her neck. It was dawn and quiet, without the battery of sliding doors. There was only the sound of the train against the rails. A finger traced the edge of her ear, then moved to a wound coil of hair, pulled out a pin, and another.

"What are you doing?"

His voice was a low whisper above her head. "Unbraiding your hair."

The railcar shook, and the space between them disappeared, removed from all directions at once. His fingers combed through her hair. Her hands pressed against his shoulders. His mouth found hers. Their weights shifted with the shifting car. What he said in the space below her ear was lost when the lock of the coupling rods screeched the wheels against the rails. The car slowed. Doors slid on tracks and passengers' voices joined the din. His hands cupped her head, the base of each palm rested against the lines of her jaw. Their foreheads touched, and she lost focus. Chloe pulled at Simon's coat when he stood, trying to keep him close, but he dragged their bags from the shelf above their heads, took her hand, and pulled.

"Let's go."

It was seven in the morning. The train had by some diabolical miracle arrived fifteen minutes ahead of schedule. He held in one hand his luggage, a rich leather satchel stamped in gold with his initials, and hers, homemade of old sail canvas embroidered with every color of thread. In his other hand was Chloe. Her hand gripped his in a vise. She had not let go since they stepped off the train. It was raining. He lacked a free hand for an umbrella, so the rain fell.

He set the bags down in front of the store and unlocked the door. He pulled the door wide and held it with his shoe, retrieving the bags and extending his arm to propel her inside. He locked the door behind them.

Her mouth stood agape. It had been opening and shutting at intervals. At the train station when they'd disembarked. At the hansom cab they'd taken from the station through the streets. At the height of the buildings and the innumerable people already bustling at dawn through the city. And then at the mammoth store building when they'd alighted from the cab. Now as she peered up eight floors, standing in the center of a Tiffany glass-covered court, her mouth opened again.

There were spots in the store where the light would hit the stained glass just right and project geometric shafts of color. Simon wished it would do it now, but instead the rain on the glass made everything appear shifting and out of focus. He pulled her by the hand across the marble floor. He could not wait for the light. He had an apartment upstairs. And a bed. It was critical that he reached it. That they reach it together. Quickly.

The marbled hall was flanked on either side by glass counters filled to bursting with every sort of feminine garnish. She half bent over the glass as he pulled her past. Hair combs and necklaces, perfumes and scarves. There would be time later to allow her to look. His objective was the elevator at the other end of the grand hall, but when they arrived before it, Chloe turned and reached for the banister that led to the second floor.

"It's eight floors up."

"I'd like to see it."

"You want to walk up every flight?"

"Can we?"

Simon pressed his lips together. It almost became a smile. "It will get us to the top."

Her hand released his, and he felt its loss. She quickened her pace up the carpeted steps. He could not deny her, so he followed, his eyes trained on the angles of her coat, the width and feminine lift at the shoulders, the narrow waist, the way the fabric swished against her legs and ankles.

They reached the second floor. Chloe's mouth dropped open again at the skirts and shirtwaists, dresses and jackets, everywhere, of every sort and color. They had purposes, every one. Walking, visiting, mourning. Each was displayed on a full-bodied figure complete with hair and hats. The faces had eyes and painted faces. She touched one.

"It's wax."

Chloe started. She'd forgotten that Simon stood behind her. He approached and stood close.

"The hair is real."

Chloe's hand, which had hovered at the wax woman's head, drew back.

"The eyes are not."

Chloe laughed at him over her shoulder.

Simon grinned. "You don't know yet what I would do to sell my wares."

She wandered through the figures, allowing her hands to touch the silk brocades and velvets. In the center of the floor was an arrangement of white wicker chairs with curved arms and backs. Wax figures were seated, posed life-like in conversation. One even held a cup of tea, the interior filled with solid amber.

"It's a replica of one of the sitting rooms on the *New York*."

Chloe's eyebrows lifted in question.

"The ship we'll be boarding tomorrow morning. The smoking and reading rooms are reproduced also. Upstairs." That got her moving again.

"Are you sure you want to cross the Atlantic? Will you be alright on a ship for…"

"Six days, seven hours, twenty-three minutes."

She stopped and turned to him. "That long?"

"Give or take a quarter hour, if the weather is good." He smiled, but his smile was grim. "The *New York* hasn't yet taken the *Bleu Riband.* That's her sister ship, the *Paris.* But she's out of commission at the moment. I'm betting on the *New York* for this trip."

She nodded, and they reached the second set of steps. The third floor was men's fashions. They reached the center of the floor more quickly this time. A series of plush chairs were connected in a row, each chair sharing the arm of the next. Two male figures sat side-by-side dressed in tweed, one holding an unlit pipe.

"We had to glue the pipe in place after several were taken."

Chloe touched the pipe, then the man's hair. "Stolen?"

His smile came more easily now. "Apparently, there are men who like to smoke."

The fourth floor was evening gowns. Crystal chandeliers hung in irregular bursts, lending occasion to the arrangements of figures. Here and there were waxed men, lounging in formal dress, each one positioned to be looking at a female form. She stopped at one figure, and fingered the fabric, wrought with miniscule gold beads. It shimmered, although the electric chandeliers were not turned on.

He might indeed be asthmatic. He was having trouble breathing again. She was touching everything. Her fingers trailed over every last piece of inventory in his store. He didn't even think she realized it. He envied each place her hand made contact.

They arrived on the fifth floor. Housewares. An arrangement of paintings hung on the walls in gilded frames. A variety of lamps with ornate shades and crystal teardrops were arranged on cloth tables. Sconces adorned the walls. She moved through, weaving in and out of the tables, peering at each painting, each fixture. At the farther end of the floor, colored bath towels heaped high on a wall of built-in shelves. Sheet linens hung from the ceilings. She moved the fabrics aside as she walked through, moving her face so her cheek was caressed by the soft cottons. She stopped at a pile of Persian carpets as high as her waist, surrounded by more lay out across the floor. She looked at him in question, and he nodded. They had time. They had all the time in the world.

She bent and unlaced her boots. It took her only a moment before she was able to sink stockinged feet into the plush wool. She closed her eyes. "It's incredible." Her hand reached out, the backs of her fingers tickling the pile. Without warning, she ascended and stood at the top. She pressed her feet into the carpet, taking small steps in place. She grinned, then bounced, tossed her legs out and fell onto the thick woven wool. Simon dropped the bags while she was still in the air, was pressed against the carpet bindings by the time she landed. Her legs fell over the side. He stood between them, shaking his head while she laughed. Her laughter died as she regarded him.

"Can you create desire?"

Simon shifted against the carpets. "What was that?" He'd heard the question the first time, but he was not prepared.

"Can you create desire?"

He didn't know the answer he should give her, so he told her the truth. "Yes."

Her brows knit together in a frown. "If you create it, it must not be real."

"Desire is the space between wanting something, and having it. It's my job to build desire by offering something just beyond the tips of your fingers, close enough to reach, but only if you lean in. Anyone can create desire, if they know how, but it's real." His shops were designed for it. "It's what I do."

She lifted her eyes from her lap. "You make women want things."

He tilted his head, but did not break her gaze. When he thought he had read her correctly, he agreed. "Yes." That she would question the existence of desire was a discredit to his reputation, and a sin. He pressed himself tight against the edge of the wool bindings, but he could get no closer. He pulled the ribbon from the hair swung over her shoulder. The unwound braids were crisp zigzags.

"Would it be more desirable if I did not…" She struggled with her words. "...if I was not...? Would it be better for you if I was not so...*willing*?"

Simon puzzled at the question for only the hitch of his breath. His hands shook as he attempted the buttons of her coat.

Her hands were faster. She pulled the shirt from his trousers and unbuttoned it, beginning at the bottom where the tails were connected. Her hands crossed his stomach. When his chest was bared, her fingers splayed across it. He'd reached only the fifth button down on her coat, had not even reached the rise of her breast, but she'd already opened his shirt; its tails were in disarray over the waistband of his trousers. The collar was still tight at his neck. She stilled, absorbed the heat of him, waited, perhaps, for the carpets to tumble down.

She pulled back and covered her face with her hands. "I don't know what's gotten hold of me."

He pulled her hands from her face. "Don't be embarrassed. I should be embarrassed. I mean, I am embarrassed. You will never know how much. But it felt good. You feel good. To me." She was almost pulled into the pattern in the carpet, but he had the good fortune of having her eyes return to his. "I would like to do this properly. Upstairs. In my apartment. In my bed." The single word thrilled her. *This*. He felt it. "Could you stop shopping for a moment and focus on getting us upstairs?"

His hands on her waist, he helped her jump down. He bent and retrieved her low boots and their bags.

Her long legs kept up with difficulty, every third step a trot across the marble to catch up. The remainder of three flights to the top floor was silent, and she did not shop.

23

They reached his private apartment, and when he swung open the door, the room crescendoed in an uproar. Simon's head bowed in resignation. It was a party.

They were greeted with mayhem. His man of business came forward and clapped him on the shoulder. "It came out with the morning edition. You're lucky you have us trained to arrive at five."

Simon felt lucky indeed.

His rooms were filled. The sound of two partnering corks welcomed their arrival. A buffet breakfast was spread along one wall. Bottles were everywhere, many open, many still to pop. Simon ushered Chloe inside. She seemed more agog than reluctant. Having arrived from the quiet of the floors below, and the intimacy of their shared goal, the bedlam was more perception than reality. In truth, the room was populated with only two dozen people. The morning shift of female clerks, his business manager, and a few men from shipping.

Simon had never been the type of proprietor to make class distinctions. He'd caroused with everyone. He grimaced and stole a glance at Chloe. She was handed a tall flute of champagne and drank it with deliberation as she surveyed the scene. He accepted a glass, and lifted it, downing the whole in one swallow.

He tugged at her sleeve. "Chloe, this is Judah Klink, my man of business. Judah, my wife." Judah took her hand and shook. Judah turned over his shoulder and shouted to the room at large. "Simon's wife!" The crowd lifted their glasses in a general hurrah.

Chloe's eyes fell on a large ice sculpture in the corner of the room, tinged through by the powder blue moire drapes. In spite of the thunderous weather outside the window, the ice sparkled. The sculpture pulled her forward through the room. She lifted a finger and ran it over the extended wing. It was a swan.

Over her shoulder, her eyes found Simon's. She was hungry. She pulsed with it. And not for the fruited confections spread down the long table. She wanted to touch him. Dear God, he had a wife, and she wanted to touch him, so badly he could read it in her eyes.

Judah's eyes followed Simon's. A raised eyebrow and a nod of Judah's chin indicated Simon's shirt, unbuttoned and disordered. "Spent your wedding night on the train?"

Simon looked down. He refastened the buttons of his shirt beneath his white jacket. One hole was missed, and the remaining line was off-center. He tucked a tail into his waistband. The other hung free, a clash of white against his black trousers. "Adjourn this meeting." Each syllable had its own weight. "Posthaste."

Judah's other eyebrow raised to join the first, but he knew better than to comment on the urgency that pervaded Simon's words. He finished his glass, set it on a nearby surface and clapped his hands. "One hour until we open." He winked at Simon, then shouted. "One last round!"

Simon glared. He would fire the man. They'd been friends since rowing the eight-man at college, but he would do it.

Chloe returned to Simon's side, two of the store's dress clerks in her wake. He introduced them, ignoring their sly looks. Though he'd debauched neither, they had assisted him in general revelry a time or two. He regarded the room. No one there was a stranger to his habits. He ran a hand over his face. He'd brought his wife to the lion's den. One of the girls nudged Chloe. "Why don't you take off your coat and stay awhile? Make yourself at home." She winked at Simon, then eyed Chloe's stockinged feet. He grimaced.

Chloe unbuttoned her coat with reluctance. "I'm not dressed for a party." The women beside her came alive. "You're in the right place for that." They turned to Simon. "Can we show her 'round?"

Simon breathed through his urgency, the hiss of air from a balloon. "We'll be gone for four weeks. She needs everything."

Chloe continued with her buttons, one by one, making her way down the blue cotton twill while they all watched. Simon counted from one hundred, backwards, while he watched her fingers work the buttons through their holes. When she was finished, he accepted her coat, and she was swept from the room. The yellow skirt of her dress disappeared around the frame of the door. He called after them. "You have one hour." Yellow buttons. He ached to unpop each one. The next hour spread before him in an agony of suspense. His mother-in-law's kitchen was the only image he could conjure in comparison.

Judah retrieved his glass and poured it full from a large magnum. Then he refilled Simon's.

"You seem a bit touched." His dark eyes held mischief. "Were you drinking on the train?"

"I'll sack you."

"You will not." Judah guided Simon to the buffet through the bodies that peppered his suite. "Fresh fruit?" He popped a grape into his mouth. "Have some pineapple. You paid for it."

Simon made no comment, but accepted the pineapple.

"Her father own a pistol?" Judah snorted. Then recovered. "So you're leaving again? Honeymoon in the Poconos?"

"Belgium."

Judah whistled. "She's persuaded your return to water? It must have been quite a visit home."

"She has a grandmother."

"I have a grandmother. Yet you've not agreed to cross an ocean for it."

Simon took another piece of fruit.

"How was the wedding?"

Simon rubbed his jaw. "Which one?"

"I suppose there were two. The paper says you were married yesterday morning." He looked at the ceiling and tapped on his fingers, as though counting the hours.

Simon chewed.

Judah popped another grape. "You want me to clear the room?"

"Please."

Judah set his glass down again, and rubbed his hands together. "I can't imagine you will ever tell the tale, but someday…"

"No."

"All right then." He clapped loudly and called, "This time I mean it. And leave your glasses behind."

In five minutes, the room was empty. Simon regarded his suite. He found the bags at the door where he'd dropped them, and Chloe's shoes. At a loss for what else to do, he gathered and carried them to the door of his bedroom. He opened it, set them on the closest chair, and was alone. No echoes of revelry, no artifacts of the morning's celebration. Or of the train ride before, Chloe's head against his shoulder, his hands unwinding the coils of her hair.

Only what had once been his room. It was familiar, but it wasn't his room anymore. He recognized each object. Nothing had been moved, but the entirety of it now was strange. He dipped out of his overcoat, sinking his knees so the sleeves would fall off. He threw it to the chair over their bags.

On his desk was the morning edition. The society pages had been lifted from the center and placed on top, their wedding portrait above the fold. A bottle of champagne in a bucket of ice wept a ring through the paper. The groom looked straight at the camera. He recognized himself with a start, and bent more closely to view the image. He'd always seen his brother whenever he looked at a picture of himself, yet here he was, only him. How odd. His bride's perfect face was blurred in motion as it looked up at him. It raised the hair on the back of his neck. He tried to pull her face into focus, until he quite lost the plot. A clap of thunder roused him.

He retreated to the bathroom. It was his favorite room, of all rooms across all eight floors. Cavernous and white, tile and porcelain. The tub was large enough for two. Once, he'd had three, although that had been more a burst of creativity than finesse.

The sink was deep and round. He shifted out of his suit coat, loosened his necktie, and pulled it over his head. He unbuttoned his collar and braced himself at the sink. He looked terrible. His eyes glowed with sleeplessness, and something else. Everything else. He closed them, and the room spun. Yellow buttons.

He splashed cold water on his face, and blotted it dry with thick cotton, smelled the laundry's scent of lavender and clove. He walked serpentine, kicking off his shoes and pulling off his socks, booting them both under the bed out of sight. He climbed atop the mattress and fell right the hell to sleep.

24

The lock made a soft catch as Chloe closed the door behind her. The buffet table in the main room was still laden with fruit and half drunk glasses of champagne. Corks were strewn across the table's cloth.

"Simon?" She spoke, neither shouting nor whispering, not expecting him to answer, but just to hear the name. "Simon?" The last few hours had been like a dream. Only the fever pitch of her nerves persuaded her she was awake. That they would be alone together made her heart race.

A harsh trill made her jump. A telephone was across the room atop a desk. The arrangement of furniture separated the large room in two: a study and a sitting room. The shrill ring came again. She ran to it and picked up the handle and crouched low to the mouthpiece. They didn't have a telephone at the cottage. "Hello?"

"Mrs. Low. It's Judah. Is Simon there?"

Chloe looked around, "I don't think he is."

"When he comes back, tell him the doctors are catching the morning train."

"For Hattie? She doesn't even know they're coming." Hattie. Thought of her friend hadn't crossed Chloe's mind for the span of several hours. Guilt weighed, then lifted. Hattie would be pleased that Chloe was having an escape.

"I'll send word," Judah assured her. "What would you like me to say?"

Chloe considered only a moment. "Let these men have their way with you."

Judah's laugh crackled through the earpiece. "Are you sure?"

She nodded at the receiver, leaning closer. "Definitely. Sign my name." Hattie would laugh at the message, and it would be like they were laughing together. "Thank you, Judah."

"You're welcome, Mrs. Low."

The name startled her, and she listened for a moment to the crackling silence on the other end of the telephone before she returned it to the forked handles of the receiver.

Chloe surveyed the scene. The windows ran thick with rain. Evidence of the morning's festivities remained strewn about the room. Water dripped from each of the swan's wings, wetting the tablecloth. Crystal flutes with varying levels of flat champagne sat on every surface. There was no hope of cleaning up. She would have no place to set the dishes or the food. There was no kitchen. She counted the doors off the sitting room. Three. Wasn't there a kitchen? Curiosity propelled her to the closest door. She pushed it open on swinging hinges.

In fact, a kitchen surprised her, a fair-sized room with soapstone countertops and a white porcelain sink in front of a pane of windows. They were on the building's top floor, high enough to look out over neighboring rooftops. Gardens greeted her, short and tall pipes, telephone wire. She pushed herself back from where she leaned over the sink. She turned the handle of each faucet until the water ran, then turned them back. She regarded the room. It was spotless. Chloe doubted that Simon was as tidy as this. Her brothers and her Da had taught her early that men were not, by nature, tidy. Simon either kept a maid, or this kitchen had never been used. She opened the pantry door and found a pound of butter and a bowl of eggs. Neither smelled rancid. That was a good sign. She closed the door again.

Beside the kitchen was a tiny water closet with a sink, and a mirror and a toilet with a high cistern and chain. Chloe caught a look at herself in the mirror as she turned to close the door. She didn't recognize herself. This wasn't her life. Already, it was getting harder to remember that fact. Her hair had been pinned up by the shop girls. They'd brushed it so the memory crisscrosses of her braids had been straightened. Pieces of hair missed the pins on purpose and had been curled in particular until they hung just right. The girls knew Simon very well. Though not, Chloe thought, so well as to be discomfited by the activity of outfitting his new wife and pinning up her hair in a flattering poof. Oh, it was ridiculous to care, but she cared. She wanted Simon to see her hair. She liked the look of it, although she couldn't fathom how they'd done it. She'd have to pay attention when she took out the pins.

The emptiness of the apartment evaporated as she contemplated door number three. She pushed it open, and there he was, face down atop the mattress, his cheek pressed into a pillow. He was fully clothed, with the exception of his socks and his collar, dead asleep. She watched his back, waited for it to rise and fall. When it didn't move, she hurried to the side of the bed and her palm hovered over his back. She felt heat even before she felt the rise of his back against her hand.

"What's that under your arm?" His back rumbled beneath her.

She looked at it and then back at him in confusion. His single eye blinked. "It's a riding crop."

"A riding crop?"

"Simon, look at this dress." She backed away and spun, the crop slapped against a lampshade on the entrance table and the lamp beneath tottered. She steadied the lamp, smiled once she was sure it would not fall, and stood straight again. "It's the most beautiful thing I've ever worn."

Simon regarded her, his approval buried in the pillow. "I'm still taken with the one you wore last night."

An image flashed between them of Chloe's dress, the mark of blood at the hem, and how it had arrived there. The bottom of the skirt had been tucked between them. There had been enough blood to reach it. It should have been a violent image, but it was not.

Chloe flushed. "I liked that dress very much, but I won't be wearing it again." Her gaze moved from his bare feet. "This is a different sort of dress. This is a dress for going out. For riding." She turned to show her skirt and revealed a set of draping folds down the back, like ruffles. They formed a triangle, pointing down. She regarded him with confusion. "Do you have a horse?"

Simon's single eye blinked again.

It was a riding costume the color of slate, gray with a tinge of lavender. A black velvet collar and nine black velvet buttons formed the closure of the tight-waisted jacket. He removed an arm from beneath his pillow and crooked a finger at her. She obliged and stepped closer. He repeated the motion until he grew impatient and his hand waved her for emphasis. She arrived at the edge of the bed, and Simon pinched her stick of wood and leather and lifted. Chloe's hand rose with it in the air. Together they regarded her raised hand and the whip.

When he spoke, the words did not make it past his throat. "I don't have a horse." He plucked the crop from her hand. His hair was ruffled from sleep, and now both eyes blinked. He settled his head into the pillow. He reminded her of a cat, a large, male cat, holding her riding crop.

"How am I to go riding if you don't have a horse?"

Simon's legs found the floor with a slow, measured sweep. A sigh hunched his shoulders as his fists pressed the mattress, and he stood. "They're having a joke with you."

"How is that funny?" She retrieved the crop with n indignant pluck.

Simon ran the backs of his finger against his jaw. The scratching noise of scruff was the only sound in the room. "The physics of…." He pressed a thumb against the dip in his temple. "You understand the logistics…" A muscle in his jaw twitched. "Men and women are engineered to…"

Chloe's eyebrows rose.

He compelled himself to finish his sentence. "Ride."

She regarded the crop. "You don't have a horse?"

"No." He shook his head. "I don't."

"Riding is a metaphor for sex?"

"Yes." He bit out the affirmation before the lilt of her question had reached its apex.

"Well, that explains my outfit." She regarded the front sweep of her dress. "Should I take it off?" Without waiting for an answer, Chloe tucked the crop under her arm, and lifted her hands to the first black velvet button of her collar. Simon watched her fingers work. It was a tight loop, and unbuttoning that button was slow progress. His look was pained. When it finally made its way through the loop, he exhaled.

She apologized, "The next one will go more quickly." She worked through the remaining eight buttons on her jacket until it was open down the front, revealing the scooped neckline of the dress beneath, and the full rise of her breasts. She was getting the hang of this. Simon's hands were balled in his trouser pockets. It was a delicious game, to see if she couldn't persuade him to touch her. She hadn't recognized the signs before, but now they were impossible to ignore. It was a revelation. She pointed the crop at his chest. "Here, hold this." He accepted the crop, mute.

Bending without ceremony, she pulled at the hem of her dress, lifted it off, and dropped it in a heap at her feet.

"Sweet Jesus." Simon's knees bent, and he found a seat on the bedside settee.

She smiled in self-satisfaction. "You're not the only one with alacrity."

"Alacrity." He rubbed the back of his neck. "That's a polite word for it."

She'd forgone petticoats and short drawers. The girls had tittered when she'd suggested them, and offered her instead a grey leather corset, lined in white lace. Although she'd not understood the joke of the riding costume, she'd understood the corset was a design meant only for the bedroom. Impractical anywhere else, it was held together between her legs with little metal hooks and eyes.

His eyes prowled the edges of the corset, where the top curved over her breasts, and where the bottoms ran across the curve of each thigh. "They dressed you in a leather corset."

"And gave me a riding crop." She took two steps to where he sat bolt upright on the sofa. "I see the full picture, now." She plucked the crop from his hand and tapped his knees with it, until she had space to stand between his legs. "The girls had to fasten me up. I need your help getting it off again."

His eyes burned, but his hands hovered beneath the juncture of her thighs. She nodded her encouragement, and he was careful not to straighten the clasps. The fabric between her legs separated. He dropped his hands and ran them along the tops of his thighs. "Can you do the rest?"

Her fingers worked down the front of her corset, separating the hooks until it opened and fell to the floor. She wore nothing but her garters and tights and heeled boots that covered her ankles in little black buttons. Chloe looked down at her boots. There would be no undoing those without significant effort. She hadn't the patience for more buttons.

She knelt between his legs, and he exhaled in a long breath. "You're not shy."

Chloe shrugged. It wasn't a question, so she didn't explain. She'd been to the Millers on occasion to prepare the bodies. What she'd seen there chased shyness away.

She tugged at the fabric tucked haphazard into the waistband of his trousers. He'd removed his collar, so only a few buttons more at the top, and she could lift his shirt right over his head. She studied those buttons until her hands moved of their own volition. Her fingers pushed ebony through white linen. Chloe sat back on her heels and pulled up the hem of his shirt until his arms lifted. She tugged it off to his wrists, and there they stuck.

He held his arms out to her, and she had to find his cufflinks from the inside out, pushing the fabric back toward his shoulders until his wrists were revealed. Link passed through cuff, and then again on the other side. She helped him toss the fabric away. She sat on her heels, the front of her bared to him; however, he wasn't looking. His eyes had not left her face for the duration of her task. She met them finally and stood, wanting him to look at her.

She touched the leather end of the crop to one breast. His eyes grew hooded, and something shifted in his gaze. The string at her belly pulled tight and hard. She dropped the end to between her thighs. "Will you touch me again here? What would happen if you did?" In a slow fall, Simon moved off the sofa onto the carpet. He captured her hand and took charge of it.

His eyes fixed on where he held the leather against her. "What would happen if I touched you here?" It stayed there, tickling and hot. "Of all things, I should have shown you that." He tossed the crop to floor. His chin jerked, and his hand passed through his hair. "Come closer." His arms rested on his knees where he sat on the floor in front of her.

She stepped between his legs. Standing before him, she felt exposed, vulnerable, but she wanted more of him. She reached down and touched his hair. He jolted. "Is this alright?"

"Closer."

"I can't get any closer." Her inner thighs brushed the sides of his knees.

His eyes warmed with promise. "You have no idea."

She moved against him and felt his arms circle her and push her against him from behind. She felt his cheek press against her, then the other as he moved his face between her legs. She felt his lips against her, and he pressed her closer from behind. She felt his breath against her, and then his tongue. Her fingers tightened in his hair. Her knees buckled. He controlled her fall. "I don't think…"

"Don't think." His words vibrated against her. His body shifted and his face was beneath her. The movement pressed her closer, and his tongue worked her slowly. His hands cradled her hips, kept her steady, then moved her. He let her go when she wanted to get away, but he wouldn't let her go far. She felt his breath until she no longer wanted to hold herself away, and she let him pull her down again. Her fingers grasped his shoulders when his tongue found someplace sweet. He moaned against it and the vibration made her wanton. She moved against his mouth, and the palms of his hands hovered over her hips and thighs, playing with the energy there, no longer controlling her. She thought nothing, saw nothing, heard only his moan and felt every lick until she felt nothing but….*white.*

When she opened her eyes, her breath came in gasps. She had *never.* His words from the night of Wolfe's wedding echoed. Simon had been right, if this is what he'd meant. She felt Simon's rough jaw against the inside of her thighs, both of them at once. His breath was warm between her legs. She realized where she was. Her body still pressed against his face. She'd braced herself against the back of the settee. Her fingers still clung to it now. She knelt splayed and unsteady above him.

The thought flashed, *how in the world was she ever going to get down?*

Balanced by a palm, she tried to push herself away, but Simon pushed up beneath her until she sat astride him on the sofa.

"I felt you come. It was the damnedest thing."

Her eyes were at his chest, and she shifted against him. "I felt it, too."

Simon wanted to laugh. She had no idea what he was talking about, had no idea that this did not happen. Sex was sex, but this was...Simon thought he might be the luckiest man on the face of the earth. He had felt his wife come. He'd actually felt it. It had coursed through him as though it had been his own. What was more, he was still hard as a rock. It had been her orgasm, not his.

She sat astride him. The feel of her above him was thrilling. His legs kept hers apart.

Her eyes were still wide with the shock of pleasure, and the knowledge made him harder. He let his hands move to her legs to run his palms along the tops of her thighs. Smooth. Long. His fingers trailed up over her knees before returning to her thighs and up her waist. He ran his hands over her hips. It felt good to finally touch her.

She placed her palms against his chest, ran them in circles across the smooth skin and hair, his nipples, down his stomach. His erection had worked its way up so the head was above his waistband. Her thumb ran over it unawares. When he jerked, she pulled her hand away. He found it and brought it back, returned it to his chest, held it there. With his other hand he opened his trousers.

He had forgotten that she was new to this. She didn't act like it when he was touching her. She was up for anything, and she moved like a temptress. If he didn't move fast enough, she pushed him along. He lifted her until she was poised above him. One hand high up on her thigh, he pressed her legs apart. His other hand he held beneath her, his fingers teasing her entrance, entering.

He wanted to get her to ride him, to make her want to do it without saying the words. He wanted her to have the idea on her own, to sink herself down on him until he was fully embedded. He ran his fingers along the seam, separating, entering, leaving. She arched her back to the rhythms of his hand. Until he withheld it, and he heard her moan. It was the first sound she'd made since they'd started. She'd been utterly quiet as she'd moved above him, her arm extended to the wall, her knees splayed and lowering her against his mouth. He hadn't needed to hear a sound.

Now, he wanted to hear her. He removed his thumb from where it had been teasing. She moaned again. She was getting close. He rubbed her wetness at his tip.

"Are you scared of anything?"

"Only that you'll stop."

He kissed her. His tongue moved in her mouth in time with his finger. He was rewarded when she pressed herself down. He was ready. She moaned when he entered her. He focused on the sound, realized too late it was not a distraction. She moved faster. He pressed up to meet her until he needed to drive down. He held her tight against him, rose from the sofa, found the bed and pushed her backwards. "Wrap your legs around my back." He groaned when she complied. He felt her coming, shifted his hips so he nudged her core, then touched her. She went off like a firework, and it took him with her.

"Oh, my God."

Chloe felt her heart pound. She had no idea sex could be anything like that.

Simon was breathing heavily, too. He rested his forearm over his eyes and took great gasps of air. His breathing steadied, and he lifted his arm.

What did one say after something like that? Chloe hadn't a clue. "Judah called." Thunder rolled in from a long distance. Simon rolled to his side and pulled her against him, wrapping her with his body. His breath moved the hair at her temple. A pin or two might still remain. His used his leg to lever her close. Chloe struggled again for something to say. She was usually so good with words. "Thank you for arranging the doctors."

His arms around her tightened, then loosened. His exhale was smooth and sweet. "You're welcome."

"My boots are still on."

His lips curved in reply. "Are you still talking?"

There was only one thing she wanted, really, to say. Her eyes grew hot. She would not even allow herself to think it. She kept her eyes open and saw when he fell asleep. The rain stopped. It had been stopping and starting all day. The sheet covered him to his waist and left his chest exposed. Her hand hovered over it, floated. She allowed an inch of space between her palm and his skin, smooth and tight, reveling in the desire to touch him. "Simon?" She tested him. "Simon?" Still he did not respond. She liked being this close to another person. She liked being this close to him. The thought intruded, and she pushed it out again.

Her hand moved to his arm, floating over his bicep and shoulder. It was no wonder women were attracted to him. He was magnetic. She felt the pulse between his skin and her hand. The pad of her thumb traced his lips in the air, and she could feel their softness even without touching him. His cheekbones, each brow, the tips of his eyelashes. He sighed in his sleep, and Chloe returned her hand to beneath her cheek where it rested on the pillow while she watched him.

Would it always be like this, waking up beside him? Thoughts of always pushed against her chest. There was no such thing. She could barely allow herself tomorrow. There was no always. She felt tears, for the first time since she was a child, burn her eyes, and she pursed her lips to keep them at bay. She rolled to her back, careful not to wake him. Sunlight lit flecks of dust in the air. She told herself again she was not in love with him, but it was getting harder to believe.

25

Dreaming again, Simon breathed underwater, swam like a fish, fast and efficient. He chased a flash of white fabric around the mast of a sunken ship. It rippled like cotton, thin and soft. He took deep inhales expecting each time to take in water, but somehow he found oxygen, enough to keep him swimming, his eyes finding what he sought anew after each turn. The material was a flag, waving him on, guiding him, always just beyond his reach, telling him to explore. He enjoyed the pull of it. His smile was broad. Under water was a new world. He reveled in the newfound power, to breathe in a place he'd never been.

Loss followed joy. Like the flip of a switch, he searched without success. The water suffocated him. He pushed toward the surface. The light above the water receded faster than he could swim.

Simon woke up with a gasp. He took deep gulps of air and ran his hands over his face. He heard the rain on the windows and roof, the sound of horses and wheels and people in the streets eight floors below and remembered.

He didn't reach out. Not right away. He left one arm flung over his eyes as he caught his breath and his heart rate slowed. He moved his hand from where it had been resting on his chest to the place beside him. He steeled himself for the connection. Empty space greeted him. His palm travelled over the smooth sheet. His arm fell from his eyes, and he rolled to his side and pushed himself up.

Gone.

He kicked his legs to the carpet and bit his tongue. He would not call out. He found his drawers among the sheets and padded barefoot across the room to the door. The sitting room was empty. He found her in the kitchen. Relief washed over him like water.

His relief was short lived. He thought belatedly he might have put on more clothes. He didn't know what was worse: her attempts to look away from his body, clad only in short drawers, or that her attempts failed. Her eyes moved from the table to him and back, landed on him at every point. More specifically, she studied his chest and looked away. A few heartbeats later, her gaze found his stomach, which he tightened unconsciously. Her teeth worried her bottom lip.

She was killing him. The women who usually saw his short drawers were sadly unfazed. Chloe was something new. Clearly, she wanted to look at him, and clearly, she was not used to it.

She smiled an apology. "I thought I'd make lunch, but I only found butter and eggs. And magazines."

His cupboards were full of magazines. A small stack was at her elbow.

"My mother has a subscription to the *Ladies Home Journal*." She lifted a magazine up and it flapped open in the air before she set it down again. "This one has more pictures."

Simon pulled out the bench and sat down at the table. The last time they'd spoken had been before… Before. The only topic she had the nerve to broach now was this. Fashion magazines.

He could talk fashion magazines, if that's what she wanted to talk about. He wondered if she might like to work at the store. He'd been joking about it before, but her taste was good, and she was an extraordinary seamstress. He pulled the magazine to him, flipped to a page toward the center, and pushed it back. "We sold this dress to a hundred different women in the spring."

"It looks comfortable." She traced the picture from the model's shoulder to her wrist where the fabric pointed to the center of her hand. "How do your customers not show up somewhere in the same dress?"

"It's a problem." Simon brought the magazine to him again, pulling it across the wood of the table. "It used to be that the modistes could prevent it, but with hucksters like me who sell ready made, it's harder to control."

"Why are your magazines in the cupboards?"

"I wouldn't know what else to put in a cupboard. "

Chloe gave him a wry smile. "How about food? I could make you something. "

"Do you cook?"

Chloe stood, and the wood chair squawked against the floor. "You haven't been very discerning in your choice of a wife."

Everything she said made him want to laugh out loud. Just being near her made him want to giggle like a schoolgirl.

She pulled a bowl from the shelf above the sink and cracked three eggs from the bowl on the counter into it. "At the very least, you could've found someone who would cook for you."

He couldn't care less if she could cook. It had never occurred to him that the ability to cook should be a requirement. Apparently, to women, it was. His mother had asked the same question. He hadn't been thinking of setting up a household. There'd been other considerations to occupy him.

She whisked, watched the eggs lift, and watched him, peered over at him around the length of her hair.

Holy hell. She wanted him again. He could feel it.

She turned her back to him and stole a glance over her shoulder. Her eyes landed on his mouth. "Can I ask you something?"

He felt frown lines form between his eyes. The backs of his fingers scrubbed a light beard. "What is it?"

She put the bowl down and added butter to the skillet she'd placed to warm on the stove. "How did you get your reputation?"

His frown lines deepened. He tried not to sound insulted. "I can understand after last night, but after earlier, I thought…"

The angle of the stove meant she could not hide her face. It flushed with heat. "I meant when did it start? Have you always had it?" The eggs sizzled when she poured them. She pulled a wooden spoon from where several stood in a jug. He'd thought until now they were for decoration.

Simon rubbed the back of his neck. "Michael was fairly inaccessible. I don't know if I've explained it very well. We were twins. I always expected that would mean something. To Michael it only meant he could never get far enough away. "

Chloe pushed at the eggs in the pan until they formed a mound. The task kept her eyes from his face.

"Women were another matter. I learned quickly enough I could please them. I could please them very well."

She lifted the skillet and emptied the contents onto a plate, which she set before him with a gentle thud. "So pleasing women became a substitute for pleasing your brother?"

Simon grimaced. "Not an exact match, obviously."

She placed a napkin beside the plate, and a fork on the napkin. She stepped back to lean against the sink and watch him. He shifted on the bench. He wasn't hungry for eggs, but he took a bite. His eyebrows shot up. "You can cook."

"It's just butter and eggs."

He ate two more bites. "What else?"

"Salt."

"What else can you cook?"

"Vegetables, fish, soups. I'm not very good with steak."

"Not a problem. There are places to go for a steak."

She wiped her hands on a dishtowel that had been also, until that moment, only for show. "And now you know where to go for eggs."

Simon tried not to make more of it than it was, but it was the first time she'd acknowledged that they would be together beyond the duration of their honeymoon, that marriage meant more than anything beyond the next step, the next day. He shoveled into his mouth the rest of the eggs and swallowed, wiped his face with the napkin and brought the plate to the sink. She held her ground, and he felt her heat against his skin when he reached around her to set down the dish.

She'd donned a housecoat, a thin white robe that she must have packed from home. The sash was tied in a bow around her waist. It was a simple design. No buttons or lace. Simon picked up the sash and fingered the fabric. "Did you make this?" Her eyes fixed at his hand on her robe.

She nodded.

They stood close, so close he worried he would touch her without meaning to. He meant to, but not until she gave him something more. "I please you." He was fishing. He wanted to hear that she liked him. That he was handsome at least, almost pretty, anything to reassure him after the previous night's inelegance. He was rewarded with a soft laugh.

"Your reputation remains intact."

He was glad she agreed with him. He'd not doubted it, but now he wanted to hear more than that she wanted him. Simon wanted to hear the words. He wasn't sure which words. He'd know when he heard them, and he had an idea how to get them, but he couldn't do it. He wouldn't touch her again until she knew what it did to him. She was fucking him, every time they touched, and he needed to tell her. He flinched. Perhaps not in those words.

A part of him was afraid that if he spoke the words, if somehow he was able to explain to her what this feeling of inordinate connection was, that it was more than a feeling, that it was an extraordinary phenomenon in the extraordinary universe, that when he heard the words, he would realize he'd been kidding himself, that the connection was merely ordinary. It was just love.

It was falling in love. Everybody did it. It wasn't extraordinary at all. That's what he feared. That he'd imagined it all, built his longing up in his mind until it had taken on a life of its own, made him believe the connection between them was more than the standard exchange of two people falling in love.

How would he know the difference?

It didn't matter.

He would eat eggs for the rest of his life. Give up steak entirely. That said something. He would give up steak. Keep chickens on the roof and lock her in the kitchen with a skillet and a pound of butter.

Her brow furrowed.

Dammit, had she heard him again? He bit his tongue and tried to think of nothing at all.

She crossed her arms. "Do you always eat in your underwear?"

Did he? He exhaled and smiled. No, he did not. "Never."

He jumped when her hands ran along the inside waist of his drawers. She tested the elastic. "I've never seen this before."

Simon almost laughed. He almost doubled over and knocked her to the floor with a hard butt of his forehead. Her second hand joined the first and pulled, feeling the material. Her knuckles brushed the muscles between his hips.

"Is this elastic?"

Now he did laugh. "You've really never seen it?"

"My mother wouldn't let me wash my brothers' drawers. Is it sewn in? It looks sewn in."

"It's done with a large machine. A kind of serger."

"I wish I had a serger."

"You have a serger. You have several, actually."

She finally noticed the tenting of the fabric between them. Simon had been waiting for her to notice, thinking perhaps she would step away when she did. He hadn't the will to do it himself. She stepped closer.

He wrested his eyes from her hands at his waist to a point above her shoulder and was rewarded with a distraction. "You've got a pin." It was clipped to her hair above her ear. His hands traveled to her hair. He'd expected to be able to remove it and move away. He'd removed pins before. They weren't difficult, but this one was stuck, the metal nicked and no longer smooth. A strand of her hair had been caught between the shards. He bent his head closer. It was no distraction at all.

"I was supposed to pay attention to how they came out." Her breath warmed the pulse at the base of his hand.

His two hands worked her hair. "Next time we'll pay more attention." He tried not to break a single strand, and he tried not to touch her.

The pin pulled free and he held it aloft between his thumb and forefinger. She took it, and put it in the folds of her robe, where a pocket must've been hidden. Her eyes found the space at his throat. He swallowed. She desired him, and she hadn't yet learned how to hide it. It would be easier for him if she had.

He tucked the stray lock of hair behind her ear and prohibited himself from running his finger along the soft crest of her ear, from following it down the side to the curve of her jaw, lower.

She lifted a finger and traced the space between his collarbones, at the dip before the expanse of his chest. Her palms flattened. Her fingertips grazed each muscle, trailed over his nipples. His inhale was sharp. He exhaled good intentions. They were lost in the thick air of the kitchen.

He was kissing her before he knew what he was doing. Her hands ran through his hair and brought his face closer. Her tongue found his.

He kept his eyes closed and tasted her. "You're so sweet."

"They left the fruit." Her hands dipped again inside the waistband of his drawers. His hands untied the sash of her robe. He pushed it aside, and there was nothing beneath. She pressed herself against him.

A plea brought his hands to the back of her thighs. He lifted her and her legs pressed against his backside, tightened around him. He took a single step to the table and pushed the magazines aside.

He thrust once inside her and stilled. Together they made a sound, and Simon wasn't sure if he'd exhaled or brought in air. He bent her leg and moved deeper, and she arched on the table. "Simon." Her hands pressed down the length of his back.

He retreated and pressed again. She held his hips close. He moved inside her. The pleasure of it almost overwhelmed him a second time. He pressed harder, slower. Her one leg cradled him, her other fell wider. Simon knew every angle, knew what women liked, what they needed. He withheld it. Instead, he drank in the vision of her, lay down on the table before him, and teased. "What do you want?"

She shook her head.

"Tell me." He waited, thrust again.

"Everything. This."

He leaned in and brushed her breast with the roughness of his cheek. He took her nipple in his mouth, sucked hard. "This?"

"Yes." She covered her eyes with her hands.

He palmed her other breast while he nipped and thrust deep. He adjusted his weight and the angle of his hips and was gratified with a moan that was half sob. He slowed his pace. She let him rock into her. He bent and inhaled the scent of her hair. His cheek rubbed the wetness of a tear where it ran down the side of her face to her ear. I love you. He thought he'd spoken the words aloud, but once the roaring in his ears passed, only their breathing filled the room. He thought the words again. I love you. It was a relief even to think them. I love you. It was impossible that she didn't already know.

He pushed deeper, put pressure where it would please her. I love you. The words came now to his mind each time he entered her. He stilled her hips so he could have her, make her come. He read the approach on her face, and when it arrived, it washed over him and through him. I love you, I love you, the words a pattern in the waves.

26

He dripped water onto her cheeks and chin from the wing of the ice swan he'd stolen from the parlor. None made it into her mouth. Though she tried to position it below the drops of ice water, Simon kept moving the wing. He laughed. "What? Aren't you thirsty?" She gave up, and the droplets landed on each cheek in slow succession.

"Why are you so nice to me?"

"I like you. I like the way it feels when I touch you. And I can't imagine anyone agreeing this is being nice." He tossed the ice to a tray on the nightstand.

"It's different then? Different than when you've been with other women?"

"Not at all the same." He half-rolled to his side, found a packet of cigarettes in the nightstand drawer. Deciding against them, he left them on the table top.

She nudged him. "You're allowed to smoke. It's your room."

He leaned back against the headboard. He cut her a look that arrived with a half smile. "I don't want to dull the taste of you." He raised both brows. "Are you hungry?"

"No." She didn't think it was hunger she felt.

"You haven't eaten anything since lunch yesterday. You slept through dinner on the train."

"I'm not hungry for pineapple." She waved at the door beyond which was the long table of tropical fruits.

"You don't like pineapple?"

She shrugged. "I've never tried one."

Simon's look was pained. "You've never…?"

He tutted and pitched his legs onto the floor. Chloe looked through the bedroom to the parlor and back at the rumpled sheets.

Simon returned from the far side of the room with a plate of yellow prickly half circles of fruit.

He held the plate aloft to her as he approached the bed. "Try it."

She held the sheet up to her with one hand and lifted a piece between two fingers, but lost it as it slid through. She tried again and regarded him, the piece held aloft before her mouth. She had been told it tasted good, sweet.

He nodded at her. "Go ahead."

She bit into it, and juice ran down her cheek to her jaw. Her eyes widened in surprise. She fed herself the second half, chewing and grinning. Simon laughed. She wiped her chin with the back of her hand. "It's the most delicious thing I've ever tasted." She tilted her head back so the juice would not run out of her mouth.

He lifted a piece of fruit off the plate. "I've never fed a woman pineapple."

"Never?"

"Never before in my life."

He lifted it for her, held it between his thumb and forefinger, just far enough away so she had to lean forward. She opened her mouth, expecting him to pop it inside, but he moved it further away. She bent closer, and when he teased her with again. Their eyes were inches from one another. His eyes were a deep blue, sparkling with mischief, and something more.

She felt relief, and something more. "We're not going out?"

"Not yet."

"What if I'm hungry?"

"We have pineapple."

She pulled at the sheet as she rolled off the mattress. Wrapping it around herself, she walked to the bathroom, looking back once at Simon, who had no sheet left to cover himself. He didn't move to find another, but rolled to his side and propped his head on his hand, his elbow on the mattress.

Her gasp, when she reached the bathroom, bounced off porcelain and tile. "This is the most incredible room I've ever seen."

Simon tossed his legs off the bed and pulled on his trousers. He followed her, for the moment distracted from what he had to say. "It's my favorite room. Anywhere."

She looked over her shoulder at him. "You do realize it's a water closet." Her hands trailed over the edge of the tub. "You are the most contradictory man. You despise the water, yet you live on two islands, and your favorite room is the bathroom."

"I love taking baths."

"Do they still call them tubs when they're this large?"

"I'm not sure." Simon frowned. "I suppose I should know. Would you like to try it? Perhaps a word will come."

"Do we have time?"

"We have all the time in the world. The ship doesn't launch until eight tomorrow, and they're always an hour late. At least." He closed the door behind them. "We have time."

She cut him a look. "Then I want a bath."

He sat on the wide edge of the tub and leaned in. The water from the taps rushed, splashed against the porcelain. Steam rose from the faucet.

Chloe watched the play of muscles on his abdomen where they dipped beneath his open trousers. "It's hot. Right from the pipes."

"Did you think I'd draw you a cold bath?"

"We don't have running water at the cottage. We boil it when we want a bath. By the time the tub has finally filled, it's lukewarm."

"Who's Luke?"

Chloe ignored him. She felt shy about asking, but she forced herself to do it. She would have to begin being more open about her feelings with Simon. He was her husband. They had passed the point of embarrassment with one another. They should have done so, at least. "Would you like to join me?"

He pulled at the sheet. "Come here, wife."

A muffled knock interrupted Simon's progress as he bent his face to hers. He tapped her forehead with his. "I'm going to fire them all."

"You're leaving for a month. Shouldn't you manage something before you go?"

"Shouldn't I manage something? Are you nagging me?"

The palm of her hand settled over his upper arm and caressed the ridge of muscle it found there. "I don't nag." She tilted her head. "My mother nags."

"Then I will be on my guard." He kissed her again, a fast, hard kiss on the mouth before releasing her. "You're right, regardless. I should manage something before we leave, or there could be mutiny." He pulled the door behind him, glancing at her before it shut. "If you keep it closed, the room becomes a Roman steam bath. You'll be able draw on the mirror."

The door made a soft catch when he shut it behind him.

Chloe dropped the sheet and lowered herself into the deep porcelain. Steam lifted itself from the water when she settled. The water covered her breasts. She eyed the drain and saw that, should she let it, the bath would reach her shoulders, sitting up with her legs extended. This was not a tub. It was its own body of water.

A stretch of mirror lined the tub just above where it met the tile. Already, it was clouded with steam. Chloe fisted her hand and pressed its side against the glass, leaving the life-like curve of an infant's foot. She dotted five little toes. All her life, she'd seen the irony of joy, the inevitability of its loss. But here and now, the sweetness of the baby's footstep refused to mock her. The prospect of this life was inviting, almost too tempting to refuse.

She ran her hand over her stomach, and pushed it out. She loved babies. Each time Hattie had been pregnant, she'd spent hours with her head on her friend's stomach listening, waiting to feel a movement against her cheek. Later in each term, Hattie's stomach had rumbled visibly with the baby's movements, evoking awed noises from them both.

Anxiety tightened Chloe's chest. Memories of Hattie gave her an uneasy feeling. She made a fist, and felt her fingernails against her palm. The warmth of her own hand calmed her. She let her stomach deflate and wiped the mirror clean. She slid down into the steaming water of the bath. A single bubble reached the surface and popped.

The knock on the door came again as Simon located his shirt.

This is what being in love felt like, wasn't it? The electrifying chill of another's touch, the way it coursed through veins and entered blood and drove a body mad with so much more than physical desire. Was that being in love? He didn't know. He damn well knew he felt something. Not being able to describe it was half his problem.

The other half was timing. Each time he tried to tell her, something got in the way.

He managed a single button as he walked back through the main room. She hadn't told him she loved him. Oh, she wanted him. There was no denying that, and the priest had bound them well enough, but it was Simon who now held them together. Chloe hadn't even put her finger on the string while he tied the bow. Meredith's words echoed. There were no tomorrows with Chloe. Leave it to him to fall in love with a woman as unforthcoming as his brother. She was forthcoming in other ways, Simon corrected himself. Thank God she wanted him to touch her. He couldn't imagine a world where she did not.

The knocking became more insistent. He shouted an irritated response and swung the door wide.

Simon pushed back hard to prevent the invasion, but he was hustled inside by a mass of dark navy wool. The chest against his hands was broad, a wall of muscle. His resistance got him nowhere. A man kicked the door closed behind him. Simon might have been able to recover, to subdue the man with agility and a heavy lamp over the head, but as Simon pushed back, he was overcome, blinded. *White.* The force of it took him back into the room.

The man was bulkier than he'd been two years ago, and now he wore a full beard. His hair was long and in his eyes. He looked nothing like his twin brother, but there was no denying it. Michael had come back from the dead.

27

A part of Simon had known his brother was alive. The other part had shuddered at the possibility that he was not. Now both parts thrilled with anger. "Where the hell have you been?"

"Does it matter?" Michael's voice held no undulation. The entire range of emotion had been wrung from it, drained away. His voice had always been like that. It wasn't his tone now that angered Simon. How could he believe it didn't matter? He'd let his own mother believe her son was dead. The man's inability to fathom their grief from their separation made Simon furious. His knuckles streaked toward Michael's cheek with a guttural noise.

Michael's own hand shot up and caught Simon's right cut with his own. Their fists were the same size. The gesture ended in an equal balanced handshake that pressure held aloft. Simon inhaled. They were no longer of equal strength. He was faster and stronger than he'd ever been. His brother could pummel him to the ground if he chose.

He'd changed in other ways that made Simon's lungs bright. His brother looked him straight in the eye. It was not something Michael did. He'd always avoided Simon's eyes, like everyone else's, choosing instead to look over a person's shoulder, at the light as it danced in the leaves, at the blue, bare sky. Anywhere else but in someone's eyes. They'd never discussed a reason. Perhaps there was no logic for it at all. Now his eyes held Simon fast. Simon saw there unfamiliar depths of blue.

Simon stepped against Michael's chest, his fist still buried in his twin's palm. His face was inches from his brother's. They were at least still the same height. "Why are you here?" The question ground out through the tightness in his chest.

Michael crafted his reply. Simon saw him edit the words in his head, reduce his message to the barest form of communication. "I need your help."

Simon's fist twitched in his brother's hand. "Now?"

Michael released him.

"Now?" The question bore repeating.

His brother had wanted nothing to do with Simon their entire lives. Michael had been an island unto himself, disconnected. He'd pushed Simon away since they were children. Simon couldn't fathom why. He'd never expressed a need, had never asked Simon for help. That Michael had feelings at all was something of a question. And now? Now, Michael needed him. Now that Simon had a wife. When, for the first time in his life, Simon wanted someone more than his brother to need him.

He took in Michael's unkempt clothes. Canvas and denim didn't rumple, but they showed signs of having been worn for a few days at least. There was grease on his trousers, and the neck of his shirt beneath his light wool pea coat was ripped. His beard was an inch beyond what was fashionable, even for men who wore canvas and denim.

Simon didn't know what had changed that made Michael come to him now. He might never know. Frankly, he didn't care. What he cared about now was the truth. If his brother needed him, Simon was going to get something in return.

"How did you do it? How did you hide yourself from me?" Simon had felt a connection to his brother, a physical connection, every day since their birth, but when Michael had disappeared into the water, a switch was flipped. Since then, Simon had felt only the lightest pulse of that connection, faint enough that he'd doubted it had ever been there in the first place, strong enough that it was impossible to ignore.

This time, Simon wouldn't let it go. It wasn't just about he and Michael anymore. Now there was Chloe, and he needed to know. "I felt you. A part of me couldn't believe you were dead, because, every now and then, I still felt you. *My body felt you.* All our lives, you tried to convince me the feeling wasn't real. You ignored me, ignored it, refused to talk about it, but it was real. It is real. I know it is."

Michael shrugged and said the same thing he always had. "I don't know what you're talking about."

Simon could return to the water now, he supposed. It wasn't the river who'd betrayed him. It was Michael. Simon swallowed his frustration and regarded his brother, at once more alien and more familiar than he'd ever been. "What do you need from me?"

"I need money. And a suit."

"What have you been living off the last two years?" Simon itched to know the details. Why would he do it? Where did he go? Had he really just wanted to disappear?

"I need more than I have. I need as much as I can get. And I need it now."

They'd need a lawyer. Simon eyed Michael, head to foot. And a barber.

Michael frowned. He ran his fingers over his beard, smoothing the whiskers down. "I'm not shaving it."

The banks weren't lending, not with the spring's financial crash. Simon had money in the safe, but he'd have to account for it, and he couldn't very well say he gave it to an itinerant dockworker. Michael had to look the part of his brother, at least. A notarized photograph might be enough to appease the Board. Simon's barber would appreciate the challenge. "I can give you three thousand dollars. Cash."

Michael's beard emerged from beneath his palm. He nodded once in concession, but he wasn't happy about it.

Simon would get what he wanted from Michael now. "First, answer my question. Where the hell have you been?" A pressure in Simon's chest distracted him. He couldn't wait for Michael's answer. Chloe was in the bath, and, Goddammit, she'd gone under again. He pointed an unwavering finger at his brother. "Wait here."

Simon was at the bathroom door in a few, quick strides. He closed the door behind him and in a half-second took in the sight of her stretched out along the bottom of the tub. Three bubbles reached the surface in slow succession. He knelt beside the bath and pulled her up from the water with a hand behind her neck. With the other, he wiped away the bathwater that streamed down her face. He kissed her on the mouth, let the water from her lips wet his tongue. "I have to go out, but I when I come back, I'll have a surprise for you."

For a moment, her guard dropped. She smiled, and Simon took note. "You like surprises?" He returned her smile. "Well, you're going to get more than your share tonight. "

He left before she had time to reply. She heard the outer door slam. Chloe pulled a cloth from a pile on a shelf behind her head and brought it to her face and inhaled. It smelled like Simon. It felt empty now that he'd gone. She'd grown used to him in the last week, even more in the last day. Used to him. It was a ridiculous thought, that she could ever grow used to him. The physical sensations were enough to convince her it would never happen. She'd never grow used to him, not his smell, his touch, the look of him. No, she'd grown addicted to him. She'd been reading about addiction in Dr. Reed's medical journals, which, as often as not, he left at the post office for days at a time. Chloe had all the signs of addiction. Though unlike morphine dependency, she didn't feel worse after being with Simon.

It was ridiculous. She should never have allowed it to come this far. It had been a subtle advance, an encroachment by slow degrees, until unawares it had overtaken her. There was no way of knowing how long it would last. The thought gave her a chill, in spite of the water that was so hot it turned her skin pink. That little tinkling bell of warning followed her everywhere, right here into the tub. Chloe pulled at the stopper and let the water drain.

The mirror along the wall reflected skin that shone with water. She'd never seen so much of her body all at once before. The mirror in her bedroom back home was the size of a small gravestone. There, she'd puzzled together her appearance in inches. An enormous mirror that hung from ceiling to floor at Wolfe Castle had given her once a full view. On one of her autumn visits there before the weather was too cold to venture across the water, she and Meredith had swung each other in circles, had tripped over one another as they tried to watch their steps and themselves in the mirror, both at once. She turned to the side and pushed out her stomach again, then shook her head. Ridiculous. She'd left her robe in the kitchen, so she donned the white sheet, tied it behind her neck and wrapped it around her waist. When she emerged from the bedroom, she jumped.

In the sitting room were two women in long dark grey pinafores tied in back over long black dresses with high necks and long sleeves. They were clearing the food from brunch. The swan had pooled on the table into the platter beneath it until all that remained was its oblong base. A wheeled cart was already stacked with plates.

Chloe didn't have time to retreat before they both abandoned the champagne flutes in their hands and advanced with excitement. One of the maids, close in age to Chloe's own mother, stepped forward with arms outstretched. Chloe thought at first she would embrace her, but the woman stopped and clasped her hands. "Mrs. Low." Her *esses* were held long, and Chloe's married name was said in the same register as the word itself. "My name is Agatha."

The second maid, younger than Chloe, stepped forward and curtsied. Agatha waved her down. "She's not the aristocracy, Margie."

"She might as well be," Margie replied. Then she looked at Chloe. "You might as well be." She curtsied again. "My name is Margie, and you'll be wanting a dress for dinner. Can we help you? Can we help you pick out a dress?"

28

Michael followed Simon's barber to a line of three chairs, each made of wood and worn mahogany leather, like he was following an executioner to the gallows. Simon has been coming to this same shop for years. The barber and he had exchanged over the course of those years perhaps seven words. Of the seven, two were simply Simon's direction, *the same.* Now Simon nodded at his brother, and added two more words to their repertoire. *Like mine.*

The barber opened the embossed steel step with a clank, and Michael folded himself into the chair. His hands gripped the carved claw hand rests. While the hydraulic press was pumped and the chair lifted higher, Michael seethed.

Everybody loved a professional shave. Simon grinned. Perhaps it was the indignity of being lifted in the air by another man, or perhaps it was having someone hold a razor to your neck. For whatever reason, his brother hated it.

Michael's face was wrapped in a turban of steaming cloth. His fingers drummed the claws of the chair. Other than that, he was still. The barber scraped steel against leather in a simple rhythm. Michael spoke through a gap in the towel. "I never thought you'd do it."

Simon didn't hide his surprise. Startled by even this small inquiry, he quipped. "Make you shave?" But he knew it wasn't what Michael meant.

"Marriage."

Simon never thought he'd do it either. It'd never occurred to him that it would be something he'd ever want to do. Why bother, unless circumstances demanded? There'd been a circumstance, all right, although there'd been no demand but his own. Simon was as surprised as his brother, but now that his demand had been met, he was sold on the bonds of holy matrimony. He understood finally what holy meant. Altogether. Of a whole.

The barber unwound the towel from Michael's face with a flick of the wrist. The cloth spiraled and snapped. He hung it over his shoulder and took scissors from his apron pocket. They snapped, too, twice in the air before they went to work on Michael's beard. Michael exhaled, loud and long-suffering. The beard landed in fawn-colored tufts on the sheet across his lap. Michael watched the trimmings fall, the clench of his jaw revealed by the shearing. He shifted in his chair, and the barber's scissors paused mid-air until Michael resettled. He landed an eye on Simon, as though remembering he was there. "You sure she won't get sick of your sentimentalism?"

Simon, on the other hand, hadn't forgotten his brother. He'd been watching the scene with pleasure. The scissors were returned to a pocket, and a mug of foam emerged from a counter behind the chair. The soft brush clacked against the sides before it lathered Michael's face. Watching his brother receive a loathsome shave was indeed an emotional peak. He grinned again. "You've got the wrong word, brother. You mean hedonism." Simon had been accused of self-indulgence by everyone he knew. This moment's pleasure was sublime example.

Michael's nose jutted from the froth. "I mean sentimentalism. You're an emotional shipwreck."

Simon's grin faltered. He was an emotional shipwreck, but Simon refused to let Michael know his barb stuck and said, "Lust isn't an emotion."

Michael parried, "But you think it is. That's your problem. You're always trying to get closer, closer." Michael held a hand up to his face, and then pressed it against his nose. He wiped shaving foam from his palm on his thigh.

"Intimacy has its advantages."

"Just fucking has its advantages." Michael looked sidelong at the barber, almost contrite.

"And I thought you weren't listening when I tried to persuade you of the value of fucking." Simon took full advantage of the razor against Michael's neck. "At least not until Virginia Waterstone." Only days before Michael's disappearance, Virginia had emerged from being alone with Michael, her dress torn. She'd explained nothing about what happened, but everyone had filled in the gaps. "You ruined her reputation, you know that? Then you left without a word of apology or explanation."

"It wasn't like that." His look at the barber now was more indignant than ashamed.

Simon of course knew it wasn't like that. Michael would never act with violence toward a woman, would never have taken Virginia, a woman they'd known since childhood, against her will. But Michael wasn't used to women. Once down, the wall Michael put between himself and the world would let loose a groundswell hard to control.

Simon pressed, two years of wondering balled into two words. "What happened?"

The barber stepped away, disappeared in a display of professional tact, leaving Michael's face clean and bare. His jaw was purpled with bruises on both sides. One bruise extended across his cheek to his ear.

"What the hell happened?" The echoed question bounced against the ceramic tile. Shocked by the bruises, Simon didn't care if Michael answered with his explanation of the affair with Virginia or of his battered face. He wanted an answer, any answer, past or present.

Michael's hand cut the air, left to right. "It was a mistake." His palm faced the ground. "That's all."

"Would you look at this?" Both brothers looked as one toward the low voice of a man who had come upon them unaware. "You weren't kidding. He's alive."

Unsurprised, Michael nodded a perfunctory greeting at the man who'd joined them. "Joe."

Joe Warren was tall and blue-black. He wore a grey sack coat over close-fitting black trousers. A watch chain ran across his belly, an upturned umbrella beneath a row of waistcoat buttons. A starched white high collar was a striking foil for the rich midnight of his skin.

Michael leaned forward. Joe took his hand and said, "I would've thought the mirrors were playing tricks with my eyes." Joe looked at Simon. "But you told me so."

Simon stood from where he lounged in a barber chair. "I told you so." Joe embraced him, and the two men clapped one another's backs.

Joe said into Simon's neck, "I'm glad for you."

Simon answered, without thinking, the truth. "I am, too." Whether Joe had offered his joy for Michael's return or for Simon's marriage, Simon's answer would've been the same.

Joe sat in Simon's deserted chair and perched his satchel on his lap. The brown leather was lighter than the dark wine brown of the barber's chair, and more worn. Joe wasn't a rich man, but had he lacked ethics, he could've been. His legal prowess was comprehensive. He knew something about everything related to the law, and, Simon had learned, how to get around it.

Simon didn't know the whole of Joe's story. He wasn't the type of man to extract the histories of men born into wretched circumstance, but he knew Joe had stowed away on one of the elder Wolfe's ships, escaped from an unlucky island in the West Indies. Joe had been young enough, when he'd been discovered and brought to the ship's captain, that the elder Wolfe had taken pity on him and returned with the child to New York. Tristan's father wasn't so progressive as to raise him as his own, but he'd found Joe a home, an orphanage in the city, and did not forget that he'd changed the course of the boy's life, as much as the boy had changed his own.

Joe removed a tuft of papers from his satchel. From the tuft, he selected a single one. "One death certificate, revoked." Joe's eyes narrowed at the bruises on Michael's face. "Although whatever got hold of him at least *tried* to kill him."

Michael frowned but said nothing.

Simon stepped behind where Joe sat in the chair and peered over his shoulder. "You're a magician."

"It's not magic. Look at the two of you." Joe waved between them with the page. "Any challenge to an expedited reversal wouldn't hold up in court." Joe cast Michael a sly look. "Unless you're planning to disappear again." He looked from Simon to Michael and back. "Twins. One legally dead." He shook his head. "You two could be brilliant together. Raid trains. Rob banks." He tucked the paper back into his bag, and said into it, "At the very least, have some fun with the ladies."

Simon and Michael eyed one another with mutual wariness, each considering Joe's meaning, until Michael kicked his chin at his brother. Simon felt shock at the mute invitation and held up his hands. He began, "I don't know what you've been up to, but we're not…" He trailed off.

Simon would agree to anything to help his twin. There was no use denying it. Already, he'd agreed to provide his brother with cash, but money was easy. Michael's return was inspired by something deeper than a lack of cash, and it was clear now he needed something more.

They'd never sported with their likeness, had never tried to confuse anyone, had never played practical jokes on their mother or their teachers, or, as Joe had suggested, *the ladies*. The appeal of that camaraderie for Simon would have been difficult to ignore, had Michael shown any interest before in such an intriguing collaboration.

Michael regarded Simon without emotion from the barber's chair. No expression marred his beautiful, beaten face. He ran the backs of his fingers of his jaw and frowned. "Fuck, that's soft." His hand dropped, and he said, "Joe's right. Don't file that paper. I might need you again." He stood, as though his words held no meaning at all. "Let's go."

Simon forced his face into a scowl. "Hold your horses." Michael had never asked him for anything before. Simon turned to Joe to hide his pleasure and asked, "Can you do a marriage license as fast?"

"A marriage license," Joe repeated. "You're not legal?"

Michael, too, showed interest. He echoed, "You're not legal."

Simon waved his brother off. "I will be." He felt a tension between his shoulders that belied a misgiving he preferred to ignore. He spoke to Joe. "Can you bring it by tonight?"

Michael's eyebrows rose. "What's the rush?"

Simon frowned. He'd wanted his brother to show an interest in him, any interest at all. Now that he had, Simon wanted to punch him in the face. "We're married, brother. I don't need a piece of paper to prove it." He hoped Chloe wouldn't either.

29

An elevator waited in the foyer outside the door of Simon's apartment. Chloe had never been in an elevator before, but the women knew well how to work it, and it came when called. It was manned by a young boy in black trousers, a white collared shirt, black waistcoat, and a jewel red newsboy cap. He lifted it and bowed with precocious gallantry when the women entered the elevator car. Agatha chided him, "You'd better not let Mr. Judah see that hat. Where's your bell cap?"

The boy frowned. "Simon likes me to wear the red one on special occasions."

"Mr. Low to you," Agatha corrected.

He closed the gate, shifted a lever, and the elevator descended. An arrow above their heads pointed at descending numbers with slow deliberation.

"Mr. Low was married." He smiled at Chloe. "And he ain't never been married before."

Chloe smiled back. She was glad to hear it confirmed.

He introduced himself, "My name is Daniel."

At the name shared with Hattie's newborn, Chloe felt a rush of longing for her friend. Hattie would've loved this, everything about it. They'd shopped for fabric together before, but never for dresses, ready-made in a department store with an elevator. She shared, wanting to talk about her friend, to bring her close through memory, "I know a Daniel. In fact, I know two."

The elevator stopped, and Daniel pulled the metal grate open and tipped his cap. "Now you know three."

Margie and Agatha ushered Chloe through the women's eveningwear department. A single clerk manned the floor. There wasn't a single customer in sight. Chloe was surprised as she looked around. "Where is everyone? I expected it to be busier."

Agatha shook her head. "It's the dressing hour. Any lady requiring an evening gown will be at home puttin' it on."

They led her to a luxurious fitting room tucked in the back of the department. A gilt chandelier with crystal drops matched electric scones, two to each wall. Two buttoned purple settees with scrolled wooden frames sat against opposite walls, and a long, three-panel mirror was established in a corner. Directly in front was a pedestal, high enough for hems to be pinned while a customer stood atop. The two woman regarded Chloe.

"No pastels." Margie puckered her face.

Miss Aggie agreed implicitly. "But blues and grays, I think."

Margie tilted her head at Chloe. "What've you got on under there?"

Chloe looked down at the dress she'd donned while Margie and Miss Aggie had finished clearing the buffet. Beneath her dress was a basic white cotton shift and short drawers. She shrugged, "Underclothes."

"She'll be needing some of those, too." Margie nudged Agatha, who batted off her elbow in disapproval before marching out.

"How did you manage it?" Margie asked, wide-eyed and curious as soon as the elder woman was gone. "I've rarely seen the man with the same woman twice."

She was interrupted when Agatha bustled in again, her arms extended with a dress hanging from each. Margie took one dress from Agatha but refused the other with the word, "Less." She returned her attention to Chloe. "Well, you look like an angel. There's a start."

Indeed, Chloe wondered, how had she managed it? Surely Simon had caroused with women more beautiful, and he'd kept himself out of feminine scrapes this long. Men like Simon learned early how to avoid them, so why hadn't Simon avoided this one? The question had repeated inside her head since the train. The only answer she could fathom was that he'd chosen to do it; he'd chosen her. *Why?*

The dresses began to arrive in twos and threes. Margie hung them more slowly than Agatha brought them in, so they heaped tall in Chloe's outstretched arms. The one that lay on top shimmered gold, and Chloe bent to place her cheek against it.

Tiny beads were woven with fishing wire until they created a fabric, fluid and soft. Chloe had seen beads woven like this, of wood and stone and shell, but never of metal. When she lifted her cheek from the cloth, Margie took the dress from her arms and hung it on a hook where it gleamed.

"You're from where he is, then?" Chloe's arms lightened again when Margie took another dress from the pile.

Chloe wasn't sure where Simon was from. She hedged, "I'm from the North Country."

"If you're from the same place, you must've known him when you were children."

Chloe shook her head. "I met him last week." It had been a Wednesday. Chloe noticed the falter in Margie's step and cringed. "I suppose I shouldn't have shared that.

"I won't tell, if you won't tell Miss Aggie I asked." Margie hung another two dresses and came back to Chloe's arms for more. Agatha returned, added to the pile and left again without speaking. The younger clerk sighed after the older woman had gone. "Love at first sight, was it?"

Chloe wasn't sure it was that way at all, but she'd already admitted she'd known her husband for little more than a week. What else could she say to explain? "Something like that."

Margie gave Chloe a sly glance from where she stood at a hook. Cast of iron, it jutted two feet out from the wall and already held six dresses. "Are you going to fish me for information on your husband?"

Chloe's attention was divided between the dresses and her husband, one in the end infinitely more compelling. She wanted to know more about Simon. Chloe straightened her spine. "I suppose I am."

"What do you want to know?"

The truth of it awed her. "Everything."

Margie leaned in. "He won't like us talking."

Chloe leaned in, too. "I won't tell if you won't."

As if in sentry, Judah walked by the open door to the fitting room. Chloe was for a moment distracted. "Mr. Klink. Judah!"

He popped his head in. "Mrs. Low."

"Is there any news?"

Judah checked his watch. "They'll arrive at the Denton station soon. It'll be another hour before the ferry gets to Grandview." He looked around the room filled with dresses. "Have you found something you like?"

Chloe looked over her shoulder. Two large hooks full of dresses baited her. Had she found something she liked? Yes, she had, but it wasn't the dresses. Therein lay the problem. She'd much prefer a sheet and longed to be wrapped in one again, her husband's hand on her waist, his thumb moving over her hip. She felt herself flush red.

Judah read her agitation. "Don't worry. The doctors Simon sent are the best in the city." He winked at her. "I'll let you know as soon as I hear something." He tapped the side of the doorjamb before disappearing from the room.

Margie closed the door behind him. "We'll work while we talk, or Miss Aggie will make us stop." She helped Chloe off with her dress, and sucked her teeth at the shift beneath. "First thing I know about Mr. Low is, he won't like that silly sack." She disappeared out the door.

Chloe stood in the shift she'd made with her own hands, embroidered in white at the hem and along the bust. She felt out of place. Of course she shouldn't be here. She should be home with Hattie, away from Simon, away from wanting anything close to what he offered her. She should vow to be on the next train north. Instead, she remembered the way Simon's hand had felt against the back of her neck as he promised a surprise, and her resolution faltered.

Margie returned and held up two garments, one in each hand. "Your husband will like these better." The first was a one-piece garment with thin shoulder straps and tight fitting pantaloons edged with wide lace. Margie ran her fingers beneath the edge and encouraged Chloe to do the same. "It won't ball up beneath your dress." She crooked her finger. "Off with that one." Chloe obliged, and once defrocked, stepped into the champagne satin. It followed her curves and cut low and tight beneath her arms.

Margie took up the second garment. "Your husband's store has the largest selection of corsets on Manhattan Island." Margie leaned in again. "He don't have to buy any advertisements to tell it, neither."

Chloe didn't have to ask how word got around. Simon was so promiscuous, his reputation came with props. His reputation alone would be enough to sell a thousand corsets a season.

After Chloe was ensconced, her waist cinched and her breasts pushed high, Margie held up a dress from the wall. "Should we try this one first?" Gold beads shimmered like heat off stone. The cut was simple and, Chloe noticed when Marjorie ran her hands up the seam, open at the sides.

Chloe balked. She understood now what Margie had meant by ' less'. "Women wear that?"

Margie nodded. "It's all the rage. It's called *side cleavage*. The men go wild for it." She leaned in. "They say the style is all over Chicago."

"Does Mr. Low like dresses like that one?"

Margie's eyes rolled. She clearly thought the question ludicrous. "He picked this one out. He picks out most of the dresses in this department. He loves to see the women dressed up."

Chloe didn't want to know about her husband's reputation, or the reputation of her husband's shops. She wanted to know about her *husband*. Here was an opening, a way into her husband's life beyond his taste in undergarments. She asked, as though the answer made no difference, "Any women in particular?"

Chloe remembered Hattie's description of the jealousy she'd felt when she and Daniel spent time in the city together. The shadow of that jealousy teased now the edge of her vision.

When Margie looked loath to share, Chloe qualified, "Other than me, of course." She'd learned from talking with clients how to be diplomatic.

The clerk looked relieved. "I'm sure you're the only one for him, now. But before you? Most came in and out." She squinted her eyes in a pantomime of thought. "But there was one you might want to look out for."

Chloe intuited the name before Margie spoke it.

"Miss Rita."

Chloe inhaled at the pinch in her stomach. Rita Smythe. The shadow of jealousy darkened her vision, and at more than just the edges. This was dangerous ground, indeed. Marriage just wasn't something she was built for. It was all too much to lose, even if it was just to another woman. Simon's loss, when it was sure to arrive, would be devastating. What would happen if Chloe allowed herself to grow attached to him? *More* attached, she corrected herself. She had to get out of this marriage, and soon, before she grew any more in love with her husband.

Margie smoothed the dress over Chloe's corset and checked to confirm that where the dress dipped low at her sides and back, the underclothes remained hidden. She pushed Chloe with a hand at her back toward the mirror in the corner.

"You want to know something about your husband? I can tell you one thing. He'll like this dress." She indicated Chloe's reflection in the mirror.

Chloe moved from side to side. Had she been the sort, she would've been shocked. The dress lacked any sense of discretion. She would never wear it outside the confines of the fitting room, but she knew instinctively that her husband would more than simply *like* her in this dress. She wanted nothing more than to please him, to wear it for him. Chloe chewed her lip. Her life was filling up with wants.

She took a last, longing look at her reflection before she shook her head. It didn't matter what either of them wanted.

She turned to Margie. "Help me take it off."

30

Simon walked Michael through the men's department, avoiding store clerks and the last customers of the day. He'd been right, goddammit. Michael was alive, but Simon didn't want to tell the tale of his brother's resurrection, not yet. He needed to tell Chloe first. And before that, Michael needed something to wear. Simon's clothes were two sizes too small for the brother that used to be his twin.

Simon snatched a suit coat off a wax figure and a folded shirt off a pile behind a counter. He opened a dressing room door at the far side of the department and pushed Michael through it. He didn't actually push him, not the way Michael had done when entering Simon's apartment an hour before. He couldn't have pushed him anywhere. Somehow his twin brother had grown twice his size. He even seemed taller, but Simon didn't need to push. He needed only to touch him, and Michael moved away. So Simon tapped Michael's back and, like a marionette, Michael moved in whatever direction Simon wished.

Michael bristled. "Let's make this quick."

Simon closed the door behind them. "Ditch the rags, and it'll go faster."

Michael pulled his shirt over his head, and Simon flinched. Bruises colored Michael's torso. They extended from each side up his back. He'd been pummeled, and the beating was recent. The bruises had not yet begun to yellow. Simon felt a wash of dread. "What's the rush?"

Michael took the new shirt from Simon. "The train leaves at eight. If I miss it, it's over."

The Rome, Watertown, Ogdensburg line had an eight o'clock express to the River, with connecting routes to Canada.

Michael turned to shrug on his shirt, and the bruises extended over his ribs. Simon withheld a wince of pain and kept his voice light, but it was impossible to remain silent when faced with the remains of the beating.

"What've you been up to?"

Michael finished buttoning the front of the shirt, which was too small and pulled through the shoulders. It would have to do. Michael's patience wouldn't survive finding the right size. "Work."

Simon doubted Michael's lashing had been about work. "If you've been working, what do you need money for?"

"I need more than I make by captaining a tug."

"You're a tugboat captain." Simon felt a rush of triumph when Michael told him what he'd wanted to know. "What's her name?" Simon didn't want Michael to disappear again. The name of his boat was a pin on the map.

Michael selected a tie from several that decorated a wooden rack drilled into the wall. He selected another, and switched the two ties back and forth under his chin. He studied the silk as though he cared, and Simon wondered if there was a woman involved. Michael had never cared how he looked, never cared about clothes. In his entire life, this was the first time he'd selected a tie. Simon clarified, "I mean what's the name of your boat."

Michael threw one tie to a chair and the other around his neck. He pulled each end until in the mirror they showed the correct length on either side. "She's in between names."

It was no doubt a lie. "You've got a crew?"

Michael lifted his chin so he could see the knot better beneath. "Just me."

Simon didn't dare to hope that Michael would give up the location of where he'd been harbored, but he asked anyway, "Where is she now?"

Michael finished tying the black Prince's knot around his neck without looking in a mirror. When he found it crooked, he glared at it in the glass as though expecting it to unknot and retie itself.

Simon stepped forward and loosened the knot around Michael's neck. "The trick is not to pull so tight." He pulled the ends through. His eyes tracked from Michael's neck to his face. "So you can just become a tugboat captain?" He crafted the knot below his brother's jaw. "Could I? Could I become a tugboat captain, if I wanted? Would anybody care if I just showed up with a tugboat? It's tribal on the docks here. I can't imagine it's any better up north. They just let you in?" He finished off his brother's tie. "And if you're a tugboat captain, why do you need a suit?"

Michael dipped into the suit coat Simon held aloft for him from behind and regarded himself in the mirror and frowned. "Every man needs a suit."

"I'm in complete agreement, but why do you?" Simon stepped away, frustrated again as always for answers.

"Why else?" Michael lifted his shoulders so the suit coat settled more easily on his frame. "To woo women."

Simon had always wanted a brother he could talk to about women. He would've loved a brother he could talk to about anything, but mostly he'd wanted to talk about women. A man couldn't learn about women without making an ass of himself, unless he asked a brother. Simon had learned this the hard way. But he and his brother never talked about anything, and of all things, they'd never talked about women.

"Here." Simon snapped his fingers. "Give me that cash. It's ruining the lines of the jacket." He accepted the rolled of bills he'd just removed from the safe in his office and placed them with an absent mind in his own coat pocket. They'd never talked about women before, but, now, Simon was married, and he loved his wife. More than love, his soul escaped from his body every time he touched her. He wanted to talk about that.

"I haven't even told you about her yet."

Michael adjusted his tie. "Her, who?"

Simon was again exasperated. "My wife."

Michael looked in the mirror and growled, pulling at his collar. "Tell me if you must."

The collar Michael had chosen as they'd walked by the counter display was the height of formality. Simon made to reach for it. "You don't have to wear it so high."

Michael brushed his hand away.

Simon growled back and instead handed Michael a lint brush. "How did you even learn I was married?"

"You told me."

"I didn't tell you." He wasn't even wearing a ring.

"It was written all over your face."

Likely it was. Simon checked his face in the mirror over his brother's shoulder. For a moment their eyes met. Simon was startled by their resemblance. He looked away. "It was in the paper." Simon knew Michael didn't read the papers. He always received his news firsthand. It was one of the things that made his brother seem so distant and untouchable, this sense that he knew everything, and before anyone else. Simon explained as though, this time, his brother didn't already know. "She lives at the river. On Grandview year round."

Michael gave off fighting his jacket with the brush and forced it back on Simon. He took a step toward the mirror, either to inspect the bruises on his face or the line of his jaw, newly revealed. "You're spending time with the locals now, are you?"

"I couldn't very well avoid it." Simon grew angry at the memory. "Meredith was there when you went under. She could've drowned dragging me to shore. And where were you?" Simon took a calming breath and raised his hands in conciliation. "It doesn't matter anymore. Did you know she and Wolfe were married two days ago?" He chucked the brush into its basket on the settee. "Then I was. We were." Simon wanted to share this much at least with his brother. "She knows you. I think you'd remember her. She's got this hair." His hand hovered at his head. "It's almost white. And she loves to dance. And she loves to…" He didn't know which details to share and stumbled over the telling. "Her name is…was," he corrected, "Chloe Swann." Michael didn't register that Simon had said anything at all, let alone had just shared the name of his bride, but Simon was relieved to be able to talk about it, to talk with someone about the urgency of his feelings. "I forced her into it. Marriage, the whole lot. She seems unsure about me, about everything."

Simon had been withholding crucial information. Of course she couldn't trust him, but he had the nerve to tell her everything now that Michael was back. There was no reason now not to tell Chloe that he loved her, that something miraculous happened whenever they touched. Whatever extraordinary thing it was, it was real. Michael was the proof.

Michael's face was impassive. "Some women have trouble committing."

Simon was nettled. "Now you're the expert on women?" It was impossible that Michael knew more about women than Simon, who'd spent his adult life learning all the vagaries of the sex.

"If I remember, Chloe was like that."

The sentence winded Simon like a physical blow. "What do you mean?" Chloe and Michael had known one another. Why hadn't he pressed for information before now? It had been irrelevant before now. Michael had been dead. "How do you know she has trouble committing?" He spit the last word out in disgust. He made himself stop talking. He had to stop asking questions before Michael would answer.

Michael faced him, each hand on a hip. "I don't think she's a good choice for you."

Not a good choice? "Why the hell not?"

Michael raised a brow. "Have you seen the size of her brother?"

Simon failed for a moment to comprehend Michael's reply. "Are you," he stuttered, "Are you making a *joke*? Eric stood up for me. I asked him, because you weren't around." It made sense that Michael and Eric would've known one another. They were of an age, and, Simon thought now, the same temperament. Taciturn sons of bitches. Michael knew Chloe through Eric, just hanging around with Eric.

"Chloe's not used to people."

"That's not true." Simon waved an invalidating arm. "She talks to people all day long."

"Sick people. Dead people."

"She doesn't talk to dead people."

"They might as well be dead. She certainly doesn't have to talk to them for long before they're dead. She's used to dead people, but she's not used to live ones."

Simon was unconvinced. So what if his wife understood and cared for sick people? It sounded to Simon like a lovely quality in a wife. "What does it matter?"

Michael threw up his hands, then brushed past Simon to leave the fitting room. "I'm telling you, she can't make you happy." He spoke his next words over his shoulder. "Someone like me would be fine with a wife like Chloe."

Simon tracked him out. "Someone like you?"

"Someone who doesn't need what you need."

Simon asked his brother's broad back, "And what do I need?"

Michael stopped moving and faced him, made certain his words were heard. "Someone who can love you."

31

"Here's a fish out of water."

Chloe recognized the sound before she confirmed its source. Rita Smythe. Chloe was embarrassed, as though Rita knew everything, from beginning to end. She felt her face flush, and her heart pounded. She accepted Rita's offered hand. "It's so nice to see you again."

Rita said, "Married. I read it in the papers this morning, and I didn't believe it." She pressed the button that called the elevator. "You can't believe everything you read these days. But Simon confirmed it. He told me himself that the deed had been done. He used those words exactly, in fact. I'm going to see him now."

When had Simon spoken with Rita? When had there been time? Chloe didn't want to show her ignorance, or that she cared.

Chloe pressed the button, too, and Rita gave her a sympathetic look that took in her dress. "Couldn't they find you anything to make sense of your hair?"

Chloe regarded her dress. Rumpled and plain, it was the same as she'd worn for their wedding, and the overnight train.

When Daniel opened the door, Rita swept into the elevator. "Up, Daniel." He tipped his cap to Rita. When Chloe entered, he said, "Mrs. Low." The salutation was the first wedding gift she'd received.

Daniel pulled the lever, and Chloe watched the arrow as it swept beneath the numbers. When the arrow passed seven, Chloe realized Rita meant to follow her to the top floor.

"He's not here," Chloe said, although it might have been a lie. Simon indeed might have returned by now, might be waiting for her in the sitting room, or the bedroom, or the kitchen. Chloe's face flushed red again. She didn't want Rita in Simon's apartment, hated the idea of her entering the rooms she and Simon had shared, hated more the idea of seeing Rita and Simon together. She remembered too well Rita's hand on her husband's thigh.

Chloe tried to remind herself that she should be leaving, that she would have no hold on Simon soon enough. She should try to let go. She should use the stratagems that had worked for her in the past, when she'd been compelled to let go, in spite of everything inside her wanting to hold on tightly. She really should, but she couldn't, not yet.

They entered the apartment together, and Rita removed her hat and set it on the desk. She strode through the apartment with a familiarity that made a pit open in Chloe's stomach.

"I understand you had a party in here. Is there champagne?"

Chloe shook her head. "They cleaned everything up earlier."

Rita was already out of earshot, through the kitchen door. "There's nothing here." It was an accusation. "Simon will want something to eat tonight after the party."

"What party?" Was this the surprise Simon had told her about?

"There's always a party." Rita strode to the phone and tapped it once. "Send up bread and a ham."

Chloe tried to interrupt. "We're leaving tomorrow morning." Now why had she said that? She should be leaving tonight.

Rita replaced the phone. "Simon loves ham, and he likes to eat late."

Without hesitation, Rita disappeared into Simon's bedroom, and Chloe heard the nightstand drawer open and shut. Rita returned to the sitting room with a cigarette in hand. She lit it and pointed at the room with it, a little circle in the air. "What do you think? How did I do?"

Chloe's heart pounded. Rita knew what was in Simon's bedside table. "Do?"

"I redecorated last year. It's the second time I've redecorated in two years. As soon as I finish, he wants me to get started again. He has an appetite for new things." Rita sat on the settee, her elbow resting on the arm of the sofa, cigarette smoke curling in the air. She regarded Chloe, another novelty before her, inhaled and blew smoke up and away. "Where is he now?"

Chloe wished she knew. Her mouth opened and shut.

Rita regarded her with sympathy. "Don't worry. It's not you. Simon's not a man to be kept on a leash. What are your plans?"

She was going home. That's what she should have said. "We're going out."

"Out?"

"To dinner. And dancing," she added as an afterthought. If she'd planned to stay, she would've loved dancing with Simon, and she was hungry. The mention of ham reminded her that all she'd had for several hours was pineapple.

"Then it must be Del's. We'll go together. There's no telling when Simon will be back." Rita reached over the desk and pulled the phone to her. The cigarette sent tendrils of smoke into the curtains. "Send up two dresses." Rita said, with the mouthpiece pressed against her shoulder, "Simon brings all of his women to Del's." She turned back to the telephone. "The red one I had on earlier."

She looked at Chloe in expectation.

She didn't want to let Simon go, not yet. Her hands shook. Later. "Tell them to send up the gold."

32

Simon took the steps up from the men's department two at a time. When he opened the door and called her name, silence greeted him.

Michael walked with more deliberation up the stairs. When he entered the room, Simon explained, "She's not here."

Michael said only, "I smell ham," and disappeared through the door into the kitchen.

Simon found Chloe's satchel in the bedroom, buckled shut and still packed. The bed had been made. He could tell by the artistry of the folds she'd made it herself. He checked the bathroom and found evidence of her bath. A towel was draped over the edge of the tub.

Michael leaned against the doorjamb, a slab of ham between two pieces of thick bread. Between bites, he said, "She didn't stay long."

Simon glared. "She's here somewhere."

Michael gestured to her bag with his sandwich. "She's packed."

"We leave in the morning."

"Looks like she's already gone."

Simon turned on him. "Fuck you, Mick. We're married. She's not going anywhere without me. Why don't you want to believe it?" Michael chewed in silence. Simon pressed, "Maybe it's because you're in love with her yourself. Is that it? Are you in love with her?"

Michael swallowed and said, "There's someone at the door." Simon brushed past him, and Michael said, "It's not her."

Of course it wasn't her. Chloe wouldn't have knocked. Simon swung the door wide. "Will." He tried to smile. "Nice cap."

Daniel tipped it and extended an envelope. Simon pulled out their marriage license. He winked at the young boy with a pretense of ease. "It's my marriage license. This is important. Makes everything legal."

"A black man in a suit delivered it. He said to tell you," Daniel looked at the ceiling as he remembered the words, mimicked the tone exactly, "Now would be an opportune time to knock over a bank."

Simon nodded and said, "That's my attorney."

Daniel stared. "I didn't know a black man could be a lawyer. Could I be a lawyer?"

Simon frowned. "This is New York. I think you could be a lawyer. You'd have to give up the red cap, at least until you passed the Bar."

Daniel took the hat and handed it to Simon.

Simon looked over his shoulder at his brother. "It's settled then. I'll call Joe and see if he could use a clerk." He studied the bellhop, his face and height indicating an age younger than any other person working at the shop. "He might start you as a runner, and you can work your way up to clerking."

"I can't write, or read."

"You can practice with the street signs." Simon returned the cap. "For now, keep this." Daniel reached the elevator before he turned back to Simon. He said in a voice of wisdom at odds with his age, "Miss Rita took Mrs. Low to Del's," before closing the gate and pulling the lever that sent the elevator down.

It wasn't terrible news, but it was close. Rita was not being kind taking his wife to Del's. Simon studied their names on the page. There was only one way to make this right. He had to tell her.

"There's still time to get out of it. You don't need to sign that."

Of course he was going to sign it. The question was, would she? He reached the phone, tapped it twice. "I'm going to bring her back." He pointed at his brother. "You stay here."

"Leave the cash."

Simon removed a large roll of bills from inside his coat and tossed it to the table beside the telephone before leaving the door open on his way out.

Michael removed the band and started counting, putting the bills in stacks of five, and crisscrossing the stacks to make a pile. He answered the telephone on the first ring and listened for a moment before speaking. It was the front office, and there was a telegram that had just arrived for Simon.

Michael said, "Send it up."

33

At just after six in the evening, the street outside the restaurant teemed with people. Chloe alighted from the hansom cab and waited while Rita paid the driver. After emerging from the cab, Rita brushed past Chloe onto the walk. Men and women lined the walk outside the entrance, where a large dome of fabric extended fifteen feet from the building to the street corner. They greeted one another in pairs and groups. Parasols shut up. Tall hats were pinched, doffed and levered, one between each man's arm and side. A patron pulled the end of his white scarf until the fabric left his neck in a flare and a swoop; then he tucked it into his hat. Three more men in succession did the same.

The air was heavy with water, and clouds raced across the sky, dousing the sun at intervals. Rita tugged at the fingers of a long glove that matched the scarlet of her dress. Chloe was jostled from behind, and the tight skirt of her dress caused her to stumble. Rita caught her elbow. "Watch yourself now." She gestured with her chin to the canopied entrance. "Go on inside and give your name at the door." Chloe's face must have shown reservation, because Rita smiled for the first time that day. "No one's going to eat you."

The building was shaped like a slice of pie, curved at the tip where it met the curb. The tight point of the anteroom compelled her entrance as people pushed from behind. She heard music from beyond a burgundy velvet curtain, before which she was asked for her cape by a man in black suit and tails. It disappeared into a room behind the wall. The noise was a frolic, the volume of which increased when the curtain was pulled away. It dropped again behind her. A man approached from behind a desk. His shoes were polished to a high sheen, and a tight black tie bowed beneath the pointy tips of his high collar. Chloe leaned in to give him her name. "Mrs. Simon Low." It couldn't be heard above the din. He bowed closer. The tilt of his head encouraged her to repeat herself. She said her name again, "Mrs. Simon Low." This time, the maître d' was not the only one who heard. Heads swiveled in her direction, the eyes sweeping up and down her body in frank appraisal. Heads came together, and words were exchanged behind cupped palms. Chloe heard the phrase in her head. Whispers and titters. "Mrs. Low. This way."

She glanced behind her for Rita, but Rita was nowhere in sight. Chloe followed him, and the music grew louder with each step. She'd read *Alice in Wonderland* aloud to Hattie's daughter just last summer. Chloe felt just like Alice.

A six-piece band played in the corner to an empty dance floor. A polished wood countertop curved its width, and patrons sat and stood at the brass-fitted bar. The reflections on the polished wood winked with the bartender's movements. He poured drinks into stout glasses that were carried away by servers. Small tables covered in white cloth dotted the perimeter of the open parquet floor. High-backed leather benches with matching leather buttons bordered the ballroom at ordered intervals and continued along the walls into the first floor dining room, where Chloe was ushered to a table. Lines of men and women being led up curved staircases on either side of the room suggested that the restaurant continued up and up.

This was more than a place for dining. Chloe looked around and intuited what she didn't know: Del's was a place for celebration. Chloe didn't know whether to be relieved or concerned that Rita had still not emerged from the crowd. The woman's presence was dangerous. Chloe bit her lip. What was she doing here? She'd vowed to leave the city that very night. The train left in little more than an hour. Yet here she was, dressed in a gold sheath that showed more skin that she'd ever revealed in her life. She would've given anything to talk to Hattie. Her friend would fall into hysterics if she saw her hair, topped now with a crown. An actual crown. Rita said it was a diadem, but to Chloe, it looked very much like a crown. For the hundredth time, she preached herself the sermon. *Don't get used to this.* She wasn't getting anywhere with the lesson. She was like the priest who lectured about lust at her wedding, a tad too late to be useful.

The maître d' ushered her to the edge of the ballroom and pulled out a small table, gestured to the leather high-backed curved bench. He tucked her in, bowed and left. Chloe rearranged the silverware and watched the door for Rita. A waiter brought her a glass of champagne, leaned in and corrected her place setting, returning the spoon and forks to their original alignment.

"Never been to Del's before?" It was more a statement than a question.

"How can you tell?" She kept her back straight. In spite of it, it seemed she stood out like a sore thumb in the crowded dining room. Men and women stared intermittently. She touched the braids of her hair.

"Most women wouldn't have the courage to arrive alone."

"I didn't arrive alone," she corrected and looked once more for Rita. She wondered anyway why such a thing should take courage. It was uncomfortable, to say the least, to have everyone staring, but it was nothing to fear. Chloe had known other fears, real ones.

"The champagne is a gift from the man over there." The waiter gestured with an open hand to a gentleman in black who raised his glass.

Chloe smiled and smoothed the tablecloth by her glass. She gave the waiter a half-smile. "I'm waiting for my..." She couldn't get out the word.

"The gentleman knows it. Everyone knows it, but he's betting the odds." The waiter cleared imaginary crumbs from the cloth with a silver butler while she took a sip of champagne. Compassion bent him close. "Your husband telephoned, and he's on his way."

She blinked. The tightening she felt in her stomach was not fear; it was anticipation. She hadn't seen Simon in three hours, and the thrill of his return made her hum. She was treading dangerous ground, but that ground felt too good under her feet. She gave her gorgeous wedding band another twist, and extended the fingers of her hand in her lap to admire how the worn gold looked against her skin. She polished the ring with the soft pad of her thumb.

As though the ring held magic, Simon arrived to fanfare and the sound of thunder. A loud huzzah drowned out the loud crack of lightning that followed. Heads turned across the room and half the guests stood to greet him. As he walked in the direction of her table, he was swatted, patted, and shaken. The men gripped his shoulders and pumped his hand. She was too far away to hear what was said into his ear, what he said in return. Every step he took, he was touched by someone new. The band started. She recognized the tune. *For He's a Jolly Good Fellow.*

When the tide of men receded, Simon became awash in ladies. Chloe took a drink of water. The women arrived in pairs, each flanking a side, touching his arms with both hands, one at his shoulder, another at his wrist. He didn't wear gloves, and their fingers rested on the sleeve of his forearm close to his bare skin. Chloe shifted against the leather banquette. This was harder to watch. He was the handsomest man in the room. It wasn't just the lines of his face, the softness of his lips, the flash of teeth and his eyes when he smiled. He glowed. They were like moths to a flame.

A single woman, uncoupled, emerged from the mass and replaced two women at once. Rita slapped Simon with the small pad of paper she wore around her neck before she withdrew a pencil and wrote on it. She tucked the square into his coat pocket. A square of paper torn from her longette had gone in, but Rita's fingers removed themselves from Simon's pocket, empty.

His foot hit the parquet that tiled the floor beneath the tables. It took everything inside her to sit still and await his arrival. The rest of the room had gone as quiet as a room of one hundred fifty could. Chloe flipped a sterling butter knife over and over on the cloth and studied the handkerchief in his breast pocket as he approached. She grinned at her plate, wanting to leap at him. In the end, she lifted her chin and met his eyes. "You've been here before."

A corner of his mouth tucked in, the other corner lifted. "This is my table." His chin kicked. "I usually sit there." He leaned forward as though with a secret. "Until now, the view has been better looking out."

Chloe ignored the way her stomach tensed at the image of the women whose backsides had pressed the red leather before hers. Simon's chair was pulled away from the table, and he sat. The bubble that held them popped, and the noise around them resumed with a crescendo. The diners no longer seemed curious to see whether or not the couple would touch or refrain. They were hidden again by the hum of the crowd, metal against china, glass against cloth.

He placed his napkin in his lap. "How many men have been by?"

"I only just arrived."

"How many?"

"Six." She made the number up.

He patted his pockets for cigarettes and found a crushed pack. He pulled one that looked like the last and placed it between his lips. The tip pointed, crooked, in the direction of the next table.

Chloe tried not to laugh. "Are you always welcomed like this?"

Simon didn't deny it. "They're congratulating me." The cigarette bobbed when he spoke.

Her eyebrows rose. He was newly married. No wonder he'd been greeted so heartily. She cast a glance about the room, self-conscious. Everyone knew. They must know what she and Simon had been doing all day.

He lifted his chin and scanned the room for a waiter. "Although they'd congratulate me well enough if someone would bring me a match." Simon's ease in the crowd had melted clean away. There was none of it left, as though the press of bodies, the ladies' fingers had rubbed it from him.

When after a few seconds, no one in the room lit his cigarette, he threw it onto the tablecloth between them and grimaced at her. It was an actual grimace. He pinched each end of the cigarette where it lay on the table and pulled it straight. "Tell me again how you knew Michael, where you met my brother."

Chloe leaned back in her chair. There were other subjects to discuss. She hadn't imagined this one and wasn't sure where to start.

"I'm curious. Did you know him a long time?"

She shrugged. "Not very long. A few years."

"A few years?" The pitch of his voice collected glances from a neighboring table. He leaned forward and asked the question again in a quieter pitch. Simon had known his wife only a few days. "How did you meet?"

"He visited me at the cemetery." Her head titled. "I was never sure why."

Simon looked at her a moment, and she flushed before he even got the words out. "You're a vision in gold. The color is high in your cheeks and it sets off your eyes, which keep landing on my mouth, telling me well enough what you're thinking about." He leaned in across the table and whispered, "I could touch the smooth skin at the side of your breasts, right here in the middle of Del's if I dared." He leaned back in his chair. "And you're asking me why my brother would visit you."

Her face felt hot. "Are you jealous?"

Simon smiled. "I'm not the type."

"Me neither," Chloe lied, disappointed at Simon's words. His entire attitude confused her. He was worried about something. A single fiddler stepped forward, and the thrill of the high single string was the sound of home, a song she recognized from her childhood. Chloe tugged at his hand. "I want to dance."

"I want to hear more about you and my brother."

"Michael and me? There's nothing to tell."

"What did you do, when he'd visit you?"

She laughed, "He taught me how to hit squirrels with walnuts."

"Is that all?"

"I promise I'll tell you everything your brother ever said, after this dance." Chloe pulled at his hand again.

Resigned, he pulled the table away from the wall and extended his hand. He walked her to the center of the floor. The rest of the band joined the high notes of the violin.

Her hands lifted before her in the air, the way she would with an absent partner. He laughed and stepped closer. His head dipped toward her. "Here." He placed her hand on his shoulder, held the other in his hand. On the next beat he moved her, and the frame of his body was a rampart against the crowd that watched. The fabric of her dress sparkled and hung, heavy and tight.

"That dress should be illegal." It was easy enough to keep the subject to her dress, where the sheer caps covered her shoulders.

She asked, "Where were you?"

"Speaking of legality," he spun her in two quick circles, then dipped his mouth low against her ear, "getting a marriage license."

"A license?" Her laughter at their spins hid her initial surprise, then the heat of his breath against her neck made her whisper, "We're not really married?"

Simon didn't answer her question directly. "I'm sorry I didn't remember before."

"Will I have to marry you again, to make it legal?"

His thumb traced the low sweep of at the side of her dress, found the skin bared there. "Would you? Would you marry me again?"

The question might have been asked in earnest or in jest. It was difficult to tell. Chloe didn't laugh, although she couldn't answer seriously. The question was too important, and his touch on her skin before a crowd of people, too distracting. "Your reputation is even worse than I'd imagined. If you asked me again, I should say no."

"You'd say no?" Simon's smile was half-measured. He wanted an answer.

Her hand felt small in his. She felt his thigh, and its small pressure, coupled with the pressure of his palm on her back was enough to spin her around the room. She wanted to tease the tension from his face. "Are you asking me?" She would say yes. She would say yes a hundred times, if he asked. She almost believed that she would.

He grinned. "I suppose I'm not." He thumb found the dip in her palm. "So, did you have fun today?"

She flushed red.

His head dipped again and he said into her ear, "I mean after I left."

"Shopping for dresses is the most fun I've ever had in my life."

His eyebrows rose.

She flushed again. "After that."

He laughed, and they danced for a minute without speaking. Simon led her through the turns, and when he spun her, she focused on his face like a lodestar, try as he might to make her dizzy. One by one the instruments of the band dropped off until only the fiddle remained, the last familiar strains of the waltz a high lament of the violin.

When they stopped dancing, Simon didn't lead her back to the table. "Listen. There's something I have to tell you, something you should know." He held both her hands, kept her in place on the dance floor with him. "It's a miracle you're here. I didn't realize a woman like you could exist in the world. You fit me perfectly. I should've told you before, but I wasn't sure."

The dance had taken her breath. Her eyes shone, and her lips parted. Her tongue wet them. "And now?"

"Now, I have no choice." His hand gripped with a firmer pressure. "I don't want a choice. I want to tell you. I want you to know. My brother…" He rubbed the back of his neck. He turned around and cast an abrupt glance toward the door. The last word was said with a mixture of relief and irritation. "Michael. Why the devil…?"

34

Chloe followed the direction of his gaze. Simon's twin was framed by the vestibule curtain. In spite of Simon's confession, it was clear only one word remained in her head. *Michael.* She cut Simon a look as though to prove he was still there, too, a fleeting look of pure joy that made Simon woozy, as though once and for all, she understood.

Then she ran.

She moved like lightning, yet, to Simon, everything next happened in slow motion. A staff of blond and gold cleared each table and chair in half circle arcs until she hit the saloon floor. He'd planned to reintroduce them, after he'd told her. That's all he had time to think before his wife ended her flight in his brother's arms.

Simon felt her vibrate from yards away, but this time, it was because of Michael. A cold tingle started at Simon's scalp and ran down his face. He felt it in his fingers. He tensed his thighs to keep his knees from buckling.

Michael touched the top of Chloe's head, a benediction. She didn't let Michael go, not for the length of time it took Simon to follow her off the dance floor. Simon watched Michael's lips move and might as well have heard the word. *Angel.* He called her 'Angel.' Michael had a name for her, one that fit with an ache.

They needed no introduction, but Simon gave one anyway. "Chloe, my brother."

Chloe's smile glowed, lit up the room. "Is this what you've been trying to tell me?" She didn't care that Michael had been beaten black and blue. He was alive.

"He's been kicking around a harbor somewhere. He's got a boat. Up north." Why hadn't he stayed north? Why hadn't he stayed at least at the apartment? The reason was clear enough. She stood before them both. Simon cut Michael a look. "Come on." Then he pulled Chloe away with him across the dance floor that surrounded the bar. "Our table is private. You can tell us all about her." He threw the last words over his shoulder, knowing that there did not exist a place that was private enough for his brother. He'd always avoided crowds. His return was a capitulation. For the money, Simon had thought. Now, he thought differently.

The band in the dining room began to play *For He's A Jolly Good Fellow*. Simon cut them off with a slash of his hand across his chest. Though Michael had come back from the dead, there was no backslapping. No one dared touch him.

When they arrived back at the table, he edged Chloe with his hip deeper onto the plush leather bench and took his place beside her. He removed the linen architecture from his plate. Chloe's arm reached across the table, and she took Michael's hand. Simon noted that Michael had no difficulty letting her do it. He stared at their hands until Michael removed his from beneath Chloe's fingers. He didn't have to be a mind reader to understand the meaning behind Simon's look.

"Where have you been?" Chloe's voice was hushed but excited. "Look at you." She admonished him for the bruises that colored his face. The beard in that way had given him a guise of, if not respectability, at least not its polar opposite.

Michael ran a hand over his jaw. His chin indicated Simon in an unfriendly kick. "He made me cut it off."

"Your hair!" Chloe continued her gentle harangue. "I've never seen it so short." Her smile was wide, and she took his hand again in both of hers.

"He made me cut that, too." The words tickled Chloe, and she leaned back and laughed, releasing Michael's hands. Simon breathed more easily.

This time, her smile included Simon. "You look almost like brothers." She leaned forward again, her hands now balled in excitement in her lap. "Where in the world have you been? I assume you faked your own death? Or have you been an amnesiac? Did you hit your head on a rock?"

The thought of Michael in the world fresh, wiped clean of his memories, almost made Simon smile. What would his brother have thought of himself?

"I've been north."

Chloe was unfazed by his gruffness. "Doing what?"

"Harbor work."

"Kingston? Montreal?"

"Yes."

Chloe laughed again at his ambiguity. "You must have a boat in your harbor. You wouldn't be without one. What's her name?"

"I call her Redemption."

Chloe was pleased at that. "Redemption. I hope it's apt. What is she?"

"A tug."

Her smile became wider. "How romantic."

Michael pulled a face. Simon pulled one, too. In a few short minutes, Chloe had seduced more information from Michael than Simon had pulled from him all afternoon.

"A tugboat. You must have adventures." When Michael said nothing, she asked, "Do you have adventures?"

Simon chucked his bent cigarette to the center of the table. "Apparently, he's in the middle of one now."

Chloe's smile grew wider. "Not only alive, but living. Wait until Hattie hears."

Simon's chair squawked against the hardwood floor. "I need a cigarette."

Chloe watched Simon's departing back. She knew the brothers hadn't been close. Simon had let on that much. Now that Michael was alive, and here, she would do everything she could to bring the two together. She wanted Simon to be happy. She wanted to make him happy, and Simon wanted to be close to his brother. In spite of the grimaces and his frowns at anything his brother said, Chloe knew this to be true.

"Listen." Michael extended his hand across the table, palm up.

She'd heard terrible things, sad things. She'd gotten used to the things people said when they were dying. She listened to everyone, all day, everyday, until she'd become numb with it, until she heard, but wasn't really listening. She'd been afraid to hear anything. But she wasn't afraid anymore. She loved him. She loved Simon. She could admit it now. She grabbed Michael's hand, pressed it between both of her own. He was her brother now, too, and he was *alive*. "What is it?" She laughed out loud. It felt so good not to be afraid. "Tell me anything."

Michael pressed a piece of paper into her palm. "Judah brought this after you left."

"A marriage license. Simon told me." She'd sign it now. She really would.

"It's not a marriage license. It's from the doctors."

Chloe felt a stab of uncertainty, the feeling stark against the blank flash of clarity she'd had less than a moment before. She unfolded the page. It was a telegram, the newsprint letters spare on the thin yellow paper. Chloe's eyes tripped over the lines, landed on prose in pieces. She read Hattie's name, and the doctor's apologies, and blurred type that met the edge of the paper, *already gone.*

Her heart thud once against her chest, a fist against a door, then pounded. "*Already gone?*" Where had Hattie gone? Why would she have left when she knew the doctors were coming? She looked up from the page. Michael's face was grim. She couldn't be sure. No one would say the words. Why wouldn't anyone say the words? The bile rose in her throat. Michael would.

He studied a point above her shoulder and pressed his lips together before she saw them move. "She's dead."

35

Chloe listened to the echo of the water dripping from the bathroom faucet, the droplets timed a few seconds apart. She counted the beats in between, always got to three, never to four.

White ceramic subway tiles lined the walls. Thousands of small octagonal white tiles made up the floor. A single mirror ran the length of the wall. Chloe estimated it was ten feet of mirror, and at least eight feet tall. The white was blinding, clean. She closed her eyes. Hattie wasn't sick enough to die. They'd been together only a day before. She thought back to the last moment with her, felt again the press of her cheek, the faint scent of milk.

Chloe bent forward with a new wash of pain. The children. What would they do? And Daniel. Chloe pressed her head against the mirror. Hattie's husband had been on the water for two months. How would Daniel know? How would they tell him? Hattie would be buried by the time he got word. Chloe pressed her fists into her eyes. The burial. Eric wouldn't allow their mother to degrade Hattie's burial to a financial reckoning, but she'd try.

Chloe forced herself to breathe, tried to turn off the suffocating emotions. After years of this moment repeating, time after time of hearing this very news, she had ways of managing. Her teeth clenched, her chest rose and fell. In and out, air filled her lungs. She crumpled again. It wasn't working. Tears burned her eyes, and she blinked them back. Tears were not an option. If they started, they would never stop. Instead of crying, she should scream. She pressed her forehead again against the mirror. Would it be wrong to strike her head against it? She tapped it once, and again, the second time hard enough for the pain to distract her. She wanted to hit it harder still, but she didn't want to shatter the glass. This was worse than when she'd heard about Michael.

Michael. A flash of hope, unreasonable, yet oddly logical passed through her. She'd thought Michael was dead, yet here he was alive. He was right outside. Perhaps Hattie, too, was alive, or perhaps she would come back. Chloe bit her lip, hard enough for it to hurt. She bit again until she tasted blood. Hattie wasn't coming back. Hope. Hope was the problem. She never should have allowed herself to hope.

"What's wrong?"

Simon's voice echoed off the tile. She straightened her spine and moved her hands behind her back. They were balled into fists, and he'd notice. He noticed everything about her. She didn't want him to notice this. If he noticed, it would be all over. The grief would spill over, drown her. "You shouldn't be in here."

"I've been in here before." He wasn't being glib.

His approach stopped before he reached her. He used the distance between them to see her face. She kept it averted. Seeing him only reminded her that, as bad as Hattie's death was to her now, it could be terribly, terribly worse.

"What's happened? What did Michael say?"

"Nothing."

"Of course it's something."

"It's nothing that you can do anything about."

"Let me try."

"I don't want you to try." But she did. She wanted him to try, wanted him to find her through the grief and save her. "You'll only make it worse."

He took another step. "Make what worse? Tell me what's wrong."

"It doesn't matter." She put the distance between them again. "I just need time."

His forehead wrinkled. "What does that mean? How much time?"

She'd seen what his life had been like before she arrived. That he would tether himself to her, to death, was ridiculous. "All of it."

The creases between his eyes deepened, multiplied. Then they smoothed with understanding. "Do you love him?"

Chloe knew what Simon was asking. He thought she loved Michael. A voice inside her whispered, *let him believe it.* It would make this scene easier. The faucet drip echoed. She wanted him to hold her. If he would just ignore what she said and hold her, she'd be able to disappear, melt into nothing.

"Did you marry me because I look like him?"

Chloe opened her mouth to protest. She had never given Michael her heart. She hadn't given it to anyone. The truth stared them both in the face. She'd almost given it to Simon, but she'd been reminded just in time. She pressed her lips together and inhaled cooling air.

"Would you have married me if you'd known he was alive?"

Her anatomy tried to take over, tried to make her shudder, or cringe, or cry. She wouldn't let it. She kept Simon out of focus, stared at a tile on the wall just over his right shoulder.

Simon considered his next question more carefully. "We were married before God and everyone..."

She interrupted him, "I thought you weren't religious."

Simon's frustration came out in a cough. "Don't you feel it? Tell me you feel it. Admit it. Michael has nothing to do with this. Whatever he meant to you, whatever he told you, it doesn't matter now."

But it did. It mattered. What Michael had told her meant everything.

They stood close. Simon leaned forward and spoke into her ear, his hands buried stubbornly in his pockets. "Can't you tell me? Just tell me, whatever you feel."

She shook her head. She couldn't. If she told him, he'd force her to stay, and she'd be blown into the wind like a pile of ash. Her hands remained behind her skirts. Behind her skirts, the ring spun, once, twice. She felt nothing, would feel nothing. "The truth?"

He nodded, his fists in his pockets.

The numbness took over, finally, by itself, a natural part of her, the will to survive. The instinct for survival flipped like a switch, and everything inside turned off.

"I didn't want to take down my hair."

It took him a moment to puzzle it out, but she saw when her meaning struck. She'd used him as an escape. She saw that the truth hurt him, noticed, too, that she did not care.

Simon replayed their brief courtship in his head. She'd warned him outright she wouldn't fall in love. Oh, there was lust.

The priest had been right about that. Chloe had wanted him, perhaps from the start, but in the end, she didn't love him.

He was the perfect mark. Rich, good with the ladies. *Pretty*. No one would ever suspect it was a local girl who'd compromised him. That was a good one. She'd compromised him.

Even Michael had warned him.

The dinner crowd had grown raucous. A wave of sound crashed over Simon, deafening after the hush of the porcelain and tile. His step faltered before he stalked across the dining room to where his brother sat. Michael stood from the table before Simon arrived and made to pass him, to move around Simon on his way to Chloe. Simon stopped him with a hand.

Michael regarded his brother's palm against his chest, the pressure of the opposition.

Simon pushed once with violent force, moving him backward the space of an inch. "No more mysteries. Why are you here?"

Michael's hands found his pockets. "I told you why."

"I want clarity. Tell me again. Why'd you come back, Mick?" It was the name their father had called him, and it never failed to incite Michael when Simon used it. The intimacy of the nickname sparked more tension.

Michael's jaw tightened, and, for Simon, it was an invitation. Simon hit him, this time connecting hard. Michael's head snapped to the side. The crowd's collective gasp was dulled by a roaring in Simon's ears. Chair legs squeaked against the wood floor. Michael stood straighter, centered his chin. He didn't even rub his jaw.

They eyed one another as a crowd formed. Simon steeled himself for a blow, but it didn't come. He waited as long as he could, then hit his brother again.

Still, Michael didn't hit back, although his hands were now out of his pockets, balled into fists at his hips. He swiped a knuckle across his mouth and smeared the streak of blood. He gestured with his head to the back of the room. "If she doesn't want you, she'll need me."

It was the violence Simon had expected; still, he was unprepared. The words blinded him. He had to get out. He needed air or he would faint dead away in front of the mass of Del's. He had to walk away from a man who would hit back only with words, and do it before a crowd of spectators. He avoided the faces of the people he knew. He didn't want to see how they felt about it. He didn't care. He waited for some poor sod to pat him on the back.

Michael had feelings, after all. For Chloe. *Angel.* He remembered the word when it had left his brother's lips.

For the love of all that was holy, he hadn't seen that coming.

Simon wished he had a horse. It would've made his exit more dramatic to be able to hurl himself atop a tall steed. The rain came down in a sharp torrent. The spray hit his face like bee stings. Hail. It was hailing in September. Steam lifted from the heat of his body. He pushed his face up, welcomed the pellets of ice. He deserved a thrashing. He'd left Chloe in there. He'd done it on purpose, just as his brother had left him. It felt god awful, but he had no choice but to walk away.

Rita Smythe's fingers appeared from nowhere and found the crook of Simon's elbow. "Now we really have something to celebrate."

In the face of the connection between his brother and his wife, Simon was glad for the dose of his former life. Simon's smile at Rita was wide as he nodded. "I'm feeling celebratory." He was good at it, smiling without meaning to.

He hailed a cab. The cabbie didn't hop down to open the side door to the carriage. He was glad for that. No niceties, nothing to chip away at the numbness, the utter absence of feeling. He'd grown used to it, the electricity. More than that, he'd grown used to her, the two notions together, his wife and the surge of feelings she evoked, but it was all gone now, as though it had never existed, had all been a dream. Without that spark, he never wanted to touch her again.

Chloe escaped from Del's beneath Michael's arm, her gaze unfocused, not hearing the sound of the band except for the fiddle strings, which she couldn't ignore. She found the spot in Simon's apartment where the memory of him was dimmest, where feeling didn't crowd in. Her towel was still folded over the side of the tub. She'd known then that happiness with Simon was beyond improbable. It was impossible. It had been hard to convince herself, but she was persuaded now. Had Simon argued against it, she might have delayed the inevitable. She might have agreed, this time, to marry him. They'd have grown closer with each passing year, until their separation would have ripped her in two.

"You married my brother."

She regarded Michael in the mirror. The thrill of his return had ebbed. She didn't turn around. "Did he know you were alive? All this time?"

"He had an inkling."

"He tried to tell me." He'd told her he'd had trouble getting used to it. What he'd meant was that he hadn't believed his brother was dead. "Where is he?"

"You said good-bye." Michael shrugged. "He heard it."

"I hurt him." Chloe breathed onto the mirror, a child's game, watched as the fog disappeared.

Michael stood stiff. "My brother can't control his feelings." He tugged at his tie, his fingers loosened the knot. "They overwhelm him and everyone else."

"Is that why you push him away? Why you left?" She breathed again until the fog collected. "You refuse to be overwhelmed?" She drew a heart on the glass, the kind that would be carved into the trunk of a tree.

"That's maybe why I did it. Why did you?"

She wiped the glass clean in a sweep with the side of her hand. It didn't really matter why. She turned to face him. "You're leaving again, aren't you? He made to leave the room, but Chloe stopped him. "Take me with you. Take me home."

Michael nodded, as though expecting the very question. "The train north leaves in half an hour." Then he left her in the bathroom.

Chloe heard the door to the kitchen open and the sound of food being prepared. The scent of ham hung sickening in the apartment, made her queasy.

With a shock, she knew she couldn't go home. It would be impossible to go back. She couldn't return to Riverside. She couldn't go back to managing every day trying to feel nothing. She could never go home again, not without Hattie. Not without Simon.

But there was nothing for her here. She couldn't stay in the city, not with Simon in it. The only thing she could do was go anywhere but here, anywhere but home, anywhere at all. She wanted to escape her own skin.

She exited the bathroom and found her small bag. With a pang of shame, she took a large roll of dollar bills banded on the desk, buried them in the deep pocket of her skirt. Then she slipped out of the apartment, down the carpeted marble steps of the store, and out the front door.

Michael emerged from the kitchen. Chewing, he gripped a half-eaten sandwich in one hand. The rooms were quiet. He found the bathroom door closed where he'd left Chloe. He knocked with a single knuckle. "Angel," he began. "It's time to go." When no answer came, he knocked again. "If we miss this train, there won't be another until morning." He waited. Nothing. "Angel?" He pounded this time, and when still no answer came, he wrenched the door open. The bathroom was empty.

He reached the center room and took two strides toward the telephone before he stopped in his tracks.

Chloe was gone, and she'd taken his cash.

Cursing aloud, he grabbed his cap from the table, pitched his food into a bin, and the door to the apartment slammed behind him.

36

The sofa was littered with pillows. The air was sweet with clove smoke and cigars. The room's centerpiece was a tall, functionless ottoman that looked like a tiered cake. Simon pulled a pillow from under him in a struggle of satin, fringe and his own backside.

Straight from Del's, Rita had brought him to a party, of all things, a celebration.

"It actually happened."

The voice came from a man ten years Simon's junior, and without his usual composure, Simon's face puckered. His skepticism could not be ignored. Resigned to engage with the storyteller, Simon tossed the pillow to the other end of the sofa. "It didn't *actually happen*."

In spite of Simon's recrimination, the man continued his story. "My cousin was *right here* in this apartment. Women less than half-dressed were dancing on this very..." The young man gestured to the upholstered cake beneath him where he sat on the first tier. "The debauchery was *spectacular*. They were in their knickers and boots, kicking as high as the chandelier and that's when Uncle was ushered in by the concierge." He surveyed his audience for a reaction. After a pause, he continued, "Luckily, my cousin was quick on his feet."

"He was a dancer, too?" The quip came from a voice behind the sofa where Simon sat. A man's hand found Simon's shoulder, swatted it once in greeting, and then became lost again in the crowd.

Rita had brought him straight to the party. Their entire set was in attendance. Simon knew everyone, but he hadn't a friend in the room. The young man pulled a sour face at the interruption but continued, "He told the concierge he had the wrong suite and demanded another. Now that my uncle had seen beneath their skirts, my cousin couldn't very well introduce the ladies as his friends. Thereby in a fell swoop, his friends were cut from the very wealth they'd been celebrating. And it all happened in this very room." He ended with a sweep of his arms that took in the party now in session.

It was supposed to be a true account, a cautionary tale, but Simon had read the story in last year's *Vogue*. The knowledge colored his mood further. Fiction told as truth. It cast his past, and his future, in the color of despair.

"Does she know?"

Simon's attention returned to Rita who sat close beside him. Her scent was familiar, floral and sweet, so different than his wife's. Chloe smelled like light. "Know what?"

"That your brother is a brute."

He remembered the bruises beneath his brother's shirt, across his face. "How could she miss it?"

"But does she know he's not a gentleman?"

Simon would have laughed, a sound of pure wit without feeling. Tonight, he couldn't find the energy. He only smiled. "Who of us is, anymore?"

"You would never try to take a woman against her will."

Simon's mind flashed, and his drink stuttered midway to his lips.

Rita noticed. "You're still protecting him."

He would have gone to war for the man. "He doesn't need my protection."

"None of us has forgotten what he did to Virginia."

Virginia was a friend, but Michael was his brother. "None of you has forgotten what Virginia refused to tell you."

"Her dress was torn. It was clear enough without her having to tell the tale. And he never denied it."

Simon wasn't the only one with a reputation. No, he hadn't told Chloe. Some said Michael had drowned himself out of shame, cowardice. "He didn't rape her." Simon caught a glitter of gold out of the corner of his eye, and his head twitched, but it was only the glint of candlelight reflected in a gilt mirror frame.

"You're certain of that? Sure enough to leave your wife alone with him?"

He wondered where she was now, where his brother had taken her. So Simon did the only thing he could. He smiled, another fiction to hide the truth. Anyway, he didn't have a wife anymore.

Chloe warmed her bare arms beneath her cape with her own hands. The warm breeze that had earlier blown through the city streets had since chilled. Now, a fog thickened the sky and hid the peaks of even the highest masts in the port of the North River.

Chloe learned from the ticket master that a ship heading for Belgium had just launched. It was a half-mile off-shore, brought out in the last hour with the evening's high tide. Rain came down in sheets before she reached the end of the Chelsea Pier. It pooled in her shoes. She wondered if Michael would forgive her for stealing the money she had now in her skirt pocket. She hoped he would.

She didn't ask if Simon would forgive her. She didn't even allow herself to think his name.

She engaged the attention of a man, one of a dozen leaning in line against a building. All wore dark oilcloth like uniforms. Chloe pointed to the ship, viewable on the horizon not far distant. "Can you reach her?" Her face was doused with rain that dripped from the eaves. The man shook his head, the water leaving his hair like a dog's. Chloe removed the roll of bills from her pocket and split it in two. Half went into his coat.

He looked up at the sky, at Chloe, then nodded. "I can reach her, once the weather breaks."

After fifteen minutes, rain ceased to pucker the harbor's surface. Chloe followed him to a nearby packet, and he waved at it, indicating that Chloe should board.

The boat lifted and sunk with each green wave. She wished she'd changed out of her gown back into her traveling dress. The captain took her bag and held her arm as she took a wide step from the dock to the boat. She had to raise her dress far above her knees to make the jump. Her hands held fast to the rail.

Clouds that had been moving as though blown by a breeze all day were now a thin, low fog. Filtered light from the moon lit the sky. The harbor water was a green that looked like seasickness. Wind tore at her cape, whipped it like a sail.

Before she was even beneath the low roof of the wheelhouse, the boat was released from the dock. It was only the two of them. The captain wound each line into a coil. Chloe clung to the handrail that continued into the tall, narrow pilothouse. Her knuckles were white, and they'd not even left port. The captain tossed a chin at her in invitation, and Chloe ducked inside. The bell above them rang clear and loud. It went through her like a warning.

The captain navigated the waves that pushed them from below. The ship they approached, even from a distance, was massive, and it was only a fraction of the size of the New York.

They couldn't talk. Their voices wouldn't carry above the din of the waves as they beat against the side of the tug, or the incessant clang of bell overhead, but Chloe could tell him to turn back. Now would be the time to do it. Turn back. If they turned back, she could find Simon. She practiced the words in her head, what she would say to him to explain why she left, why she'd come back. Her lips moved like a prayer, until wet and cold fell away and was replaced by something deeper: loss. She wouldn't turn back. She would lose him, now or later, and now was already hard enough.

Rita held Simon's left arm prisoner. Beside him sat a woman to whom he'd been introduced an hour before. She inched closer. He watched one hand on his trouser, halfway between his knee and his thigh and wondered that he couldn't feel her touch. His skin failed even to register it.

Rita lifted her glass with both hands. "A toast!" She angled her glass at Simon, her voice loud enough to fill the room. "For escaping the marriage noose." Her glass lifted higher.

"Here, here!" Glasses were raised and a cheer made its way through the room. The mass drank with a flourish.

Simon disentangled his arm, stood, and walked to the windows. Three in a row stretched from ceiling to floor, each trimmed at the corners in scrolled molding. Down each length of sill, thick geometric patterns had been carved into the wood. Surrounding buildings stretched out below them. The sky was murky and green, the color of water when it reflected a storm. He could hear the wind through the glass.

A young bachelor raised an empty glass at Simon. "What made you do it in the first place? Her father have a pistol?"

Simon raised his glass back at the boy and remembered Judah's jibe from the morning. It seemed like a lifetime away. He turned his back to the room, making a show of interest in the night sky. He wanted to leave, but where could he go?

Behind him, Rita spoke to the room at large. "You should see her brother." She shivered with dramatic flair. "Even I'd be tempted by something that *large.*"

Simon squinted through the glass while the storm howled. A newspaper page was caught in a swirl of wind. It twisted on itself, up and up, until it hovered a hundred feet above the street.

Simon only half heard the banter, hypnotized by the paper that hung immobile. The page was torn suddenly from its place in the air and carried as though a solid object, until it was flattened against the window of a nearby building.

"What the hell is going on, Simon?" Judah's voice barely reached him through the storm. "I had the devil of a time finding you. They told me at Del's that Michael's alive. I had to see him to believe it."

Simon tracked the newspaper until it was gone. His forehead leaned against the glass. "It was going to be a surprise." He should've told Judah. He'd been absorbed by the chaos of the day. Now, Judah forced a new page on him, and Simon was compelled to accept it.

The flag that had whipped with fury since they'd boarded the tug fell without reason or warning. The stillness caught Chloe's attention in a way that even the storm before had not. She gripped the rail, but the captain pulled at her arm. He shoved a life vest into her chest. She tied the belts with calm fingers. She'd had practice dealing with crisis, moments of emergency that, though not always as violent as a storm, always presented her with death. Chloe's body had grown accustomed to urgency, habituated her to be calm in the face of terror.

Chloe was pulled from beneath the shelter of the bridge into the rain that fell on deck. Away from the railing, Chloe clung to the man, whose frame gave her the steadiness required to make it across the length of the boat. He unlatched a door and pushed

Chloe through. He followed her down the narrow passageway, hustling her faster than she would have made it down herself. From nowhere, a match illuminated the space. A lantern arced through the air from where it hung from a loop in the ceiling. The light was shorted to a small, safe flame. Without even a command to stay, the captain returned to the steps and took them all at once.

The door shut behind her with a slam of metal against metal, finished with a water-tight hatch that sealed her in. It was the captain's berth, a living area that included a bunk, a bench and a table, all bolted to the floor. The pitching of the boat made it impossible to sit and threw her from side to side. Her shoulder hit the wall. Her gasp of pain was deafened by the waves that beat and roared against the hull. She found a railing, and held it fast with both hands while the boat roiled from the waves.

Judah gestured with his chin to the page in Simon's hand. "I'm afraid this one's bad news."

It was from the doctors Simon had sent north. Hattie Blount had died before they'd even arrived. It was terrible news. The loss made his flesh tingle with cold.

"Where did you get this?"

"It came through at the front office."

Michael hadn't come to Del's to steal Chloe away, but to tell her Hattie was gone. Hell, he could've let Simon deliver this news, but of course Michael wanted to prove his point. He'd wanted to show Simon that he'd chosen the wrong wife. Indeed, he had. Instead of turning to Simon, Chloe had pushed him away. He stuffed the page into his trouser pocket. It might've helped Simon to know the news earlier. He might have chanced upon the right words, convinced her to stay, but it didn't change anything now. Michael had proven his point rather well.

"How'd you escape, Low?" The voice was from one of the elders of his set. "I'm surprised your wife agreed to let you go." The man slapped his back twice in passing.

Judah looked sharp. "Chloe's not with you?"

Simon shook his head. "I left her at Del's with Michael."

Judah's concern deepened. "The porter saw Michael leave the store alone an hour ago, and I just left your apartment. She wasn't there. I thought she'd be with you."

Simon's skin grew colder.

Across the tight room, Rita leaned forward and refilled her glass from a decanter on a table strewn with crystal. She called out loud enough for the room to hear, "I still can't believe you married the Angel of Death."

A bird smacked the window level with Simon's eyes. He jerked backward in surprise. Then his arms flew up against an oncoming mass. A flock of birds hit the glass as though thrown by an invisible hand. The room stood as one, squawks of alarm drowning out the sound of heavy crystal dropping onto carpeted floor. In quick succession, the thuds of the birds overlapped one another until the barrage ended with a few disparate thumps.

His head spun. *Angel.*

Simon emerged from a crouch to a room energized by the storm, as though lightning had struck the center of the room from the inside. Voices overlapped like dying birds. Simon pushed through the bodies and pulled Rita close with a hand on her upper arm. "The Angel of Death?"

She leaned into his hand. "The girl from the cemetery. Your *wife*." She said the word with distaste. "Everyone calls her that, all the locals at least. Didn't you know?"

He shook his head, thick with revelation. The Angel of Death. She was like a ghost herself, little pieces bid farewell and buried until what was left? There would be nothing of her left if someone didn't collect the pieces and hold them tight.

"My God." Rita's voice was soft in the din of the room, but he heard it. "You love her."

He swallowed. "There are no words."

He pulled at his collar. Goddammit. He tried to find air, but there was none. He set Rita aside with both hands, found the door, and ignored Judah's call, the nodding heads of good-bye.

37

The lantern swung in precarious arcs at the rear of the berth. The violent motions of the ship slowed, then ceased. The squeaks of the lantern's arc slowed, then stilled.

Chloe removed first one hand, then the other, straightening her fingers to stretch muscles that had seized with the rigorous exercise of holding on. She looked up and strained her ears for information from aboveboard.

"Captain!" She tried again, "Captain!" As she called, she reasoned that he wouldn't forget her. With the intention of returning up the steps to the hatch in the hopes she could get his attention through a vigorous pounding, Chloe grabbed the rail.

It was lucky she'd held onto something. In a single heave, the boat was lifted in grotesque imitation of its earlier roiling. The bow was propelled into the air by the sinking weight of the engine. The floor slipped from her feet. Chloe's second hand found the rail and clutched. Her golden slippers kicked, until her fingers lost their purchase, and she dropped, landing on the bulkhead.

She heard rushing water, and looked for it. There was none pouring into the berth, but she heard it nonetheless. She wondered where it was making its way in. The industrial steel of the tug was sound, but it was heavy. The ship groaned, nose in the air. Two loud thumps reverberated beneath her feet, above her head, everywhere, and her feet grew lighter atop the bulkhead that had been the wall. It was sinking. She scrambled to the bed and up it, thinking only of escaping the berth before she was taken down with the ship.

The gold of her skirt was tight around her legs, and she tore at the fabric until it reached above her knees and she could climb the wood frame of the berth that now stood upright. When she reached the top of the frame, she slipped and kicked the mattress, and it toppled to the wall beneath her. She couldn't reach the rungs above her head, knew in an instant it was hopeless. She'd never reach the passageway, and if she could, never unlock the hatch.

The boat shuddered with the impact of the harbor floor. She fell to the mattress ticking below where it had landed folded against the wall.

The sound of water echoed off every surface. The noise of the engine had ceased, so she could hear the bulkheads creak and moan. Chloe also heard her own breathing, fast and hard.

She wasn't. She couldn't be.

She was not buried at the bottom of the North River.

38

Simon jumped from the cab and scanned the mass of buildings, pink granite facades with tall black lettering. The mercantile was closed, but market carts still sold oysters, fruit, flowers, textiles, anything that could come off of a boat.

Scores of people sat atop trunks, hunched together beneath tarpaulin when they had it, their own coats when they didn't. No more ships would be leaving tonight. It was too late for departures. Anyone here was here for the night. Simon turned up his coat and walked toward the pier. The concrete pilings were all different heights. Some pitched in disrepair at odd angles, others looked newly poured.

Simon was ambivalent about storms, ever since the day of the squall. Tonight, he felt the familiar misgiving, the unsettling sense that something was off.

Who was he kidding? It was all off. He'd learned from his store's commissionaire that Chloe had requested a cab to the docks. She'd wanted the place where people left on ships. That's what Chloe had told his doorman when he'd requested her direction to tell the cabbie. *The place where people left on ships.* The information inflamed Simon's apprehension to fever.

Down the pier, a crowd had formed. The bell of a watchtower rang deep and slow. It could've been a fire, but Simon smelled only the rain, and the wet wood of the docks, the salt water of the harbor.

The *New York* had not yet arrived port. Simon saw it and, as if in reply, it gave off a horn. It couldn't be called a wail, that sound. There was nothing high-pitched about it, but it was a lament. In a few hours, he was supposed have boarded that ship with his bride. A honeymoon. The word made him look into the sky. The small sliver of crescent Chloe had been marveling at two nights before was now larger, playing peek-a-boo with clouds that moved fast in front of it. Simon walked further down the pier, until he saw his brother. What had merely felt wrong turned inside out, and he ran. The slick flat soles of his shoes gave no traction, making his run precarious and awkward. He slid through a puddle and caught himself forward on one hand, the knee of his trousers taking on water from the wood.

39

"Captain!" It was pointless to call him. He'd been above deck when she'd been thrown to the floor. Where was he now? Was he alive?

The boat had flipped onto its side. She stood on what had been the bulkhead wall and took stock of the hatch, now high overhead, where she'd entered the cabin. There was no way to reach the door even to attempt an escape, but it was designed to be watertight, and it was serving its purpose. Water leaked around the edges and fell to her feet in a steady but slow stream. The sound was like a well pump releasing its last.

The lantern stopped its squeaking arc. The small flame would extinguish itself when the air ran out. She wondered how much air she had left, but what was the point in even wondering? There was no way out. The snuff of the lantern would be her signal. Until that time, she would contend with a final truth. She'd been buried alive.

She sat with her hands folded in her lap on the mattress, the metallic fabric of her dress pulled tight across her thighs. There was nothing to do but wait. She scanned the room for something to do, but it was as bare as the inside of a barrel. Perhaps a full library would've been too much to hope for, but a single book, a good romance for example, would've made the wait more palatable, kept her mind from watching the flame use up the rest of the air. Now she had only her own epitaph to distract her.

The ones she wrote for others used to appear in her mind already carved into stone. Hers had always been a work in progress. It was too bad. Even if she came up with something brilliant, someone else would choose what her headstone would say. Would it be Eric? His would be to the point, at least. *Daughter. Sister. Wife.* Or some such nonsense. He wasn't very good with words. Her mother's would be worse. Her grave would read simply, *Chloe*. They charged for headstones by the letter. Chloe hoped her father had more sense than to allow her mother to write her epitaph. An image of her father flashed. She'd never imagined putting her father in this position, carving her headstone.

In spite of it all, she'd never imagined herself in this position, never truly believed she'd be compelled to face her own death. When a person finally came to terms with death, there was a standard set of emotions. She'd found the patterns years ago. She mentally ticked off the first on a finger. Bitterness. She'd met quite a lot of people who grew angry. They were angry at God, or a family member, or all of them, resurrecting old offenses to create new grudges. Chloe considered the possibility. No, she wasn't angry, not at any one at all. She couldn't remember a day she'd been angry in her entire life. *Here lies Chloe Swann. She was never angry.* It was not her best epitaph.

Chloe ticked off a second finger. Denial, escape, a refusal to accept what was really happening was another pattern. Chloe recognized this one well enough. Odd how she'd tried to help people work through it, but had never tried to feel anything, for herself or for them. She'd felt so wise. She was only twenty-four, but she'd always thought herself wise beyond her years. She'd been told as much a hundred times. All the time she'd cajoled people to grief, counseling them to accept what was coming, the sadness that followed, but she'd refused to feel it. She'd left them alone, when what they'd really needed was to connect.

And there it was – shame, regret. Chloe had heard a lot about regret, and she was ashamed now, of so many things, but mostly of the way she'd held herself apart, of the way she ran from her feelings like she'd run from Simon. When faced with love, what had she done? The same thing Michael had been doing to Simon his entire life. She'd pushed it away. She'd pushed him away, and Simon had let her go. What did she expect? That after a lifetime of failed connection, he would fight when faced with her denial? She understood him now. Perhaps if he'd not left her, she might have realized how wrong it was to withhold herself from him. She might have told him she loved him, that she was willing to take the risk. The danger all along had been living life without him. Running away had gotten her nowhere but the bottom of the North River.

Chloe hiccupped. She was at the bottom of the North River, and she was going to die.

Tears flowed then. Two decades of dammed up tears flowed more freely than the water seeping through the hatch above her head to the bulkhead below. On the mattress now folded in half, bent against the wall, she buried her face into the ticking and cried.

40

Simon drew himself up from the wet wood and started again, fast yet wary. A small tug reached the edge of the pier. Michael commanded a small crew of men who surrounded him, ran each in a direction, following the gestures of his hands. Simon pushed himself easily through a line of dockworkers, spectators. None looked anxious. They'd seen their share of catastrophe, the loss of fingers and limbs, the burning and drowning that came from wrecks.

"What's happened?"

Michael wasn't surprised to see him. He waited until they stood close before speaking. "Your wife took my cash." Michael's jaw twitched. "All of it. She wanted on that ship." He pointed to the horizon. "Then she went down."

The ship where Michael pointed wasn't the *New York*. What ship? Why? Where was she going? Simon rubbed his temples, and it made his wet hair stand on end. Where was Chloe? And why was Michael now calling her his wife? Nothing made sense to him. It was a dream, garbled and disorienting. "Mick?"

Michael hugged the back of Simon's neck and pulled his head in closer, touched their foreheads together. "We've got to bring her up."

It would have stunned Simon had his mind not been already inert. For the first time in their lives, Simon knew what it was his brother wanted, and it was the exact same thing he did. His wife was at the bottom of the river, and they had to bring her up.

Michael released him and steered Simon to the waiting tug.

Simon's heart thudded. He tried to blank his mind, not feel what terror Chloe would be feeling. And she was feeling. This much he knew. She was alive. It was as clear to him as the bell on the bow that rang as they launched.

The air misted Simon's face as they left the harbor. He shrugged out of his suit coat and let it drop to the deck. "How far out?" Simon unknotted his tie, pulling at it in wide arcs until the knot was free. He kicked off his shoes and tugged at his socks.

"They didn't get far. Less than a half-mile." Michael cut him a look. "You'll tell me when."

It was the closest thing to an admission Simon had ever gotten from his brother. "You feel it? Now's the time to tell me."

"Of course I do."

Simon kept his gaze on the water, tense and waiting. He let his brother distract him for the few seconds he needed to pass before he'd know. "Why did it feel like you were gone? Why couldn't I feel you anymore?" After the storm, a nagging sense of life, almost a memory, was all that had remained.

Michael pushed his hands into his pockets, and his shoulders hunched against the mist. "I turned it off."

Simon would've been angry, if there'd been any space for emotion left. Michael not only had known about their connection, he'd been manipulating it. Simon asked, "How long have you been turning it off?"

"As soon as I learned how." Michael pointed at the water. "As soon as she taught me." He gripped the rail. "I knew it was the last thing you wanted, another person who could flip that switch."

Simon inhaled. He finally understood. Michael had come home to warn him, and maybe for the cash, but as much, if not more, for him. The realization lifted Simon's heart, the physical sensation of lightness reminding him his heart was, in fact, there.

"Here." Simon gestured to the captain, and the tug stopped. They peered into the water over the side.

"She's alive. That much I know." Simon felt her. It was so easy now to believe what he felt was real. He had one last question. "Why didn't you tell me sooner?"

Michael shrugged. "What would've been the point? It doesn't matter what we feel."

Simon shook his head. "That's where you're wrong, brother." He pulled in a breath, pitched himself into the harbor and sank like a stone.

41

Chloe wiped the back of her hand across her face, rubbed her eyes with both palms and dried her tears on the fabric of the mattress. There. That actually felt better.

"Of course it did, you dim-witted fool. Crying always makes you feel better."

It was Hattie. Chloe smiled. She loved her friend so well, she knew exactly what she'd say. Now that Hattie was gone, it was easy to imagine that the words came right from where Hattie lived in her heart, that her friend was making sure she wasn't alone.

Chloe said into the empty space, "We never decided on your last words."

"It doesn't matter what the words are. I'll tell you a secret." Chloe imagined Hattie's wide smile. "I put in an order for pink marble."

"Pink marble. Why didn't I think of that?" In spite of herself, Chloe grinned. "Ma will kill me when she hears that the Dooleys scooped you up."

"Not much of a risk anymore, I'm afraid."

Chloe laughed out loud at the thought. Hattie could always make her laugh. Meredith had said about her mother that she was with her all the time. Chloe knew now what she'd meant.

Hattie would say, her eyes sparkling, "You can't tell me having a husband wasn't fun. Keep the best details to yourself," Chloe flushed at the thought of telling any, "but give me what you can."

In flashes, the details whooshed by, memory after memory, and just like she felt Hattie with her, she felt Simon there, too. Only love could do that, only extraordinary connection could allow you to carry another person around like your soul was a little purse.

His words arrived in her mind as though conjured.

"What would you tell her, if you had the chance? I'm afraid to hear."

Chloe flushed hotter. "I didn't have to tell her anything. She knew all about you. She thought I'd swoon."

"I didn't realize that should've been my goal. I thought ladies didn't like to swoon, anymore. Give me another chance."

She imagined he touched her, pulled her close with a hand on her neck until his forehead pressed against hers and she could feel his breath on her lips.

"How about I tell you something that makes me swoon. See if this works for you. His lips moved to her ear. You invade my mind, envelope me. It's never happened to me before."

Belief in him flooded her, filled her mind, heady and full.

"We are connected. You're a part of me. You're inside me right now. Do you understand?"

She nodded as though Simon was there with her. Yes, she did.

"I didn't believe, not in anything until I met you. If God exists, then this would be proof of it."

"This. What is this?" Her voice echoed in the cabin.

"Us. The way I feel about you. The way I feel you. The way you move through me. Remain inside me, whenever I touch you. It makes me want to be inside you, too, every moment."

Her lips parted.

It was exactly what her husband would say.

She twisted her wedding ring from her finger. She was glad she'd not decided to leave it behind, to give it to Michael to return. She felt sorry that the heirloom would be buried with her, but it comforted her to have it now. She held the ring up to the dim light and noticed for the first time that there was an inscription. *You inside me, me inside you.* She dropped it in surprise. The words had been Simon's inside her head only moments before. How could that be? He couldn't have had time to engrave a ring, or find one with those words, the very words her grandmother had chosen. How in the world had he gotten it? Where had it come from?

Metal scraped against metal above her head. She knew what it was, *who* it was, in an instant. The bulkhead pushed open with a rush of water, and Simon was born through it.

The foot of water at her feet was enough only to make a large splash as his body hit, but not to cushion his fall. Simon landed with a thud. Water poured over him from above. Chloe expected him to have been knocked out by the crash of his body against the bulkhead, but he didn't stay down. He pushed himself to his knees. It took him less time to find her across the hull than the time it took for her hands to travel to her mouth with a surprised gasp. The water gushed from the now-open hatch. It hit the wall beneath him, and showered him with spray. His eyes locked with hers. He certainly wasn't surprised to find her there, underwater in the hull of a tug, dressed in a gown of fool's gold.

What's more, he wasn't surprised she was alive. The revelation was slow. He'd known she was alive, and just where to find her, so he'd come. He'd found her. Now he waited while the spray of the water hit him from behind, and New York's North River emptied itself from above.

His chest lifted with breath. It had clearly taken a toll for him to reach her. She wondered how far he had to swim, imagined the maze of the boat's decks and rails, inverted and confused, negotiated in the dark, without breath. What it took to bring him here, for him to find her. It wasn't just a strong set of lungs, or an understanding of the ship's insides. It wasn't religion, superstition, or stupid luck. It was Simon. He would always come for her. He would know where she was, whether she was safe or in peril, whether she was alive or dead. He would know.

He didn't move to get up. His eyes surveyed her, assessing first her body, then her face. He'd known she was alive and exactly where she was, Chloe realized, but not that she loved him. It was another revelation. How could he know so much and not know that?

She grabbed at him, found him through the water that rushed over them both and pulled him away from the crush of it.

"What are you doing here? You're going to get yourself killed."

"Me? I'm going to get myself killed?"

The tenderness in his tone brought Chloe once again to tears, but not all of them were grief. "Hattie's died." The water rose at an alarming rate. "She was my very best friend."

Simon thumbed water from each cheek. His palms cupped her jaw. "I wish you'd have told me."

They were buried alive, and she felt a bubble of joy. "I'm telling you now." She'd been buried her whole life. But now, at the bottom of the New York harbor entombed in two tons of steel, she'd never felt more alive.

"I'll never leave you again. Not even when you tell me to." His mouth was against her ear to make himself heard over the rush of water as it poured in through the hatch.

"I love you. I'm sorry I didn't tell you before. I just didn't think it was a good idea."

He released her and opened his arms to the water rising beneath them. "Clearly, you found a better one." He looked at the rush of water, the rising line now past Chloe's knees. "We have five minutes, tops."

"Five minutes until what?"

"The water will lift us to the hatch. Then we swim to the top."

"Just like that?"

"Just like that." He tugged at her. "We need to get off your dress."

She blinked. "If you think there's time."

Simon hung his head. When he lifted it again, he grinned like a madman. "Is it really necessary that I adore everything you say? You're wearing the heaviest gown in the shop. You'll sink to the bottom as soon as the water is above your shoulders. How do you get it off?"

She looked over her shoulder then showed him her back. A long line of tiny citrine glass buttons ran from the middle of her back to the hem where it hung below the water line.

"Blasted buttons. It's like they have their own life force."

"They're just for decoration, but you can still rip it off."

"Rip it off?"

"Yes, just tear it. Right down the center."

He tried, but the beading did not budge.

"Maybe it's cut on a bias." She actually laughed. They were caught under water, so deep under water, she had moments ago feared her own life, and now she laughed because he could not rip open her dress.

"Pay attention. I'm coming up with your skirts." Simon reached to their feet to find her hem. She felt him pull it away from her ankles and shimmy it up her legs. When the fabric reached her hips, he grasped the fabric at her thighs. There was not much to grab. It was beaded and wet, and the fabric was thick and stuck. "Hold onto my shoulders. I'll steady you." Eye to eye with her, he tugged the fabric up, and now she bobbed with it. The water line had already brought them higher. The hatch was only a foot above, and not much room was left after that. They hadn't time for a recalcitrant dress.

His hands shimmied the fabric, small fractions at a time. "I've had to wiggle a few tight numbers on the mannequins in the dead of night between shifts." The water had brought them level with the hatch, but his meaning was clear to Chloe. He would not fail.

Finally, the dress bunched at her waist. His hands rested on her bare hips. Chloe felt the electricity. She wanted to ask him if he felt it, too, and wished they could be alone together. It was the most ridiculous thing she'd ever thought in her life. They couldn't have been more alone, but they could be more alone, together. He read her mind. He brought the heavy beaded fabric in a wet, scratchy sweep over her head, and it sunk when he dropped it. Chloe's hair had long since fallen down, and two braids hung into the water above each shoulder. She looked into his eyes and bit her lip. Simon laughed. "I'm glad we're in accord. Definitely later."

Only half of the opening was not submerged.

Chloe looked to the hatch, quickly disappearing beneath the waterline to Simon. "I love everything about you. I haven't found a thing about you I don't."

Simon grabbed the hatch door with one hand. His other arm held Chloe fast around the waist. "I'm sure you'll find something. For example, I leave my socks strewn about the floor."

Chloe pressed her forehead against his chest. "I don't want to hear it."

Simon grabbed the back of her neck and said in her ear something she did.

She kissed him.

"Was that a good-bye? It felt like a good-bye."

Chloe nodded. "I'll see you at the top."

Simon practiced deep inhales, encouraged her to mirror him by holding her gaze fast. The third time, they took the deepest breath, and the water swallowed them whole.

* * *

Simon hadn't told her.

She swam beside him in the silks she'd worn beneath her gown. Even without light, the fabric shimmered iridescent, flowed and pushed loose and tight against her skin and away. He timed the strokes of his arms to match hers. He steered her through the tunnel of stairs and wrapped an arm around her waist when they reached the lip of the next door. He wrapped his fingers around the edge and pulled through, launching their bodies in a burst. He released her after she'd been launched with him.

He hadn't told her that she didn't have enough air to reach the top.

They reached the deck of the sunken ship, and now faced a long expanse of the ocean. Simon's count reached thirty-two. Their ascent was simple. Up. Chloe chose long strokes of her arms. Her legs kicked. The filtered light from the sky above had not reached them, but Simon saw the bubbles when she started to exhale.

His count reached forty-five. At fifty, he slowed his pace, and positioned himself beneath her. Her kicks slowed with her bubbles. When she stopped kicking, his palms found her feet. He kicked his legs and punched his arms. Every bit of him focused on the shot of her like an arrow to the surface. His own body pushed backward as he gazed up, up until there was only *white.*

Michael glared at the water, trying to distinguish the waves from the chop. The distinction wasn't useful, but the process of separation gave him something to focus on other than the reason he was aboard this grimy substitute for a tug in the aftermath of a muggy September squall.

He would've preferred to glare at his brother instead of the water. He was angry with his twin for getting him into this mess, angrier still for feeling angry. He hated the emotions his brother aroused. Useless, distracting emotions weakened a man until nothing was left but a pile of sentiment, steaming in a heap.

Worse than anger, he felt fear.

Michael pulled his hat low over his ears. Fucking hell. Why weren't they coming up?

The green harbor water ate the moonlight and burped bright spots of foam. Without a doubt, the boat had been dragged to the bottom by the weight of its engine. Nothing would have prevented its descent. Less than an hour after the boat had gone down, his brother had gone down after it.

Michael didn't blame him for it. Simon's choice to join his wife at the bottom of the North River made sense to Michael. He understood that a woman could compel a man to such depths. It was why Michael himself had emerged after two years in hiding: two women, each devilish good, it turned out, at getting him into trouble.

Now, one was at the bottom of the New York City harbor and would not come up. The thought arrived at the same time a woman's body, head-first, emerged with a speed that raised her hips above the waterline and bobbed her like an apple.

Chloe thrashed the water and spun around. The surface in every direction was empty save for the gentle waters of a passed storm.

Her eyes found Michael's aboard the unnamed boat. She looked him dead in the face and said his brother's name.

She'd come up alone.

Fucking hell. Michael threw his hat to the deck and dove in.

42

Chloe watched while Simon did push-ups. The linen fabric of his trousers outlined the backs of his thighs, and his shirt hung undone to the floor whenever he pressed up. Her eyes moved from his shoulders to his hands, where they splayed on the slats of hard wood. "Your brother saved your life. You can't still be angry with him," she said gently.

While Chloe was being hauled aboard the tug, Simon had shot out of the water like a cannonball. Michael had gone in when Chloe reached the surface, but after Simon emerged, he'd not come out. The giddy relief of her husband's survival remained light and full in her chest.

The train chugged and rolled a rhythm north, metal over metal. Simon made his own rhythm, pushing out breath with each exhale. He spoke with sarcasm from the floor. "I'll try to thank him." He paused his presses with extended arms. "Although I'll get in a punch or two first. What kind of person just swims away? Twice." He looked up at Chloe as though for sanction. "Twice he's done it now."

"You don't really intend to fight anyone, do you?"

"No," Simon's sarcasm was aimed again at the floor. "I'm just going to bring him a new suit." He pressed up twice and cut her a serious look. "Did you see the trouble he'd been into?"

Chloe trusted that Simon was sensible enough to come home safely, with the exception of when he was with Michael. She understood competitiveness between brothers, and, in only a day, the two had given her ample evidence that it was true enough for them. Should Michael and Simon get into trouble, neither would walk away without the other. She tried reason. "You think a few days of push ups will help?"

Simon's head shook once. "They can't hurt."

"They could tire you out."

Simon stopped, arms extended, and grinned at the floor. "You weren't worried about that before." He leaned to his side and sat. His arm rested on his knee.

"Simon, this is serious." Chloe ignored his teasing. "At least, this time, you know he's alive."

Simon regarded Chloe on the white-sheeted berth above him. His fingers curled against his jaw, concealing his mouth. "You believe me."

His voice hadn't risen in question, but it hung between them with both surprise and gravity. Her reply was too important to leave open to possibility. Chloe reflected on the events of the last few days. Did she? Did she believe him?

It was extraordinary how Simon had found her in the channel. He hadn't been at the shore when she entered the water the night of the wedding. He'd swum to her, knocked right into her, even though the water was dark, and she'd been deep.

Then later, after they came together at Frederik stone. He'd found her at the bay where she'd been wading. She'd expected that he would wait for her, or never come back. She hadn't put the two events together, but he'd done it again. It had never occurred to her that he'd know where to find her. Yet he had.

And, to top it off, there was last night. Her skin tickled with goose flesh. He'd found her, buried alive. What person could deny even the most extraordinary notion after that? There was no denying it. How could she? Why would she want to?

Chloe found the pulse at his throat where his collar was open. The beats kept time with her heart. "I believe you." Simon blinked, so she answered again for emphasis. "I believe you."

This time, he heard her. He ran a hand through his hair. "I didn't believe it. My whole life. But I met you, and I believed." Simon joined her on the berth. "I should have told you from the first. The way I feel about you. The way I feel you. The way you move through me. Remain inside me, whenever I touch you. It's like you're physically inside me. It's the most erotic thing I've ever felt. I'd only ever felt this way with Michael." He looked sharp. "Not the erotic part." He made another face. "Speaking of which, I can't stay with your mother. Eric will smother me while I sleep."

Chloe ran her hand along the length of his arm, where the muscles stood out after his exercise. "We can stay with yours."

Simon flexed his arm beneath her fingers. "She'll like that." He sobered. "I'll stay a day, then I have to find him."

"I understand. I have things to take care of, too." Chloe ached to touch the arch of the baby's foot to her lips.

He rolled to his side and reached deep into his pocket. "I have something for you." He opened his palm. In its center was a small but wide band of gold.

Chloe gasped, "I thought I'd lost it." She remembered the inscription that had surprised her, the sense of physical connection she'd felt upon reading the words right before she'd dropped it. "How did you find it?"

"When I went down to pull up your dress, it was wedged in your slipper."

He'd found a little band of gold tucked into the toe of her shoe. Chloe's eyes met Simon's, hers cornflower and questioning, and his dark sapphire in answer.

The ring balanced now on his palm. He closed the ring in his hand and pretended to pull it away. Chloe grabbed his wrist and pulled it back. She took the band from his hand. She'd considered it lost, like so much else. She felt the tug of a string at her belly, the hard pull toward her husband.

She slid it on her finger. "This is mine."

The relief was like the lifting of twenty pounds of stone. Simon moved his mouth across her hair, pushed it away until he found her ear.

He bit it. "That's what I've been trying to tell you."

THE END

If you liked *Swan Bay*, try the first book in the series, *Wolfe Island.*

Be sure to leave a review – good or bad – at Amazon (even if you didn't buy the book there), or at Goodreads. Reviews sell books!

Sign up for updates on the next installment of the *Diamonds on the Water* series at giuliatorre.com. Michael's story is coming up next.

Thanks for reading!

GT

60925186R00144

Made in the USA
Middletown, DE
17 August 2019